A trilogy of Revelation Cove novellas

Hollie Porter
Gone Wild!

Hollie Porter's Hat Trick Christmas
Open Me First
Hollie Porter Saves the Planet

ELIZA GORDON

SGA
BOOKS

Also by Eliza Gordon

Planet Lara Series:

Welcome to Planet Lara (Book One)

Planet Lara: Tempest (Book Two)

Planet Lara: Sanctuary (Book Three)

The Revelation Cove Series:

Must Love Otters (Book One)

Hollie Porter Builds a Raft (Book Two)

Love Just Clicks (Standalone, Book Three)

Standalone novels:

Dear Dwayne, With Love

I Love You, Luke Piewalker

Books written as Jennifer Sommersby (YA):

Sleight (Book One)

Scheme (US) / *The Undoing* (Canada) (Book Two)

Fish Out of Water

Land Acknowledgment

I would like to acknowledge that I live and work on the traditional, ancestral, and unceded territory of the **Coast Salish**, **Kwikwetlem**, **Tsleil-Waututh**, **S'ólh Téméxw (Stó:lō)**, and **Qayqayt** people. I am grateful for the privilege of living in this beautiful place.

Join the Raft!

Do you want to be the first to hear about new books, upcoming releases, exclusive sales, and/or life and publishing news? Then **join the raft**! I can also guarantee pictures of my very spoiled tuxedo cats and granddog, Pippin Took.

Sign up for Eliza's occasional, not-at-all-annoying newsletter.

Welcome aboard. So glad to have you. Can you pass the Dungeness crab, please?

In the wild, sea otters hold hands so they aren't separated in the tides. These groups of floating otters are called rafts.

About the Author

A native of Portland, Oregon, Eliza Gordon (a.k.a. Jennifer Sommersby) has always lived along the West Coast. Since 2002, home has been a suburb of Vancouver, British Columbia. When not lost in a writing project, she works as a freelance editor (via Plumfield Editing), mom, wife, bibliophile, Superman freak, and humble servant to three pampered tuxedo cats (@tuxietrionurojo on Instagram).

Eliza writes women's fiction, romantic comedy, and enviromance; Jennifer Sommersby writes young adult fiction. Both personalities are represented by Stacey Kondla at The Rights Factory.

Want to buy direct from Eliza? Visit the SGA Books Shopify store!

Hollie Porter's
Hat Trick Christmas

A Revelation Cove novella

ELIZA GORDON

For my Raft sisters,
Deb, Katie, Katrin, and LJ

Welcome back to Revelation Cove!

It's been a while. I know.

A little secret between you and me—this is my *first novella ever*. Crazy, right? I have this problem where my characters are always like *Yeah, we're in charge, not you*, and then the short story becomes a long story and forget it, now it's a novel. The author is never really in the driver's seat.

I'm excited that *this* time, I kept my eye on the prize. I decided I would write a little something as a Christmas present for my dear Rafties, a small gathering of women who cheer me on with every single word, every single rejection, every single vent session wherein I complain about life and related topics.

As a result, you, too, get a wee, adventure-filled catch-up to reacquaint yourself with our beloved Hollie Porter and Co. up at Revelation Cove.

And thank you to all the readers who have checked in on upcoming Eliza Gordon books. Two new projects are with my agent at the time of this writing, and I *do* have others on the go. I know, I'm slow. But I work full-time as an editor, so my writing time is precious. Plus, it's been one *hell* of a year with the months-long Hollywood strikes (remember that Mr. Eliza is a sculptor in the film biz. Follow his awesome TikTok: @practicalfilmmaking). I have SO many book ideas and not enough time—maybe someone has an RX for an immortality pill they'd be willing to share? I'll pay in bad jokes and sweaters knitted from cat hair.

Anyhoo, I love that we wrapped 2023 by hanging out with Hollie and Ryan. What do you think? Should I keep going?

xo,

Eliza

1

I 'll have to slip Tanner a twenty so he doesn't narc on me to his brother. If Ryan sees how many of these packages have my name on them, I'll never hear the end of it.

"Glad we brought the big boat today." Tanner winks as he pushes the wheeled blue bin down the dock. He doesn't complain about the subzero temperature or the brisk wind. He laughed when I said the sporadic scant snow looked like Zeus had scratched his scalp and then shook out the dandruff over the western British Columbia coast. He called me weird. I thanked him and boarded the Revelation Cove aquatic limousine.

"Most of these are Christmas presents. They're just addressed to me." I accept one of the bulging canvas totes as he hands it over the boat railing. As I lack the Fielding brothers' beefy biceps, the bag does not have a soft landing on the floor.

OK, so maybe I went a little nuts this year.

But can you blame me? Ryan looks hot in this particular brand of Henley I found so he needs one in every color; Miss Betty has been not so subtle in her hints about new kitchen gadgets all year (we probably should not have introduced her to the cooking influencers on Instagram), plus she has no chill when it comes to buying toys for Acorn, Chef Joseph's golden retriever who actually prefers Miss Betty to everyone else; we're doing a Secret Santa so most of the staff have sent their orders care of our P.O. box; and I do have the World's Most Incredible Niece, Elsbeth, who deserves all the latest and greatest in books, My Little Ponies, and STEM games. I'm gunning to be first on her list of thank-yous when she's accepting the Nobel, the Pulitzer, and the Fields Medal.

"One more," Tanner says, hoisting a third (fourth?) tote over the side. "Jeez, Hols, what is in this one?"

"That might be my cauldron," I say. Tanner lifts an eyebrow and wipes his bright red nose.

"This better not all be stuff for my kid."

"*Your kid* is a genius. I will do everything in my power to make sure she obliterates the competition."

"She's barely started preschool."

"Never too early to get started on that world domination, bro."

He laughs and signals that he's going to run the cart back up to the dock shed. Because Revelation Cove is nowhere near a package distribution center—and last I checked, the gray and blue Amazon trucks are not amphibious—all our online retailer orders are sent to a commercial post office in Victoria. Every few weeks, one or two among us take the three-hour boat ride south from our island, rent a ride-share vehicle from the harbor (we had an old van for such purposes, but it was stolen from the storage lot two years ago and we opted not to replace it), and empty our pickup locker where all non-food deliveries collect and wait to come home with us.

Home to *the* most beautiful place in the whole wild world. Emphasis on *wild*.

This week's load includes extra food—enough to feed half a major junior hockey team made up of seventeen- to twenty-year-old players who regularly eat double their weight. Hockey players clean out pantries like a locust swarm. I'm just glad the organization gave Ryan a per diem to feed the lads he's flying up.

Last count, at least eight of the twenty-four players will be at Revelation Cove for Christmas, along with a few members of the coaching staff and their significant others, as applicable. On top of the guests who've already arrived, we will have a very full house.

A wind buffets the side of the boat, and the water chops underfoot in our harbor moorage slip. I smile to myself as I push and pull bags and boxes into distinct piles—and maintain my balance. Over the last four and a half years of life at Rev Cove, my sea legs have grown in nicely.

Tanner unties us from the dock and then hops onto the rear deck. A shiver of excitement runs through me—after a busy morning and early afternoon of errands, pickups, and banking, we're heading north, and that means only one more sleep until the man of my dreams floats back into my life so I can unwrap my Christmas present of a different sort altogether.

2

I ate too much breakfast. I'll be burping scrambled eggs with fresh crab and onion all morning.

And I keep looking at the clock but not paying enough attention to the numbers to note the actual time. According to my clipboard of checklists, written on paper instead of one of those apps Tabby keeps bugging me to try, everything is under control.

Checklists written on paper never lie. Unless they're written in Ryan's messy script and then who knows what the hell they say. Don't tell him I said that—his handwriting sucks, but fortunately, he has other hand-focused skills that are *much* better.

Thank the gods he's coming home today. Every thought running through my mind is tainted by perversion, my dirty little mind twisting regular words into innuendo no matter the topic. It's not gone unnoticed by Tabby and Sarah, but that's only because I have zero control over my mouth when it spouts "That's what she said," à la Michael Scott of *The Office*, whenever remotely applicable. It's not my fault. I have not seen my gorgeous husband in a whole month, and I have *needs*. I can't help it if someone mentions a "poke check" while watching a hockey game and all I can think about is Ryan poke-checking me, naked. Or when they talk about excellent stick

10

handling and I mention that Ryan has top-notch stick-handling skills.

And if all goes to plan and that float plane arrives on time, Ryan Fielding, my sex-on-a-hockey-stick demigod life partner, will earn himself a hat trick before tomorrow comes.

Heh, heh, heh, you said comes. *Get a hold of yourself.*

I glance at the clock again. "Four minutes later than the last time you looked," Miss Betty teases. She has flour on her cheek. Again. Still. She hasn't stopped baking for a week. No complaints —'tis the season of elastic-waist pants, plus the lodge's air is redolent with the heavenly aroma of gingerbread, pies, cookies, and every kind of sweet bread imaginable. My darling mother-in-law has baked so much that at least three of us have made emergency runs up the strait to Smitty's to strip his general store shelves of flour. And at least twenty pounds of yesterday's Victoria-to-Revelation-Cove cargo was baking supplies.

"He's been gone for a hundred years," I grumble, easing onto a padded stool. Miss Betty snickers and slides over a chocolate chip cookie, still melty and gooey from the oven. We are in the resort's commercial-grade kitchen, stainless steel everything, triple sinks, ferocious dishwasher that has burned me at least a dozen times, and yet, with Miss Betty here in her Christmas apron and her silver hair newly coiffed (thanks to Tabby, our resident über-stylist), this could be a scene right out of a cozy, teeth-achingly sweet Hallmark flick. (Most of which are filmed in this beautiful province, I will have you know, so yeah, we kind of have the edge on the whole Christmas vibe.)

But despite this glorious, decadent setting, my body feels like I've been caught in an on-ice melee. Between the bazillion Christmas decorations we've installed over the last three weeks and moving all those bags and boxes with Tanner yesterday and then tackling whatever was on today's to-do list (including a deep clean of our apartment since a hurricane known as Hollie lives like a single girl when (former) Concierge Ryan is on the mainland acting as (current) Hockey Coach Ryan)—yeah, I will be swallowing my Advil with a gin & 7 tonight.

But the lodge looks incredible, and thanks to my mad skills as Revelation Cove's director of marketing, we are booked solid through Valentine's Day. Mmm, Valentine's Day. Ryan's favorite holiday . . .

"That smile looks wicked," Tabby says, sliding onto the stool next to mine. Her cherry-red hair, twisted in a stylish updo, looks almost as festive as some of Miss Betty's baked delights.

"She's willing the clock arms to spin faster," Miss Betty adds, turning to slide another tray of cookies into the top of her double ovens.

Tabby leans against me and whispers close to my ear. "She's willing her husband's plane to fly faster so she can get a sweaty, hot dose of vitamin D for dinner."

I grin and nudge her back but not without the *Hello, no dick jokes in front of his MOM* look. Tabby sticks her tongue out at me, hoists onto the footrest of her bar stool, and steals a cookie of her own from the cooling rack.

"Speaking of vitamin D, Tabby, please remember that the young men arriving today are basically *children* and therefore unavailable for any one-on-one sessions in your salon."

"Hols, I am a grown-ass woman. The last thing I want is some tender-hearted man-child reeking of hockey gear demanding my attention." She pops the last of her cookie into her mouth. "I have better men to do." She winks and hops off her stool. "Toodles!"

And by better men, I'm pretty sure she means Nils, one of Ryan's assistant coaches. He and Tabby met at a preseason barbecue back in August, and let's just say my BFF has had an extra spring in her step these past few months. It's good. Thomas, a former member of our security team, broke her heart when he accepted a job in personal protection back east. After she fell for Thomas, she tabled her big Hollywood plans and focused on building something here. But he needed more adventure than what our quiet island had to offer. Last time we heard, he was taking bullets for dignitaries and loving every minute of it.

I'm glad to see that sparkle in Tabby's eye again. And Nils is certainly worth the sparkle.

Miss Betty hums Christmas tunes while the mixer churns with her next creation. I turn my phone over on the counter and about jump out of my skin when I see a new text.

I open it.

It's a shirtless picture of my husband.

"T-minus four hours, Porter. Comin' in hot."

That's what she said.

3

I make a final circle of the property, inside and out, because sitting in the lodge is about to drive me insane. It's effing *cold* out here but not as windy as it was in Victoria yesterday. Zeus's aforementioned dandruff floats by in half-assed flurries now and again, but nothing sticks. You'd think we'd get more snow—we are farther north, *and* this is Canada—but we're at sea level here on this rocky outcropping shoved forth from the ocean depths. If it's snowing at our lodge, you can bet the mainland is getting walloped.

This year we installed a temporary, covered outdoor "rink"—it's made of fake ice, which is probably the weirdest thing I've seen outside of one of my ex-stepmother's mescaline-fueled drum circles —but you can actually skate on it. In the long run, it was cheaper than building a proper rink with hockey-grade ice, which costs a fortune to maintain. I still have not mastered life on two blades, but at least I've provided comic relief for everyone else. And so far, knock on wood, I haven't broken my ass and required yet another emergency boat ride south for a shiny new stamp on my Island Health Authority Frequent Visitor card. (Would it be arrogant to suggest they invented that in my honor?)

Ryan hasn't seen the finished rink—or the miniature Christmas train that circles the lodge and takes riders through a forest of LED reindeer, bear, raccoon, one dog that looks a little like Acorn the dog, and yes, even a raft of otters—since we finished everything. And I have forbidden anyone from sharing photos with the boss. I want it all to be a surprise for when he flies over.

A few years ago, we halved our golf course due to environmental and financial concerns. Keeping eighteen holes of greens *green* year-round is a tremendous drain on resources, and even though we're surrounded by water, it's ocean water and we don't have the infrastructure (or space) to build a desalination plant. The islands off the coast of BC grapple with water shortages pretty much every year nowadays, which is nuts considering our location.

With a grant from a Vancouver-based eco-first company two years ago, we underwent a "rewilding" process wherein we tore up the greens (made of very dense, non-native grass) and then planted new trees, area-specific grasses, gravel and mulch walkways, and pollinator-friendly wildflowers. Miss Betty and Chef Joseph have a decent plot of garden now, Acorn has plenty of space to bury soup bones some archaeologist will uncover in a thousand years and wonder what kind of beast lived here, and guests are welcome to unwind by digging in the dirt during their downtime spent with us, weather permitting, of course.

Yeah, we took a hit with some of our golf-loving regulars since we now only have nine holes, but if I get my way, we eventually will have no holes at all.

Stop thinking about holes.

My phone buzzes in my ass pocket. A text from my sister-in-law:

> "Hol, can you come up to the office?"

If Sarah's here, Elsbeth is too, and if there's anyone in the world I love as much as my dad and Ryan Fielding, it's Elsbeth.

I mean, come on, we've been friends since she squirted free of her mother's nether regions into my hands on the floor of their cabin and then held her breath for the longest minute of my entire life. She didn't die during my first and last foray into obstetrics, and I survived the existential crisis that came in the wake of her birth.

Our bond is sealed for eternity.

I zip my coat against the biting wind and hustle back up the trail, gravel crunching under my well-worn Timberlands.

4

"What does that mean?" I ask, balancing a very heavy Elsbeth on one hip as she attempts to braid my hair while the grown-ups talk. Bill, our facilities manager, and Tanner, Elsbeth's dad, are at the radio desk, all of us crowded into the back office. Wall-mounted computer screens monitor our security cameras, local weather patterns, local twenty-four-hour news, and communication channels for our passenger vessels, both water and air.

"It means they're grounded until this weather clears," Bill says, pointing to angry, multicolored blobs dancing across the weather screens.

"How could the weather change so fast?"

Bill shrugs. "These are the forecast models. Whichever comes true, it looks like we're getting a white Christmas."

Elsbeth whoops too close to my ear. "I love snow!"

I offer her a tight smile and kiss her still-pudgy cheek, hoping she doesn't sense my anxiety. "But tomorrow's Christmas Eve. Will they be able to fly tomorrow?"

"Environment Canada has issued a snowfall warning and travel advisories. This is a big storm. Arctic outflow is colliding with a stronger-than-expected low-pressure front moving in from the Pacific—"

"Bill, *English.*"

"We're about to get dumped on. They can't fly."

My eyes sting. "What about by boat? Tanner and I can leave now."

"I wanna go!" Elsbeth sings.

Bill's already shaking his head. "Not safe. Gusts are up measuring upward of 60 km/h along the strait and running south. And with the freezing level at zero, you'll be in white-out conditions on the water."

The room gets very quiet, other than the low buzz of radio chatter from the two-way.

A tiny, slightly sticky hand grips my chin and turns my head. "Unca will be here for Christmas, Hollie Cat." I love how she adopted my dad's pet name for me. "I asked Santa."

I squeeze Elsbeth in a tight hug and hope that Santa listens to this kid who's in the top 1 percent of the Nice List.

5

After what feels like a million tries, Ryan finally picks up. "Sorry, babe. It's a mess over here. Trying to figure out who's going where since some of guys, their billet families have already left town."

"Are you back at the apartment?" With the hockey club's help, Ryan rented a place near the Langley arena for him to live during the season. Even though I miss him desperately when he's off island, it's nice to have a landing pad on the Lower Mainland when I need to take meetings, do supply runs, or have nekked alone time with the world's hottest hockey coach.

"Yeah. I've got five kids with me. Nils has three at his place. The roads are chaos."

"The storm hasn't even hit yet."

"You guys don't have snow?"

"No."

"It's coming down pretty good here," he says. "But you know how Vancouverites are in the winter."

"Laughingstock of Canada, I know." I want to be lighthearted and positive that Christmas isn't a total wash, but at this point . . . "Do you have enough food to feed all the guys?"

"I'll send them down the block to the store. It'll give 'em a chance to burn off some of this energy."

"Do we even have enough blankets for everyone?"

"We'll figure it out," he says. "I can hear the worry in your voice, Hol. I promise I will get home as soon as I can."

"Yeah, no, I know. It's just . . . it's Christmas. I was looking forward to seeing you."

"Me too. But as soon as we're given the all-clear, we're out of here. Promise."

"'K . . .'" *Don't be a baby and cry about this. Suck it up. Safety first.* "Elsbeth said she's asked Santa to bring Unca home for Christmas."

"Well, if anyone can get through to that old jolly bastard, it's Els."

We talk about lodge business for a few minutes, how most of our holiday guests have already arrived and checked in, so we have an almost full house. The few cancelations we've received have been tentative only, as in if the storm disappoints the glee-riddled meteorologists and the passenger shuttle is allowed to run again by Boxing Day, the guests would still love to come up and spend a few days between then and New Year's.

I'm midsentence when the back office goes dark. "Shit."

"What?"

"The power just went out."

Ryan is quiet for a beat. "I'll let you go. Call me with updates. I love you."

"Me too," I say, disconnecting. For the first time, I realize that ache in my chest isn't just because I miss my husband—it's because I'm pissed off that he's not here to deal with this, that he's hours of travel away from *his* lodge and family, that I am not in Portland with my dad this year since Ryan and his business partners wanted to do something "big and special" for Christmas, so I've worked tirelessly over the last year putting everything together, creating dream packages for guests, running very successful ads campaigns, and pulling off the impossible with Bill and Tanner to organize the fake-ice rink and the ride-on train and the stupid light-up creatures that cost a fortune and took forever to arrive.

For the first time since Ryan Fielding and I crossed paths four and a half years ago, I want to punch *his* lights out.

6

I slouch in the comfy wheeled chair, the back office dim save for the single battery-powered LED camp lamp and the glow of only two of the eight computer screens. A beefy biomass generator hums along the western exterior of the building, delivering enough juice for the bare necessities. Weather and security feeds, refrigerators, the walk-in freezer, one heat pump to keep the main dining room and ballroom warm, interior safety lights now that the sun has gone to bed, as well as the electric fireplace inserts in the guest rooms. On the monitor tracking the incoming storm, that menacing red clot grows closer with every Doppler rotation, and I stare at it as if I possess some magical telepathic ability to change the will of the weather gods.

You will turn to rain. You will stop blowing boats around for your perverse amusement. You will bring Hollie's hot hubby home. Weather gods, hear my plea.

The door bursts open, startling me from my tired trance, and Tabby stands with hands on her shapely hips. "Everyone's waiting in the ballroom."

"For what?"

"It was your idea to put on a Christmas pageant."

"It's a talent show."

"Whatever it is, it's time to pay the piper."

"What does that even mean?" I whine as she pulls me out of the chair.

"It means if you don't get in there and start bossing people around, they're gonna start drinking."

"We have guests to take care of. I can't have the whole staff drunk."

"Then move your butt."

"I should've taken Smitty up on that offer for a living nativity."

"Yes, because nothing says Merry Christmas like three blind sheep, an earless donkey, and a gnarly alpaca dressed as a camel."

"Yeah, what happened to the donkey's ears?"

She stomps her foot.

"*Fine.*" I stop resisting and allow her to drag me toward the ballroom just off the main lobby and down the hall. Before the door is even open, we are blasted with the discordant sounds of a not-great cover band warming up.

"You should not have told the maintenance crew they sound good when they make those noises," I say.

"Those noises are a guitar, drums, and bass."

"And the song they're murdering? We should plan a funeral."

We pause outside the doors. "You're right. Eddie Van Halen is rolling in his grave." Tabby crosses herself, as if she weren't the *least* Catholic person I know. "We are sorry for what they're doing to your music, Mr. Van Halen. Amen."

"Amen," I echo.

She opens the door and the "music" hits me smack in the face. "How do they have power for the amp?" I ask.

"Brad has a battery pack," Tabby yells, pointing at the raised platform that serves as the ballroom's stage. Sure enough, our maintenance lead is scratching his pick across the strings of his guitar with such vigor, I will have workers' comp claims for hearing loss within the hour.

"Maybe this was a bad idea," I yell back to compete with the din.

"You think?" Tabby loops her arm through mine and drags me

to the stage, drawing a finger across her neck in the universal sign to the "musicians" to STFU. Even with the battery-powered camp lamps on every other circular banquet table and the auxiliary emergency lights burning a muted yellow from soffits around the room's edge, it's a little creepy in here. And once Brad stops molesting his poor guitar, the wind's ferocity becomes more obvious, howling like it's interested in booking a spa day.

I step onto the small stage, heart skipping every third beat from my thinly stretched nerves. I'm not great with public oratory. And every time I'm in this room, I think of my first time at Revelation Cove when I partook of my patio hot tub, inadvertently locked myself out of my room, stark naked, and ended up in the lobby where Concierge Ryan took great joy in offering me a woefully tiny dishtowel. I then happened upon a banquet in progress wherein I provided comic relief for a room full of horny businessmen before yanking free a tablecloth to stand in for evening wear. Heat prickles the back of my neck revisiting that fun night.

"Hey, everyone." Thirty or so faces smile, smirk, or stare back at me. Not everyone is Team Hollie. That's OK. As long as they're Team Get My Job Done, that's all I care about. (It's taken three long years of therapy via Zoom to be able to say that and *almost* believe that I don't need everyone to like me.) "So, Ryan and his guys are stuck in Vancouver until the storm lets up. Bill and Tanner are keeping an eye on the weather reports, and thanks very much to our fix-it crew for getting the generator up and going so fast."

Brad bows to whoops and hollers, his right arm draped along the top of his electric guitar. Behind him, Lawry does a one-two tap on his middle drum. A chuckle murmurs through the crowd.

"Until the power is restored, we will run on a minimal operations schedule. The guest-room fireplace inserts will work as long as we have generator fuel, but if we can coax folks to gather in the main dining area or in here to conserve resources, we can then offer free drinks or coffee and tea and whatever holiday delights Miss Betty has been baking up for us—" Another round of hoots and applause interrupts me. *Everyone* here is on Team Betty, as it should be. She waves her appreciation from her padded banquet chair, her flour-splattered apron still tied around her front. Acorn, yet another Christmas-print bandana tied around his golden neck, barks his approval.

"Chef assures me we have plenty of food on hand, including fruit and veg that can be prepped and served without need to turn on the ovens. I don't think this storm should last more than twenty-four hours. This *is* the Pacific Northwest, am I right?" I smile, hoping to see it reflected at me.

Instead, another gust slams into the building, the wood and concrete and stonework structure groaning against the blow. "Um, yeah, so I think we should postpone or even cancel the talent show to save—"

The rest of my sentence is buried under an avalanche of disagreement.

Tabby hops up onto the stage next to me and whistles between her fingers. Damn, I wish I could do that. "Listen up, dorks. Let her finish."

The crowd quiets again. I need to get this out quickly—we only have five staffers minding things while the rest of us are in this superfluous meeting. "We don't know what the next twenty-four hours will bring, how soon the power will come back, how long this storm plans on hanging around, how much snow—"

"All the more reason to do the show!" someone chirps.

"Yeah, we can entertain the guests and keep their minds off everything else. It will be like summer camp, except it's winter," someone else adds.

Tabby turns to me, eyebrows raised in question. "That's not a terrible idea," she murmurs. The room chatter increases again, everyone expressing opinions about why the show must go on.

"I'm not trying to be a party pooper," I say, raising my hand in the hopes they will shut up. Tabby tucks her fingers into her lips, threatening her deafening whistle again. They shush, although the wind has now added a new ingredient to its smacking against the double-paned, east-facing windows: snow.

Like, a *lot* of white. A proper blizzard.

"Um, so my biggest concern here is the comfort of our guests. We need to ration our generator power so we don't end up running out of the fuel that feeds it."

Brad raises his hand, but the look on his face tightens my throat. "Um, about that . . ."

7

Since I primarily work in marketing these days (and still offer my wildlife education tours to our youngest guests), I don't have my finger on the pulse of everything in the operations department. That's a Bill and Brad and Tanner thing and a Ryan thing when he's here. This is not a Hollie thing.

Which is why Brad telling me in front of everyone that we have enough biomass fuel for *maybe* two days, tops, is not awesome. "We were supposed to get another fuel delivery for the genis two weeks ago, but our guy had a disruption in receiving the stuff we use from his supplier. These biomass generators are getting really popular."

I know nothing about biomass generators, other than they're better for the environment. I didn't think I would ever need to know anything about biomass generators because *it's not my job to know about biomass generators*. I know how to create lookalike audiences and interpret analytics and target my demographic on ads platforms and I know a thing or two about *Enhydra lutris* and *Orcinus orca* and how to stop a gaping wound from bleeding out, none of which requires a degree in biomass generators.

"Well, now we definitely need to cancel the talent show. We

27

cannot waste an ounce of electricity on anything not considered a priority."

Bill, seated at a front table, raises his hand. "We have about five cords of wood dried and stacked for use in the fireplace in the dining room. Let's keep it stoked so we can conserve geni power by not heating that huge space."

"Great idea. Thank you. Anyone else?" I scan the room, looking for more suggestions, but I receive only dour, disappointed faces. "We can totally reschedule the talent show once we know our guests won't freeze to death. Also, if you haven't picked up the gift you ordered for the Secret Santa, pop by the break room and have a look in the totes. There are still quite a few unclaimed packages, and everything needs to be wrapped and labeled for tomorrow's gift exchange. OK, thanks. Send any relevant updates or concerns via the group chat."

The head housekeeper lifts her phone above her head. "The Wi-Fi is out. And I only have, like, one bar from the cell tower."

Tabby and I exchange looks. *Shit.* I forgot about Wi-Fi. Few years back, the country's biggest wireless provided installed a cell tower a few miles from here, camouflaged in the vast forest and meant to improve communications for boats, ferries, planes, and local residents, but it's temperamental during inclement weather, despite us paying a king's ransom in monthly fees.

Miss Betty stands and faces the group. "Long before we had all these fancy devices, we used a message board and *wrote* down our dispatches to one another. I'll wheel it out of storage and set it up behind the concierge desk so we can post notes and updates and that sort of thing to keep everything moving smoothly."

Great idea, except I don't think Miss Betty realizes they stopped teaching handwriting in school years ago. Good luck interpreting the chicken scratch of our team members.

"OK, let's pause the show plans for now, focus on our guests, and man those battle stations!" I try to sound chipper and not freaked out. Tabby hides a smirk behind her hand.

Amid grumbles and commentary I can't quite hear, the staff push in chairs and collect whatever props they brought along for today's rehearsal. Brad lifts his guitar over his head and shuffles toward his amp, a shriek of feedback echoing through the room. I follow as he kneels to replace his instrument in its case. Bill and Tanner clomp onto the stage behind me.

"So, this seems kinda bad, right?" I ask. The three men look at one another, though Tanner speaks first.

"Nah. We've seen worse. We'll be fine."

It's almost as if Fate was waiting for someone to say that out loud.

Because all the lights powered by the generator blink us into near black.

8

Our big plans for the generator to keep the guest rooms warm —ha ha ha ha ha—yeah, no. Bill and his team bundle up and head out to diagnose whatever the hell is wrong with the super fancy, *very* expensive biomass geni while Brad and his guys trudge to the maintenance shed to retrieve the two smaller gas generators we retired but hung on to for this very reason.

We have to keep the fridges and walk-in working, no matter what. The one hundred and twenty-odd people currently under our roof will likely not appreciate crackers and granola bars and warm beer for Christmas dinner, plus losing thousands of dollars' worth of food was not on this week's handwritten to-do list. I know because I double-checked my clipboard and *nope*, it wasn't there.

The lobby fills with guests who we direct into the main dining room where a huge fire blazes in the hearth. We're lucky in that the people staying with us aren't high-maintenance whiners—at least not yet. Let's see what happens if the guys can't get at least minimum power flowing again. Not sure how patient everyone will be about sleeping on the dining room floor just to keep warm.

The most popular question after "Does BC Hydro service this island?" is "Do you have any way for us to charge our phones?"—a question I have also pondered in the last hour or so after noticing the dwindling battery icon on my own device. I have a pocket charger bank thingie that Ryan bought me last year as a stopgap as I am constantly dancing on the brink.

Do I know where that charger is? No. Will it be charged even if I do find it? Absolutely not.

Whereas before I was worried about Wi-Fi, now I realize that Wi-Fi doesn't matter if your phone is dead.

Wait—Brad has the battery pack he was using to power his guitar. We can use that!

Except Brad has disappeared, likely to throw on his winter gear so he can head into the whiteout to deal with the generators.

An actual whiteout. HOW did that hit so fast?

I check my phone again. Battery's at 16%. It'll be fine. Besides, the guys will have us up and running in no time. Right?

"Hollie," Miss Betty calls, waving to me from behind the concierge desk. She's talking to Cam, a strapping young lad who took Ryan's spot as concierge as she fiddles with a giant key ring to open the storage closet. While we keep life jackets and safety equipment for water sports within, I don't think we have toboggans or sleds. Seems a little dangerous since sliding down a snowy mound will likely deposit a person into the frigid waters of the Salish Sea.

"What can I do for you?" I ask, right as she finds the correct key and swings open the door.

And is met with angry chitters and hisses from a *very* large momma raccoon standing on her hind legs, claws readied for battle.

9

"How did they even get in there?" Miss Betty asks, her hand flattened over her heart as she leans against the hastily closed door. Acorn's unceasing bark echoes in my skull.

"I saw at least three babies," I say, kneeling to calm the dog.

"I counted four," Cam adds.

"OK. This is fine. They're just cold and scared. They must've wandered in when the doors were propped open or something." I close my eyes and push my fingers against my eyelids, hard enough that a constellation bursts in my blackened vision.

"How did they get past Acorn? And how will we get them out of there without raising a ruckus?" Miss Betty asks. The tone of her voice unsettles me—Miss Betty is usually a pillar of strength, the Every Mom who has all the answers no matter the situation. Sprained an ankle due to poor choices in footwear? Here's some ice. Broken fingers after an attack from a protective daddy crow? Here's a couple aspirin. Delivering a baby on the floor of a nearby cabin? Grab some towels and hot water. Miss Betty just *knows* stuff. She says it's a mom thing.

The only thing my mom knows is how to disappear and break

laws and crash weddings. Although I hear in her new digs, she's learning how to make license plates.

Tanner blows through the front doors like the Abominable Snowman. In his right hand, the scoopy part of a snow shovel; in his left, the shovel's broken-off wooden handle. "Snow's heavier than it looks," he announces, stamps his frosted boots on the huge industrial door mat, and freezes. "What's wrong?" He looks first to me, then Cam, then his mom and Acorn. "You look like you've seen a ghost." He drops the dearly departed shovel and removes his gloves. Tanner doesn't have Ryan's bulk, but they have the same walk, the same mannerisms when worried.

Seeing his face as he looks at his mom zaps me with a fresh jolt of melancholy—and frustration—that Ryan isn't here.

"A family of raccoons has taken up residence in the storage closet," Miss Betty offers. Tanner pauses to pat the dog on the head and accept obligatory slobbery licks to his sweaty hand and then wraps an arm around his mom's shoulders.

"Is that all? You look a lot more worried than some misdirected trash pandas."

Miss Betty looks up at her son. "I hid everyone's Christmas presents in there. And I still need to wrap everything."

Above us, the lights flicker back to life, the massive lobby Christmas tree blinking awake in all her twinkly glory. A round of cheers echoes through the building.

"OK, Mom, don't worry about the raccoons. We have power!" Tanner says, thrusting a fist skyward as if inviting his personal lightning bolt to high-five him. I wish he wouldn't tempt the gods, especially after I just made so many demands of them about the weather.

"Miss Betty," I say, stepping beside her, "the communication board can wait. We probably won't even need it. If we have power, we have internet. We can message the guests in the lodge group chat with whatever we need to announce. Everything's gonna work out."

She nods, but Tanner's right. She looks more worried than normal.

Then again, Christmas Eve is in a few hours, we have raccoons in the storage room, Ryan is AWOL, and we are under fearsome attack by Mother Nature's tempestuous middle daughter, Frosty McBitchface.

"You still have that stash of Bailey's in the back office?" I ask her. "Come on. Let's go see if we can find it."

10

With the power partially restored, the wall of monitors is again lit up like our own personal Times Square. Feed from the regional news station shows intrepid reporters standing like bent trees on darkened street corners, clutching their mics close while broadcasting about the ferocious winds and white-out conditions. A chyron rolls across the bottom of the screen that reads "Transport Canada is asking motorists to stay home unless it's an emergency. Road conditions are treacherous."

My heart plops into my gut to feel sorry for itself.

With Miss Betty nestled into one of her floral-print wingback chairs that look like they belong in an English teahouse, a steaming cup of Bailey's and coffee in her grip, *Downton Abbey* on one of the monitors, and Acorn curled at her feet snoring away, I check my phone. Battery is at 12%. But we have power, so I can charge it. Duh!

When I plug it in, low power mode disengages, and my notifications light up on the group chat we use for guest communication. Since I'm the one who lured so many of our current residents to Revelation Cove with the promise of a magical

Christmas getaway, my DMs have way more messages than the other channels:

Hi Hollie, any idea when the power will be back?

I'm in room 28 and the fireplace insert isn't working. It's freezing. Can you please send someone over?

Is dinner still on for tonight? We have to EAT something. A little communication would be great.

The kids were really hoping to go on your Christmas train. When will that be an option?

Hullo? I keep calling the front desk to have champagne sent to our room but no one's answering. Does anyone work here?

Plus another twenty or so messages asking about how to charge their devices if the power doesn't come back on, two asking if they will be given a discount or refund due to the inconveniences, and—not even kidding—the couple in one of our suites asking if we can fly them back to Vancouver because "you didn't tell us there would be a blizzard."

That thing I said about no high-maintenance guests?

I lied.

I'd rather check in an entire gaze of raccoons.

11

Chef and his small but talented team whip together a sumptuous late dinner, served in the dining room for everyone to partake of. A few whines are uttered about the limited menu, but thankfully, the stink-eye from surrounding tables when seen harassing a member of the waitstaff amid these insane circumstances keeps everything to a dull roar. People are braver in the comfort of their rooms—they can send snarky messages without having to look me in the eye. Here in the public forum, bitching and moaning about this unexpected weather tantrum earns the bitcher and moaner an unfriendly eyebrow hike from those within hearing range.

Good.

Our forward-thinking Chef preps breakfast and lunch for tomorrow while we have electricity, his kitchen a well-oiled machine. Christmas Eve dinner is supposed to be a massive charcuterie spread—much of it already prepared and resting in the walk-in—so we should be able to feed people through tomorrow, knock on wood. When I asked him about Christmas dinner, touted in my Christmas package sales pitch as "the biggest feast of Pacific Northwest delights this side of the Rockies," Chef handed me a steaming twice-baked potato on a cake plate and told me to get out of his kitchen.

I guess that's a wait-and-see, then?

With full bellies and beer-soaked brains, our guests return to their quarters with instructions to remain inside the lodge until the storm settles. Bill and Brad and Tanner found the reason for the biomass generator's hiccup—wires chewed clean through—but that doesn't eliminate the problem of us running out of fuel by the twenty-sixth. And Bill talked to his guy at BC Hydro who said it could be up to a week before they get to us.

A week. *A week?*

This is not ideal. We will have to empty the lodge if we can't get power back on before the generators run dry.

Tanner will know what to do.

He and Sarah and Elsbeth live in a cabin a few miles south on another island, but obvs they're camped out here with us until further notice. Miss Betty's suite has enough room to accommodate, and there's little she loves more than having Elsbeth as a roommate. And Els, drunk on sugar when Sarah scooped her from the posse of lodge kids playing in the main dining room, shrieked her goodbyes to her new friends from her perch over her mother's shoulder as they traipsed down the main hallway. One would think she was about to board a spacecraft for exploration of distant galaxies, never to be seen again. "Goodbye, my friends! I love you! I will miss you!"

Tanner vows to get his little family settled and then return so we can see about reintroducing Momma Raccoon to her natural environs—except the snow is still sheeting down, the wind still yelling at our doors and windows. I counter that we offer the raccoons a free night's lodging right where they are, safe and warm, and that Tanner go to bed and let me handle things for a while. He is slow to agree, but judging by his wind-burned cheeks and bright red nose that won't stop running, I'd guess he's too exhausted to risk any further threats to his well-being this evening.

I absolutely can appreciate that.

And in all honesty, I'll take a family of trapped raccoons over an agitated cougar (or demon goat) any day.

"Don't tell Elsbeth about the kits. She'll want to make friends with them," he says, scrubbing a hand through his hat hair.

"They are pretty damn cute."

"Have you not learned your lesson?" He snorts. "See you in four hours." Tanner mock salutes me and disappears down the hall toward his mom's suite. We've decided to monitor the front desk in shifts to give everyone a chance to rest. Though the lodge typically has a night agent, Hannah, she's in Ontario visiting family until the second week of January. And since I can't sleep because I'm worried about Ryan and Christmas and electricity and raccoons, I volunteered for the first shift.

Upon checking the lodge messages, it appears everyone has been placated with complimentary bottles of whatever they wanted, and the most urgent demands have been met. Again, it's always funny to see how aggressive people can be from behind a keyboard but then in person, they're like, *Oh, no, don't worry about it.* Another thing I've noticed in my almost five years in Canada? Canadians tend to back down when confronted. Some will bluster and gripe until you stand up to them or give them lip back, and then the passive aggression clicks on: *Now don't get so angry, I didn't mean to upset you.*

I've only ever had one woman clap back at me—in a Canadian Tire parking lot when she wouldn't get out of the crosswalk, so I squealed my tires at her. She startled so hard, she dropped her cigarette and came after me where I parked. It felt good to be American again for a few minutes of heated parking-lot screeching.

And then when we passed each other in the housewares aisle inside the store, you'd never know anything happened. Well, except for the matching middle fingers we raised like flags at each other. Ryan was so embarrassed, he sent me to the car to wait for him to finish his shopping.

Speaking of Ryan, I should call him. Check in. What time is it?

My phone sits in the charging dock at the front counter, and I am SO thankful to see that red battery icon replaced with its healthier green comrade. It's quiet down here now with only an hour left before it's officially Christmas Eve, everyone else snug in their beds. The LED Christmas tree lights are on a dimmer, giving off a muted reflection against the howling night just outside the huge west-facing wall of double-paned windows. Since we're on generator power, any unneeded lights and electronics are off, the lobby and entry area cast in eerie shadow. With so much silence, I can hear Momma Raccoon chittering to her babies in the storage closet. Probably telling them to go to sleep or Santa won't come tomorrow night. Maybe I should go to the kitchen and get them something—

My phone buzzes with a call, and I about jump out of my skin.

"Babe!" I answer.

"Hey, Porter … you OK up there? Everyone safe?"

"Yeah, the guys got the geni back up and running. Looks like something chewed through a few wires. Oh, and we have raccoons living in the storage closet, but other than that . . ."

He snickers. I hear a rousing game of something in the background. "Hold on a sec—" The sound fades and a door clicks closed. "I forgot how much energy teenage boys have, especially when they can't burn it off on the ice."

"You guys are all right, though?"

"We're fine. They're eating everything in sight, Skip the Dishes has been here four times, and they're playing video games. Aggressively. At least three neighbors have knocked on the door to complain about the noise."

Despite this, it's quiet for a beat. "I miss you, Ryan Fielding."

"What are you wearing?"

I hear the smile in his voice. "Revelation Cove khaki."

"Mmmm, I love it when you talk dirty."

"I'm minding the front desk. We're taking shifts."

"Can't people just chill out long enough for you guys to get some sleep?"

"You'd think." I sigh. "I wish you were here."

"I know. I will try everything in my power to get there for Christmas Day. This storm can't last forever."

"Feels like it."

"Aww, someone sounds like they have a case of the sads."

"More like a case of *where is my hot husband because he's not in my panties.*"

"Ohhhh . . . more of that, please."

"Seriously, Ryan. This is dumb. I've been counting down the minutes until you were gonna be home."

"I know. I have too, babe. The guys have been teasing me about being an asshole lately, saying they can't wait for me to reunite with my woman so I can get my happy back."

I stand and do a quick scan of the foyer and attached hallways to make sure no one is on their way to complain about the towels not being soft enough or that the moon is hidden by the storm clouds. All clear, so I set the shiny service bell on the counter, open the door to the back office, and tiptoe in. No one else is here, but I'm afraid to make too much noise. Might disturb the raccoons.

"Call me back on FaceTime," I say. "Give me two minutes to set up my laptop."

"I like the sound of that."

"And when you call, I want you naked," I demand.

"I have an apartment full of teenage horndogs."

"So go into the bathroom and lock the door." He starts to protest but I cut him off. "If you don't do as I say, you'll regret it when you finally do reunite with your woman."

"Yes, ma'am. Two minutes. Naked. In the bathroom."

My cheeks ache with a wicked grin. It's not the first time we've had cyber marital relations, and it's nothing like the real thing, but if seeing my husband's shredded form sans clothing, his various parts happy to see me, even from a distance . . . I'll take whatever I can get on this cold winter's night.

I grab my laptop from my backpack, open it on the painted antique desk, then lean over to flip the lock. We don't have security cameras back here and this small room has no windows and only the single door, so I'm safe from intrusion. With all but two monitors dark—the weather one and the main security feed—I click off the second lamp so I'm lit only by the one behind my computer on the desk. I turn on the laptop's camera to check my position and lighting, my heart racing as the two minutes tick away.

Ryan's profile picture—him in full hockey regalia, an action shot from when he was playing with the Canucks—lights up my screen. I click on it, pleased to see he followed my instructions.

"You're still clothed," he growls.

"I am. I thought you might want to watch that part."

"You thought correctly."

I click play on my Music app. Chris Isaak's "Wicked Game" starts, and Ryan laughs on the other end of our connection. "Fuck me, Ry, I have missed that smile." My eyes sting. Then Chris's sultry voice floats from the speakers and I remember my mandate. Slowly, I untuck my forest-green Revelation Cove shirt from my beige uniform cargos, lifting it just enough to show my belly button, gyrating as I unhook my black leather belt and pull it from the loops, folding it in half and slapping it against my palm before dropping it to the floor. Slowly, I lift the shirt above my head and whip it around once before tossing it over my shoulder.

Ryan laughs again, but he has that look on his face he gets right before he heats up. Pupils dilating, the way he bites his lower lip, runs a hand through his dark brown curls. I love that look. I *live* for that look.

I play with the top button of my pants, unbutton, and turn a slow spin to make sure he has a clear picture of my backside.

"Is that a new bra?" His voice is husky.

I face front and lean close so he gets a better look at the lace. I'm not busty, but this bra does my existing boobs a real favor. "Consider it an early Christmas present."

"Tell me it's a matching set," he whispers. I step back and slide my pants down over my hips. "Jesus, Hols . . ."

It is indeed a matching set.

As Chris Isaak croons about not wanting to fall in love, I turn away from the camera again, reaching behind me to unfasten the lacy bra—*sproing!*—a peek over my shoulder, throw in a little ass wiggle. My bra is only held to my body by my right hand, and I slowly turn to face the camera again, letting one cup drop to reveal some boob. Ryan's answering smile is molten, and from the slight shimmy of the camera on his end, I know he's handling a job I usually enjoy.

"Naked," he demands. Chris Isaak fades out but restarts—I knew this might take longer than the song's duration—and I don't miss a beat, doing my best to look sexy. Hand lifted, my bra tumbles to the floor, and I slide a finger along the waistband of my lace panties, daring to push one side down to give my husband a glimpse of his personal playground.

His smile has grown serious, his breaths shortening.

I ease my hand under the left side of my panties and slide them down, bending so he gets a full view of my top half while I step out of my underwear, pluck them from the floor, and give them a playful twirl above my head. No idea where they land once they fling free.

Ryan and I have done this before, and while my shyness about undressing on camera has not completely disappeared, we do have a line. Nothing too explicit, no spread-eagle chach shots. Who knows who might be hacked in and watching from some dank basement in Calgary.

I gyrate and spin and wiggle through another minute or two, touching parts unknown off-camera since, after nearly five years together, I know what Ryan likes—

Ding.

I startle but resume my rhythm so my handsome partner doesn't detect a thing.

"*What a wicked thing to do … to make me dream of you …*"

Ding ding.

Shit. That's the front desk bell. *Keep dancing.*

"Damn, Hols, you are so beautiful …"

Ryan is getting closer, so although the sensuous bubble on this side has popped, I want him to—

Ding ding ding ding ding ding ding.

Fuck!

Whoever is molesting the bell will wake the raccoons, if not the entire lodge. If Ryan doesn't speed things up, who knows how long this dinging will go on. I ease into another slow hip-rolling rotation to surreptitiously turn away from the camera, scanning for my far-flung garments—

Whoever is at the front desk is now dinging *and* hooting. "Hello? Is anyone back there?"

Come on, Ryan.

Ding ding ding ding ding is followed by a *knock knock KNOCK.*

Ryan pauses, face flushed but not quite the flush I was going for. "Hollie, is someone in the background?"

"A guest is banging on the door. I am so sorry—hang on. I need to find my underwear—"

The door to the tiny back office opens, light from out front flooding into my darkened love den. I shriek and attempt to cover myself with my hands. "I'll be right with you!" I yell at the boomer-aged dude gawking at me, his hand still on the doorknob.

"Oh! Sorry! We just need—"

"OUT!" I yell.

He splutters and backs away from the door, though he leaves it open. I bound after him and slam it closed.

"Did you not lock it?" Ryan barks.

"Of course I locked it!" I scurry around to collect my clothes, throwing my arms through my bra, shirt over my head. "Where are my fucking panties?" I search in the dimly lit space and in my haste to click on another lamp, I knock it over and the bulb smacks, breaks, and blinks out. "Shit!"

"Damn, Hols, slow down and don't cut yourself. Get dressed first and deal with the broken glass after."

"I can't find my underwear," I spit. Fuck it. I pull on my cargo pants, commando, and gather my hair into a ponytail at my nape. "I'm sorry. I'll call you back."

Ryan has now stood and turned on the shower. "Go deal with your intruder. I will call you at first light with an update."

"Shit, this whole thing really sucks, Ryan. FaceTime sex once every two weeks is not conducive to a happy marriage."

Ryan's expression sours—I know that look. Even though we both agreed to this living arrangement while he's coaching, it doesn't mean I haven't bitched about it on more than one occasion.

I can't help it. I miss him. He's my best friend. I miss everything about him, and this longing only intensifies knowing he won't be home for Christmas.

"I'm sorry, Hols. I'll call you in a few hours. Love you." He hangs up.

"Bloody hell . . ." I mumble, throwing open the back-office door.

The guest at the front desk better be here to report a goddamn earthquake or volcanic eruption because his interruption of my happy funtime with my stud lover boy has resulted in some serious seismic fallout.

12

"He walked in on you?" Tabitha asks, voice lowered as she hunches over her cup of Matcha.

"Stark-ass naked."

"Did he see anything?"

"Pretty sure he saw everything." I sip my black coffee, not because I love the taste of motor oil after four hours of not-great sleep but because I'm too effing tired to walk back to the kitchen and find sugar and creamer.

"And Ryan was on FaceTime?"

"Yes." I cringe.

"Was he—"

"Stop." I shake my head at my friend. Tabby and I are close, yeah, but I don't have to share every morsel with her. *No, Tabitha, my husband was not able to reach fruition of his one-handed carnal adventure because Ivan Interrupter from room 34 decided he needed more freaking bath towels.*

We're sitting in the almost empty ballroom at a table nearest a roaring wood-burning fireplace that hardly ever gets used. It's Christmas Eve, the main dining room across the lobby is packed with guests who've decided they do indeed still like us, and yes, the worst of the storm has passed. That's not to say we're out of the woods yet. We're still running on generators, and BC Hydro has not moved up the estimation of when they will restore us. While the blizzard has stopped, the wind picked up where its flaked sibling left off, hitting about 35 knots along the coast, which means vessels of the air and water variety are still not cleared to operate.

I've already done a walkabout this morning with Bill and Tanner. We have almost two feet of snow and the temps are subzero, the wind chill bitingly colder. The cloud cover will break open now and again to reveal stunning hints of blue, but then more threatening gray and white pillows blow in, as if to say, *Nope, you've looked your fill of the turquoise hope, back to despair you go.*

I think if Ryan were here and not stuck in Langley, I would be thrilled about being snowed in.

But he's not, and it's too cold and brisk for Elsbeth to make a snowman or for the other lodge kids to skate on our stupid fake-ice rink or for Tanner to dress in his conductor's hat and drive guests around in circles on that ridiculous train.

"OK, that's it," Tabby says, slapping her hand on the table. I jump in my seat, splashing coffee onto my pants. "You're being a total Grinch, that Bah Humbug guy—what was his name? Cratchit?"

"No, Bob Cratchit is the good guy. He has the sick kid with the old-fashioned crutch—Jimmy. No, Timmy."

"What's the bad guy's name? The dude who bitches about Christmas so all the ghosts come and chew him out."

A couple seconds pass while we dig through memory banks.

"Ebeneezer!" / "Scrooge McDuck!" we announce in unison.

"His first name is Ebeneezer," I clarify.

"Whatever. Scrooge. You're being a lame-ass Scrooge. Yeah, your man isn't here to tickle your fancy bits, but there are a ton of other people who would be really happy about some Christmas entertainment."

I know where this is going. I shake my head. "We can't. Generators will run out of juice."

"Bullshit. The big expensive one, maybe, but we have enough

gas to keep the other two going to get us through the First Annual Revelation Cove Christmas Pageant Extravaganza!"

I do not like where this is going. I don't want to be happy. I want to pout and feel sorry for myself.

"What about the raccoons?" I ask.

"Do you want to invite them to perform?"

"Smart-ass. I mean, all the noise might freak 'em out?"

"Now you're grasping." Tabby leans forward, relieves me of my coffee cup, and grips my hands. "The show must go on, Hollie Porter. It's time for the Christmas Pageant Extravaganza."

We lock eyes for a few beats, and I know the battle is lost. "It's not a pageant. That makes it sound like we'll have scantily clad women sharing their views on world peace. Or worse, toddlers in evening gowns."

"OK, gross on that second visual, but considering how Mr. Richardson in room 34 found you last night, I'd say we could probably work in an act with a scantily clad woman, if you're up for it."

I yank my hands free and stand. "I hate you."

"You love me." Tabby stands and slides her phone into her back pocket. "Are you going to make the announcement, or shall I?"

"I should probably run it by Bill and Tanner first."

She flaps her hand at me. "They already said yes. You're the last blockade on the road to Pageant Town."

"It's a talent show."

Tabby whoops and pulls out her phone, hitting the preprogrammed number for who I assume is one among the proper management team. A male voice echoes through her speaker. "She said yes! We're on!"

She disconnects and throws an arm around my shoulders as we approach the doors that will release us back into the fray.

"Did you just call Bill? You should've let me talk to him about the raccoons."

As we exit the ballroom and round the bend to the concierge desk, a small crowd has gathered—Tanner, Bill, Cam, and Miss Betty—just outside the open doors to the storage room where our fuzzy, masked friends spent their evening. Acorn's inside, sniffing and snorting as if he were a bloodhound and not the Chef's overfed dog child.

"What … is going on?"

"Good news!" Tanner says, the grin that reminds me so much of his brother puncturing his cheeks. "The raccoons are gone!"

"Oh. OK, that is good news. Um … how? Where did they go?"

Tanner's glee melts like an icicle. Slowly, one muscle at a time until the worried grimace is back in place. "Well, that would be the bad news. We have no idea."

13

The whole vibe in the lodge changes once word gets out that Mean Hollie changed her mind about the talent show. As I have zero talents to share—unless people want a tutorial on CPR from my long-ago days as a 911 dispatcher—I will man the door and fetch drinks and snacks and smile with every "Hollie Berry" joke, *et cetera*. I've had my fill of dancing after last night's performance for Ryan (and an unwitting Mr. Richardson from room 34). And I'm pretty sure there's a law fresh from the provincial legislature down in Victoria that strictly prohibits me from singing anything other than the national anthem, and even then, I must be supervised.

With the storage closet vacated of last night's guests, Miss Betty was able to drag out her communication hub (a giant dry-erase board on wheels) so the show tunes nerds in residence could plan tonight's lineup. Guests are invited to participate if they have a bona fide talent. Last thing we need is a bunch of drunk hosers taking the stage to tell off-color jokes. No guarantees that won't happen among the staff who've already scribbled their names on Miss Betty's lobby playbill.

For now, I'm outside with Sarah, both of us bundled to the ears, shoveling snow off the pool tarp so it doesn't tear. We've already been down to the fake-ice rink to attempt to clean the fake ice of snow—a futile effort given the wind's refusal to menace someone else for a while. I think Bill reassigned us up here so we'd at least have the shadow of the lodge to protect us from the buffeting gusts. Bill's a nice guy. Like everyone's extra dad.

Although I don't need an extra dad because I have the best OG dad already. He called this morning to check in; they're encased in an ice storm down in Portland, so everything's jammed up there too. He filled me in on his big holiday plans—covering shifts at the hospital where he works as a nurse supervisor—and promised we would get together in the new year when everything thaws out. We talk at least once a week and throw memes at each other's phones on the daily, so Dad knows how much I miss him, how much I miss Ryan during hockey season. And he knows how much of a brat I can be when I don't get my own way.

On our call today, however, he was relieved to learn we're all safe and sound and warm, and he told me to toughen up and not make his awesome son-in-law feel bad about missing Christmas when "he's just out there earning an honest living like the rest of us."

That's my dad. Always the voice of reason. Except I threatened that if he decides he likes Ryan better than me, I will only invite Lucy Collins to use my friends-and-family discount. We had a good laugh because Lucy Collins can no longer darken my Canadian doorstep due to the wee little felonies attached to her passport.

Thank the Mounties.

"Hollie! I've got it!" Sarah pauses scooping, leaning on the handle of her shovel. She's not broken a sweat, whereas I am damp from head to toe, panting like I've run a marathon in weighted boots. Maybe if I were a cold-water, long-distance swimmer like my sister-in-law, I wouldn't look like the ill-formed, half-melted relative Frosty the Snowman doesn't like talking about. "You can dress up in the sea otter mascot costume and hang out with the kids for the talent show. Elsbeth would love that. We could even pin a Santa hat onto the head!"

"Fun idea, but the costume is on the mainland undergoing repairs." Couple years ago, we got a deal on a walk-around sea otter costume from the same company that made Fin, the Vancouver Canucks mascot. And then last summer, one of our guests helped himself to it, tried to wear it waterskiing, and screwed up the head. It's been at the mascot vet ever since, awaiting rescue by one of the Revelation Cove raft members.

"Oh, right. Damn it. That would've been fun." She resumes her work. The pool water under the tarp is not frozen solid, so we don't dare step on it, but Bill gave us this plastic rake thing with an extendable handle to scrape off layers to lighten the weight on the tarp. The snow's heavy, so it takes both of us to get a good pull, and even then, the pool deck is also buried in white, so there's nowhere to pile the scooped snow and yeah … it's a mess. While I'm a staunch feminist and stand in my luscious female power, yada yada yada, I'd really love it if a gallant dude with muscles and a hero complex would come outside and offer to finish this job for us so I could grab an Irish coffee and search the back office for my missing underwear.

An hour later, we declare the job "good enough" and trudge back indoors.

Miss Betty rushes at us down the hall, past the mini gallery of framed, signed hockey jerseys from a variety of NHL teams. She pauses before us, the sleeves on her Christmas cardigan pushed up to her elbows, her right hand fidgeting with the locket hanging around her neck.

"Mom?" Sarah asks. "Something wrong?"

"Have either of you seen Elsbeth?"

14

It's not unusual for Elsbeth to play hide-and-seek in the lodge with her grownups, even when said grownups don't know the game is afoot. But Miss Betty works herself into a righteous froth, terrified the child has wandered down to the docks and fallen in. It's a legitimate fear when the ground is bare of snow, and Elsbeth has been told at least a thousand times to not go near the boats without her "life jackie" on.

I will not allow myself to worry more than is necessary, at least not yet. Especially since Miss Betty is practically hyperventilating. She was watching her granddaughter, who was happily sprawled on the back-office floor coloring in one of her activity books, and stepped out "just real quick to put together a snack for Els."

First thing, we check the walkways to and around the docks, looking for tiny footprints in the white powder, quickly realizing that the snow is so deep in spots, it would be practically impossible for Elsbeth to wade through it without getting stuck or giving up. And her little otter-print boots are still in the office—she's absolutely obsessed with them, as she is with most things I buy for her (which is a lot, yes, I know, I can't help that she's so cute, I'm compelled to reward her simply for being alive). We're confident she wouldn't go outside without her otter boots from Hollie Cat.

Since we don't want to panic anyone—we've already done enough to traumatize our guests in the last thirty-six hours—I post a gently worded but urgent inquiry on the resort group chat, just in case Elsbeth has decided to follow one of her new little friends when Miss Betty popped into the kitchen. Any staff who are not busy with guests are searching; Sarah runs to Miss Betty's apartment while Tanner checks all the potential hiding places in the main dining room and ballroom. I've checked the storage closet and back office twice, my pulse ratcheting up with every cupboard opened and every box moved that does not reveal the tiny form of my niece.

I move into the lobby, hands on hips as I turn slowly in a circle, trying to imagine where I would hide if I were five and full of mischief. According to my father, I *was* five and full of mischief at one point. "Elsbeth! Where are you hiding? Come on out so we can grab some of Gramma's Christmas cookies!"

Tabby opens the door to the spa and salon on the northernmost end of the lobby and shakes her head. "She's not in here either."

"Els, sweetie . . ." I move around the front desk to the sitting area with the plush couches, rich area rugs, and our giant Christmas tree. "Elsbeth, where are youuuuuu?" I sing.

"Do you think—"

I lift a hand to quiet Tabby. "Shh. Did you hear that?"

We freeze, ears perked.

A tiny giggle. It's close.

"Elllllsbeth . . ."

Another giggle. Tabby and I both spin toward the Christmas tree, and it's then I notice that one of the ginormous prop presents is tipped over near the back. I snap once at Tabby and point, mouthing *She's over there.*

Slowly, I tiptoe around the side of the tree, cooing my niece's name. "Princess Elsbie, have you escaped to your castle? Who will I share these delicious cookies with if I can't find you?"

"BOO!" Elsbeth jumps out from the red-wrapped appliance box.

Except she's not alone. In her arms is one of the raccoon kits, and behind her three more squeak and squeal as Momma Raccoon flies out of the tree at my head, hissing all the way.

15

Elsbeth, freshly bathed and in her tiny bathrobe after thorough inspection by both her mother and grandmother for ANY sign of broken skin, sobs in Sarah's arms about why she can't keep the baby raccoons. They tag-teamed and asked her a dozen times if any of the little critters had given her a bite or a nibble or a scrape or a kiss, and little Els cried and said, "No, they're my babies, they would never hurt me." We called the nurse helpline and then talked to a doctor at the ER in Nanaimo, and after two hours of consultation and another inspection of every inch of her extremities, it's decided we could wait for the winds to abate to take her in. We don't play the "fuck around and find out if you have rabies" game with raccoons.

Miss Betty tends to the impressive scrape on my face, earned when I tumbled into our plump Douglas fir to avoid the raccoon. The latest oozy insult to my person extends along my right cheek, eyebrow, and nearly into my hairline. After I came to live at Revelation Cove, Miss Betty took a bunch of first aid courses online and even did a week-long "citizen medic" workshop in Victoria, to become certified as our official Emergency First Responder. Given the amount of trouble I got myself into during my first year here, it seemed like the smart thing to do.

It's certainly come in handy today.

At first, they thought Momma Raccoon's claws or even teeth had carved the mark in my face. There was quite a bit of blood, as would be expected with an injury involving yours truly. However, I did not recall the furred outsider clutching my fleshy bits at any point, and upon closer inspection, including review of security footage, it was declared that I was, in fact, attacked by a rogue branch on the Christmas tree. How rude.

And yet I am grateful it didn't blind me, despite the unsavory gouge now decorating my otherwise unmarred complexion. Bummer thing is, my skin is only unmarred because I'm in that blissful week when my cycle-related acne takes a breather. (You'd think that by thirty, zits would be a thing of my distant past. *Au contraire!*) As Miss Betty inspects the damage and sets to cleaning my wound, she vacillates on whether we should head into Nanaimo immediately, just in case it was the raccoon. I reassure them I'm fine and remind her that until the wind calms its shit, we cannot go anywhere, and calling the Coast Guard for a scrape is probably not cool, given the likelihood they're dealing with *actual* emergencies.

"Maybe it's a good thing Ryan won't be home tonight. Who wants to look at *this*?" I joke, sucking air through my teeth as Miss Betty presses the ointment-covered Q-Tip too deep.

I'm seated at the breakfast bar in my mother-in-law's kitchen, her industrial-grade first aid kit sprawled open on the countertop. My ringtone interrupts the quiet, earning me a side-eye from Sarah —Elsbeth was almost asleep in her mother's arms, but Els knows Ryan's ringtone, so her head pops off Sarah's shoulder. "Unca! Unca! I wanna talk to him!"

"Sorry," I whisper, then hop off the barstool and move toward the bathroom to answer.

"She's awake now. Just answer it so she can talk to him," Sarah says, sighing as she plops onto the couch and releases her squirming daughter.

"Hey, Ry," I answer.

"Porter, seriously? Is everyone OK?"

"Everyone's fine. Elsbeth is completely unharmed, other than a broken heart that she can't keep her baby bandits. And your mom is tending my wound—"

"Wait—you're wounded? Tanner didn't mention a wound."

"I scratched my face on the Christmas tree."

"Are you sure it wasn't from the mother raccoon? Hols, you know we do not mess around with rabies."

"Babe, I know. It's not from the raccoon. I kinda fell into the tree when the momma launched—you know what, it's fine. I'm *fine*. Your mom is fixing things, and we'll go to Nanaimo as soon as we're not at risk of checking in to Davy Jones' locker should we embark upon an aquatic voyage." I'm trying to speak in euphemisms so Elsbeth doesn't pick up any unnecessary fear about going in the boat.

Ryan responds, but I can't hear him because Elsbeth is losing her ever-loving mind about talking to her favorite uncle. "Ryan, gonna ask you to pause whatever you're saying and talk to Els first before her head explodes."

I hand the phone to my niece who puts it to her ear and then tucks her shoulder close to hold it. She's a pro. At five. And with her tiny rainbow-painted fingernails and the terry-cloth robe, her little mouth chattering as fast as she can form words to regale Unca with how mean we all are for not letting her keep the "rancoons," my mind does that fast-forward glimpse thing where I see her as a teenager, phone propped against her head as she unloads about whatever recent injustice she has suffered at the hands of her very uncool family.

"Unca, why can't you come home for Christmas? We have lots of snow and we can make a snow family and Gramma made SO much cookies. Can't you just fly your plane? The water doesn't have snow on it, so why can't you land Miss Lily like you always do?"

Ryan's voice buzzes low through the phone's speaker as he talks to his niece, and it dawns on me as I watch her that she looks so much like her dad . . . which means she looks so much like Ryan.

Maybe what our baby girl would look like.

Uh, what the hell, Hollie . . . Where did that come from?

"OK, bye, Unca. I asked Santa to bring you home for Christmas, so I'll see you soon!"

She drops the phone on the couch and launches into a solo performance of original choreography that mostly involves hopping and spinning and singing at the top of her lungs.

I scoop up my cell. "Whatever you said, she's dancing now. Thank you."

"I *am* her favorite."

"You're her favorite *uncle*. I'm her favorite Hollie Cat." I lift a finger to indicate a pause and wander into Miss Betty's bedroom for a moment's quiet. The view from this window is never not impressive, but right now, with the blanket of white covering everything and the sky purpling toward dusk, I again whisper a quiet thanks to whatever deities conspired to plant me here.

"How are things on your side of the strait?" I ask. "How are the roads?"

"Dumb. And the winds are picking up. Power's out in White Rock, Richmond, and parts of Surrey."

"Shit."

"The lights have flickered a few times. Worst-case scenario, the five boys here will head over to Nils's place. He has a generator. And his mom and sisters are in town, so they're better equipped to feed a hockey team than I am at the moment."

"Right." Nils has a house. A nice house with acreage and lots of space. Ryan and I have talked about houses, but the market is utter madness and we can't justify a mortgage if it's just him living on the mainland, especially since the hockey club covers half the rent on the Langley apartment *and* we live basically for free at the Cove.

"I'm sorry, Hollie. I know you're upset."

"It is what it is," I say, trying to hide the emotion burning my throat. "We'll see each other in a couple days. This shit can't last forever."

"You didn't just say that out loud, did you?"

I chuckle to hide my sniff. "Did Tanner tell you the talent show is back on?"

"He did."

"It's like herding cats in this place sometimes."

"You mean all the time?"

The line is quiet, and I know I need to hang up before I start bawling. "Um, I gotta go so I can get a Band-Aid. I love you. Call me with any updates."

"I love you too, Hols. So much."

"'K, bye." I hit the red button, pluck a Kleenex from the box on Miss Betty's dresser, and wince as the first salty tear rolls into the raw, open wound on my cheek.

16

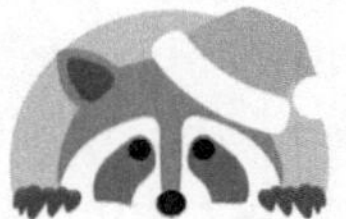

The talent show is as chaotic as I expected it to be. I had my jokes at the ready about how loosely we use the term "talent," but I was pleasantly surprised. So many of our staff can sing, play, dance, do magic tricks, and tell way better jokes than I could ever come up with. And among the guests, we have two *very* accomplished pianists who wowed us with Christmas songs; one of our regulars, a lawyer in real life, has a voice like velvet and showcased his talents with multiple selections from the rather un-Christmassy *Les Misérables*; a Vancouver Symphony Orchestra violinist had her instrument with her, so she played a piece from *The Nutcracker*; and her wife, a soprano with the Vancouver Opera, jumped up to duet with the singing lawyer on a *Les Mis* song that choked up the whole room.

I had *no idea* I was surrounded by such talent.

Consider me schooled.

The talent show I thought would be a total waste of resources turns out to be exactly what we all need. While we still don't have electricity, the generators are cooperating in their task of providing lights and heat, the fireplaces are continuously monitored, fed, and stoked, our creative bartenders have outdone themselves with clever

Christmas cocktails, and Chef has set up a charcuterie buffet for the ages.

As the last performers take their bows—Brad and his not-terrible band who call themselves the Garden Gnomes—one of the pianists resumes her seat behind the baby grand and begins a rousing rendition of "Santa Claus Is Coming to Town" while the singers gather onstage and invite everyone to join in. As bummed as I've been with the storm stress, last night's *very* embarrassing cybercoitus interruptus, Raccoonageddon, and the reality that my fifth Christmas as a married woman will be without the other half of my heart, even I am not immune to the infectious spirit overtaking the ballroom. Sarah and Tanner and I trade off dancing with Elsbeth who sings at the top of her lungs, making up the words as she goes along.

The song reaches its crescendo, and from behind the makeshift curtain prances Santa Claus—Bill in an amply padded Santa costume and long white beard, accompanied by Acorn outfitted in his own festive red suit and an impressive set of antlers. Santa waves at the kids, ho-ho-ho'ing above their excited shrieks, a bulky sack thrown over his shoulder. Acorn barks his seasons' greetings, although I'd guess he's probably yelling in dog language that it's really damn loud in here and can everyone just take it down a notch, *thanks very much.*

With the singing concluded, the pianist continues with a quiet serenade as Santa seats himself on an overstuffed chair and calls up the kids one by one to receive whatever presents their parents secretly stashed within his burgeoning bag of joy. When Santa calls Elsbeth's name, she sprints forward and then stops to straighten her Christmas dress before taking the two small steps up with all the grace of a princess. You can tell we're not related by blood—she doesn't trip and break her nose while collecting her present from the giant red elf. And when she steps close and throws her arms around Bill's—I mean, Santa's—neck, a collective "Awww!" echoes through the room, punctuated by the blinding flash of Miss Betty's camera.

After presents have been distributed, Santa stands, offers warm Christmas wishes, and tells all the kids he has to get back to his sleigh so he can visit the rest of the world before the sun comes up. Everyone waves him offstage, and the pianist wraps up with "We Wish You a Merry Christmas" as guests gather their things and their children. Thanks and hugs are exchanged, and more than a few revelers are a little wobblier on their feet than they were at the outset of our Christmas Pageant Extravaganza.

Pageant. Talent show. Whatever.

The fun's not over, though, as much as I'd like to go back to my cold, lonely bed and uncork a bottle of Prosecco and pop in the Blu-Ray of *It's a Wonderful Life*. No, ladies and germs, we still have the Revelation Cove Staff portion of this evening's fete. I fear that means more noise from the Garden Gnomes, so in preparation, I step behind the bar cart and help myself to an unopened sparkling wine. It's warm, but I'm not a fancy girl. Plus, maybe the 12.5% ABV will make me forget how much my serrated face stings.

Brad and two of his guys move one of the festive round tables onto the stage where Tabby and her salon assistant, both dressed as sexy elves, make quick work of unloading two totes of Secret Santa presents. Brad then sets up his iPhone in a dock and blasts hard rock, but only until Miss Betty points at him and shakes her head. Anyone who's lived and worked at Revelation Cove for more than a couple hours knows that look. He rolls his eyes and grabs his phone to find a playlist more suited to the occasion.

As Bing Crosby croons the first notes of "I'm Dreaming of a White Christmas," Miss Betty's eyes widen and sparkle, her hand flattened over her heart. Yeah, Brad's got the boss's number.

With the guests cleared out, we've all gathered around the front near the stage, each person waiting until their name is called to collect their gift and then we'll all open them together. Some debate circulated in the group chat about whether we should play Vicious Christmas, but thankfully, the idea was vetoed by a wide margin. People wanted to get real presents for the coworker whose name they drew, not throwaway garbage or jokey stuff that could be plucked or traded. And since people are already three sheets to the wind, the last thing we need is a barroom brawl over the most prized gift in the room.

"Hey, Hols, do you want a glass for that?" Tanner asks, nodding at the bottle clutched in my fist.

"Nah. I'm good." I take a long swig. He shakes his head at me and laughs.

"Hollie knows how to handle her liquor," Sarah says from my other side. I lift my hand for a high five. Elsbeth, sitting at the table just behind us, runs a comb through the pink and purple plastic hair of the My Little Pony she just opened from Santa Bill. She's again singing an original Christmas composition, lost in her own world. This kid, man—she's absolutely wrapped in family who loves her. She will never want for anything, never wonder if her mom loves her or know the hollow pain of thinking herself not good enough, not worthy of her mother's love.

Shit. I lift the wine bottle in front of me. How much have I drunk already?

"OK, that's the last one!" Tabby hollers, tossing a wrapped present toward Tanner and nodding at me. He hands it over. I look down at the tag—*To Hollie, from Your Secret Santa*—the scrawl nearly illegible. "One, two, three! Everyone open!"

The room fills with the sound of ripping and tearing, followed quickly by laughs, hollers, and hoots. I slide into a chair adjacent to my niece and set my wine down long enough to open my present.

"Whaddya get, Hollie Cat?" Elsbeth peeks over her pony.

I laugh. It's a three-pack of Band-Aids printed with sea otters. I hold them up so Els can see.

"Hey, you can use those on your face right now! Do you want me to help you?" She drops her plastic comb and jumps out of her chair, eager to play doctor.

"Thank you! Whoever these are from!" I announce, lifting the box over my head before Elsbeth tears into it and slathers me in adhesive strips.

The music cuts out midsong, eliciting groans that maybe the power is failing again—but then the room fills with a new tune, this one very much not a Christmas jingle.

A slow guitar lead-in. Sultry, haunting, but sensuous. I recognize that riff.

Because I played it last night.

The crowd silences, and stage left, a giant sea otter in an ugly Christmas sweater slinks and shimmies from behind the curtain.

I mean, it's not a *real* sea otter but rather someone dressed in a sea otter costume. *Our* sea otter costume. The one that's been at the mascot vet for months.

When Chris Isaak's voice slides through the speakers, the sea otter gyrates, turns, and wiggles its butt, then spins back around. My work family is no longer docile but raising the roof with their catcalls and whoops.

I don't dare get my hopes up . . .

Then the sea otter pulls something from the pocket of the Christmas sweater, slowly, teasing it free. Pinched in its fingers, the otter spins it above its head, thick midsection rotating in what I think is supposed to be an Elvis-inspired hip thrust.

And then it hits me: THOSE ARE MY PANTIES.

From last night.

If I weren't cackling to the point of breathlessness, I'd be mortified.

The otter slows its awkward mating dance and shuffles to the stage edge, right arm outstretched with furred paw pointing straight ahead, its left hand still twirling the panties like the starting flag at a NASCAR race. The crowd parts as the otter hops down—

And drops onto its knees right in front of me.

Everyone erupts into applause as I lift the sea otter's huge head from its shoulders.

And underneath is the world's most beautiful, wonderful, adorable Ryan Fielding, grinning at me with that look that says he knows he's a man who is getting laid tonight.

"Hi," I say, his cheeks cupped in my shaking hands. Fresh tears sting my owie, but I've never been happier for pain.

"Hi yourself," he says. "I think these are yours." My panties hang from his outstretched finger.

I snag them, stuff 'em in my pocket, and throw myself onto my human sea otter for a not-safe-for-work kiss.

17

I wait long enough for Ryan to greet and hug his mother, brother, and sister-in-law, and of course, Elsbeth who jumped up onto one of the banquet tables to announce, "See, Hollie Cat? I TOLD you Santa would bring Unca home for Christmas!" Ryan circulates for handshakes and half hugs, and when Bill tries to loop him into a conversation about the generators and how we will probably be out of fuel by morning, I intervene, emboldened by the twenty or so ounces of Prosecco sloshing around in my gut.

"No. It is Christmas. My husband will be available to talk about biomass bullshit in the morning. GOOD NIGHT, EVERYONE!" I grab Ryan's right arm with both hands and pull, walking backward as I tow him from the ballroom still in the otter costume (sans head) as he waves to his adoring crowd. Once we're in the lobby, he scoops me into a bridal carry and runs down the hall toward the residence wing, practically bouncing me out of his grasp more than once. I hold tight, squealing the whole way, not even caring if I wake the entire island.

Ryan stops in front of our door, releasing me only long enough so I can dig out my key card from my borrowed, sequined clutch.

66

He again lifts me off my feet and glides over the threshold into our love nest, but instead of hightailing it to the bedroom as I'd hoped, he slides me onto the kitchen island. The marble is cold under my ass—I'm dressed in tights and the closest thing I have to Christmas attire, some green and black plaid minidress Sarah dug out of the back of her closet.

Ryan turns around so I can reach under the hideously awesome Christmas sweater and unzip the otter costume. He shimmies free as it puddles on the floor and faces me again.

"You're wearing a tuxedo?" I ask.

He smiles like a cat who just swallowed an entire pet store of canaries. "I wanted to look pretty for you." He then moves between my knees, his warm hands sliding up my thighs, under the hem of the dress, until he reaches the crease where my legs join my torso. I shiver from head to toe.

"And the otter costume is fixed." I nod at the furry pile.

"Indeed. We will be keeping that locked in a safe." We share a quiet laugh.

Ryan then extracts his left hand to tip my chin slightly. Without touching, he inspects the Tannenbaum's terror stretched along my right cheek. He smirks, shakes his head, and tucks my hair behind my ear.

"Am I too scary to look at?" I ask.

"Never." His left hand journeys under my skirt again, this time heading right for the honey as his lips meet mine. "Goddamn, I've missed you, woman."

Grateful the tree didn't scrape holes in the parts of my face I use to kiss and lick my husband, I wholeheartedly follow Ryan's lead in the tongue tango I've been dreaming about for weeks.

He leans back, his breath sweet and hot on my face. "I have it on good authority that you have been a *very* naughty girl this year." He reaches back and pulls the clip from my hair, releasing the dirty-blond waves around my shoulders.

"Pretty naughty. But not nearly as naughty as I'm going to be once I extract my sex machine from his tuxedo." I reach between us and flatten a hand over his crotch. Yeah, the sex machine is definitely fueled and ready to go.

No generator needed.

18

"Porter . . . wake up." Warm, full lips kiss my neck, across my collarbone, down my boob. A tongue flicks my nipple.

"Keep doing that and I'll wake up."

He leans over and administers the same care to my other boob. "It's snowing again," he whispers between licks.

I crack my eyelids and look toward our huge window. A gap in the curtains indeed reveals chonky white flakes drifting slowly earthward, the atmospheric backdrop a muted midnight gray. "What time is it?"

"Just after two." Ryan ceases the careful lavage of my nipples to slide from the bed and throw apart the curtains. He stands with hands on hips looking over his domain, silhouetted against the falling snow, his thirty-six-year-old body still a work of muscled art. Evidence of our run-in with Chloe the Cougar a few years ago is still prevalent, but between reconstructive surgeries and countless hours of top-notch physiotherapy, he's recovered about eighty percent strength on that side.

"Come back to bed. I require affection."

He turns wearing a wide grin, my favorite grin, his teeth practically glowing in the ambient light spill. "*More* affection?"

"Yes, Coach. All the affection."

He slides under the covers and pulls me against his chest, tugging to make sure I'm covered with the blankets. He buries his face in my hair and inhales. "Thank you for dealing with everything. I'm sorry I wasn't here."

"It's fine. We have an awesome team. We handled it."

"I knew you would. You always do." He kisses the side of my head. "The storm and power outage, the guy from room 34 walking in on us last night, the raccoons today . . . you know what that is, don't you?"

"Another day in the life of Hollie Porter Fielding?"

He snickers. "That, my dear, is a hat trick."

Three goals, one game. A hat trick. He's right. "Except I think more than just three things went wrong."

"Still, you handled it. I am so proud of you, babe."

"Thanks . . . and I'm so happy and proud of *you* for finding a way home to me."

"Yeah, not gonna lie. The boat ride here was scary as fuck."

"You're an idiot," I say, pinching his side under the covers. He jerks and laughs.

"The winds had died down enough on the mainland that the ferries were running again. I wouldn't have tried it otherwise."

"You couldn't fly?"

"Miss Lily is in Victoria, and I didn't want to waste the window of calm by stopping there first, fueling up, all that."

"Right. Wait—" I lean up on my left elbow. His eyes sparkle in the dim light. "Whose boat did you use?"

"Nils'."

"Doesn't Nils have a *speedboat*?"

Ryan shrugs and pulls me back down to him. "I made it just fine. At least I didn't take a rowboat out in a thunderstorm to commune with orca like *some* people I know."

I pinch him again. He yelps and flips me onto my back, my wrists pinned above my head on the pillow as he eases his body between my legs. Again. "What did I tell you about pinching?" He crushes his lips to mine and grinds into my pelvis before pulling back.

"Tease."

He snorts. "I am anything but a tease." He releases my wrists and leans on his left arm so his weight is mostly off me, our bodies still touching. I drape my left leg over his hip in encouragement. "Hols, maybe I should hang up my skates. Come home. I can't stand being away from you so much."

"Ryan, no. Babe, seriously?" I flatten a hand against his cheek. His beard is so soft. "If you quit coaching, you'll regret it. You are giddy when you're behind that bench. And those kids *need* you."

He pulls my wrist from his face and cradles my hand in his much bigger one. His thumb caresses the bracelet I haven't taken off since the day he gave it to me at the Vancouver Aquarium after I pulled a runner, days before our wedding.

"Our raft, our rules." He whispers the words engraved on the silver surface. He lifts my hand to his mouth and kisses my palm. "I would do anything to make you happy, Hollie. And I know how miserable I've been over in Langley without you. Yeah, I'm fine on the ice, but when I get home and it's so quiet and our bed is cold and lonely . . . I don't want to be one of those husbands who makes his wife mold her entire life around his career."

I laugh and look at the beautiful room around us. "Yeah, 'cuz it's been a real hardship so far, let me tell you."

He intertwines our fingers. "You know what I mean."

"Rafts float together. I float where you float and vice versa. Watching you coach is basically the wind beneath my wings, so you're not giving that up."

He leans close and gently nips my lower lip with his teeth. I pull my hand free and lace it through his dark waves, deepening the kiss. Ryan moves over me again, preparing to prove he's not a tease.

"Ryan . . ." I mumble against his lips.

He unseals his mouth from mine for a beat, our eyes locked in the sensuous dark.

"What about if I come ashore for a while . . ."

His eyes widen and he eases back, adjusting his weight ever so slightly. "What do you mean?"

"I mean . . . I can do my job from anywhere. Maybe we should pick up that conversation about, you know, a house. Maybe a house with a couple extra bedrooms, just in case."

"Hollie . . ." My name floats on his breath. "Are you serious?"

I move my hips just so, lining up his stick with the mouth of the goal. "What is that you mentioned about a hat trick?"

Ryan's eyes glisten with what I suspect is emotion, his smile so wide I'm afraid he'll pull a muscle as he drives himself home. "Porter, you know I always shoot to score."

Follow the clues.
Win the prize.

Open
Me
First

A Revelation Cove Valentine's novella

ELIZA GORDON

Authors, find and nurture bookish friends like Deb and Katrin and Katie and LJ, strong, damn funny women who provide much-needed comic relief and subplots AND give you the kick in the pants to believe you can do hard things.

1

Chef Joseph is trying very hard not to lose his patience. I warned him cookie decorating would not be a skill in my wheelhouse, that I don't understand how to *flood* my icing without it running over the sides and onto the parchment paper. When he demonstrates *wet-on-wet* technique, everyone at the stainless steel prep table gets it to work for their heart- and flower-shaped sugar cookies except me, and then Tabby starts making crude jokes about *wet on wet*, followed by another line of inappropriate banter when Chef encourages us to use the *luster dust* on our creations, only Tabby misheard him and thought he said *lusty dust*, and yeah . . .

Poor Chef. I would be frustrated too. Last I checked, teaching cookie decorating to grown toddlers was not in his job description.

But we have two Valentine's Day events in the next ten days, so he recruited help to make a bazillion cookies and I got caught in the dragnet when Miss Betty lured me into the kitchen with a plate of fresh brownies. She held it right under my nose and *mmm*, so fragrant and delicious, I had no choice but to put down my pen and follow her from the back office into the kitchen where the door was locked behind me, precluding any opportunity for escape.

Paint cookies or no brownies, my mother-in-law said. So mean.

Alas, here I am. The upside: I get to eat the cookies I screw up. The downside: My eyeballs are doing the Glucose Boogie in their sockets.

Midsession, my phone rings, and all the luster from floods of royal icing disappears because it's Nils, Ryan's assistant coach, calling me at 2:30 p.m. on a workday, and I'm pretty sure he's not after a recipe.

"Hey, Hollie. Don't freak out."

My heart thuds. "That is a shit way to start a phone call, Nils. Where's Ryan? Wait—is that a siren?"

"Sorry. You're right. Um, he's fine. I mean, mostly fine. Other than the bone sticking from his arm, and he probably has a concussion, but yeah, you know how tough he is."

"What is going on?" I don't mean to yell. It startles the sous-chef next to me and she screws up the intricate floral design she's spent the last ten minutes piping.

"In practice, a couple guys got a bit aggressive and lost track of their positioning and Coach just happened to be in their way, so boom!"

"Boom? That's it? Nils, did you mention a bone? Let me talk to Ryan."

"Hang on—the paramedic is poking him with a needle for an IV and pain medicine."

The kitchen has stopped moving, everyone's widened eyes on me. Miss Betty is immediately by my side. Yeah, sure, I'm worried, but Ryan is her *child*. I rest my free hand on her forearm in reassurance.

"Here you go, Hollie, here he is."

Shuffling, followed by, "Hey, babe."

"Ryan, what the fuck? Are you OK? Is there really a bone sticking out of your arm? Oh my god, which arm is it?"

"The left."

Shit, that's his cougar arm.

"But the nice man in the dark blue coat just gave me morphine, so can I call you back when we get to the hospital and I know more?" I hear the pain in his voice, morphine or not. "Hols, don't worry. I'll be OK. I don't need you to swoop in and save me this time."

"The hell you don't."

He snorts. "Hollie, I swear, I will call you when I talk to a doctor. Everything'll be fine. It always works out, doesn't it?"

Miss Betty leans close and talks into the phone's speaker end. "Hi, Ryan, it's Mom. I love you. We all love you." Her voice cracks.

"Babe, tell my mother I'm fine and I'll call you guys back. Love you too."

Beep beep beep.

The eight or so cookie decorators stare back at me, the kitchen silent other than the soft whirr of the ventilation hood. I pick up another messed-up heart and bite into it. Chef shuffles over to the walk-in and pulls out cold butter to make another batch of dough.

An hour later, my brother-in-law Tanner, Miss Betty, Tabby, and I are in the apartment I share with Ryan. I'm pacing a path in the area rug while Miss Betty tidies, because that's what she does when she's anxious, and I am embarrassed but also relieved that there's enough disarray in here to keep her occupied. Tanner has a DVR'd hockey game muted on the TV, though he's hunched over his phone, no doubt updating Sarah, his wife, while Tabby, the dear, makes tea and coffee and throws together a quick chicken salad to counteract all the sugar I've consumed today.

I call my dad and update him with as much as I know. He says he's packing a bag and is on his way and will meet us in Vancouver. It's about a five-hour drive from Portland to the truck crossing in Blaine, Washington, longer if Seattle traffic sucks or with heavy border lineups. I try to insist that Nurse Bob stay home until we know more, but he refuses, says he'd rather come on up now instead of waiting for his planned trip next month "because someone's gotta make sure that boy listens to the medical professionals."

That's my dad.

Finally, an ER doctor who sounds like a fifth grader calls to double-check medication allergies before Ryan's taken into surgery. Dr. Puberty also provides a more detailed account of events: Ryan was on the ice, near the boards, overseeing a drill when several players collided and piled into him, which wouldn't have been that big of a deal if he hadn't impacted the ice with his *and* their body weight on the arm Chloe the Cougar mangled, the one Ryan has had multiple surgeries on to reconstruct and months of physiotherapy to regain use and functional strength.

But he landed hard on that patchwork appendage and snapped the humerus with enough vigor that it punctured the skin, making it a compound fracture—*and* he smacked his head on the wall as he tumbled, splitting open his eyebrow, and then bounced his un-helmeted noggin off the ice, so he definitely has a concussion. Ryan Fielding never does anything half-assed.

"How long will he be in surgery? I'm about three hours away, maybe more. You're in Langley?"

"Yes, Langley Memorial. I'm not sure when your husband will be going in or how long it'll take—I do know, however, that it'll be a complicated repair. I can have the orthopedic surgeon call you before they get underway, if you'd prefer?"

"Yes, please. Thank you." I rattle off Tanner's and Miss Betty's numbers as backup before Dr. Puberty hangs up. "Who's up for a trip to the big city?"

2

Tanner is our primary pilot, and a floatplane is the fastest way to get from this rocky outcropping to the bigger rocky outcropping known as Vancouver. So he packs a change of clothes from the stash he keeps in his mom's apartment here at the lodge and then smooches Sarah and little Elsbeth farewell and barters that he will bring home Els's favorite person in the world if she will just let go of his leg.

The plan: We'll fly into Vancouver Harbour and then take a Lyft to the hospital in Langley. It is my sincerest hope that by the time we arrive at our destination, I will have received word from the surgeon that Ryan's bone is tucked back inside the fleshy bits, zipped up where it belongs, and that my best friend with benefits is in recovery, sleeping off the anesthesia.

Until then, however, I shall bring my iPad so in flight, I can clean up my inboxes, a tedious, loathsome task but a great distraction. And since I am already tearing holes in my cuticles (a habit I cannot break despite Tabby's efforts to beautify my fingers with sparkly gel polish that I peel off within an hour of application), sorting through email will give me something benign to focus on and thus settle the Chicken Little voice in my head yelling about surgery complications and/or floatplane engine failure.

Before we even lift off the surface of the Salish Sea, I'm fretting about how much Ryan will fight me about coming home to the resort for postop R&R. He'll want to recuperate at our Langley apartment so he can report to the arena every day and carry on his duties as the head coach of the Giants, a major junior hockey club. Admirable? Sure.

But I know Ryan too well. If he stays on the mainland, he'll refuse to take it easy because he loves his job, he loves his players and his coaching staff—he won't want to do anything to disappoint them, especially since the team is at the top of the standings as we near the second week of February. They are gunning for a playoff spot, and losing their head coach weeks before the end of the season was definitely not on management's agenda.

And yet, my husband losing use of his arm or suffering lasting problems from the concussion because he's not properly rehabilitated is not on *my* agenda. Five-plus years in, we're still technically newlyweds; I, Hollie Porter Fielding, have *needs*, and my husband is the only man I want servicing those needs for the rest of my life.

As such, I will invoke the "in sickness and in health" clause and demand he come home to the Cove for a couple weeks where he shall allow us to dote on him for a change. Ryan does everything for everyone.

Not on my watch, sir. Not this time.

Plus, with Nurse Bob on the job, Ryan won't have any choice but to comply. It'll be nice to have the old man around for a bit. I miss him like crazy.

Am I happy my better half was injured to the point of requiring general anesthesia and scalpels and probably even more hardware that will trigger metal detectors at airports?

Absolutely not.

Am I sad he will be with me over the next ten-plus days and that Valentine's Day is next Thursday so I will be able to make him forget about his sore arm and brain for a few hours via my naked feminine wiles and a generous sprinkling of lusty dust?

It's almost like I'm an evil cookie genius or something.

3

Ryan's surgery was long—he was still in the OR when our hired car pulled curbside in the hospital turnaround—but it was a success, thank all the deities. They opted to keep him overnight with the tentative promise they'll discharge him today, depending on the head CT, for which we are awaiting his turn. The neurologist is confident Ryan has a grade 2 concussion, but the doc wants to make sure there's nothing more sinister going on underneath the cranial eggshell.

My dad arrived last night right as my groggy husband was rousing (and ralphing) from the anesthesia, and though I tried to keep my shit together, I melted into tears when Dad, bathed in heavenly light, strolled into the room. Can't help it—I will always be a daddy's girl. When my father is around, I can relax for a second, let him be the adult. And he speaks fluent Doctor, so when is that not helpful?

I am beyond grateful he dropped everything to hurry north. Dad and Ryan are thick as thieves, so in the coming days when Nurse Bob explains to my beloved former concierge why he can't go play hockey coach with his friends, Ryan will listen. Dad will diligently check the bandaging and positioning of the busted arm, plus he can eventually pluck out the eyebrow sutures so I don't have to. *Ewwww.*

Midday, the neurologist returns with news that nothing freaky is happening in Ryan's gray matter. However, with his assessment, he delivers the stinging blow: "No stress, no yelling, no ice time, no overthinking, no meetings, very limited screentime …" The list includes more than this, but Ryan has long tuned out by the time the short bald guy in the white lab coat and expensive loafers shuffles from the hospital room.

When the orthopedic surgeon comes in to recheck and sign off on discharge, she basically reiterates everything the brain guy just said about taking time off work and resting as much as possible. My darling husband actually sighs and flops his head into his pillow upon hearing this proclamation for a second time in under an hour.

Like I said, good damn thing Nurse Bob is here.

Truth be told, this isn't Ryan's first or even third concussion. The arm will heal as well as it can, given the former Chloe-delivered trauma that will certainly mess with recovery. But smacking his brain against its case, a brain that has a history of smacks throughout a prolonged hockey career—yeah, Ryan needs quiet time. Even if he doesn't like it.

"I guess I'm the boss for a few days," I say, gently removing a flake of dried blood from his forehead. Whoever sutured his eyebrow did a fantastic job.

"When are you not the boss?"

I plant a gentle kiss on his lips. "Good boy."

4

With enough medication on board to make it look like we tipped over a pharmacy, we're at last en route back to Revelation Cove. Tanner's piloting, talking via the headsets with my dad while I make sure Ryan is as padded as we could get him in the airplane seat.

Knowing he'd need extra comfort, Tanner and I flew down in the air taxi we use almost exclusively for guest transport. Couple years ago, we added a second plane to our tiny fleet—more guests means more trips back and forth—and Miss Lily is *not* a bird I would offer to paying guests, even with the duffel bag of travel-size liquor bottles Ryan keeps tucked behind the front seats.

"How are you feeling? Can I get you anything?" I ask.

My gorgeous husband rolls his head against the headrest. "Stop. Asking. Me."

"Babe, I just want to make sure you're all right. I know you won't complain, so I have to ask a thousand times."

"If I promise to complain, will you stop hovering?"

I lean across the armrest that divides our seats and smooch his bearded cheek. "I will never stop hovering. You are my love god."

His grin lights a nuclear reactor in my chest. I shall never tire of it.

"Hols, I promise I will let you know if I need something."

The plane shudders; I clamp down on Ryan's thigh. Maybe I should sort some more emails. I only got halfway through my Promotions tab.

"Sorry," Tanner says. "All good. Everything's fine."

I look ahead through the windshield, then through the porthole-size window on my left. The sky is a rich blue, no clouds, a fantastic February day. We had a vicious storm at Christmas and pissy weather lingered into the first couple weeks of January, but since, it's been like spring can't wait to bust free.

Another wind buffets into our flying tin can.

"Tanner . . ." I lean forward and poke his shoulder.

"We're fine. Just a bit breezy in through here."

Ryan taps my foot with his. "Babe, tell me what I've missed. What are you working on these days?"

He knows how much I don't like the floatplane, how I will always choose the boat if offered the choice, no matter how much longer water travel takes or how many statistics he shares about how safe air travel is *blah blah blah*.

"Um, so, I just started a course on how to improve SEO and ads campaign strategies for the website. I signed up for a series of beginner illustration classes so I can learn to use the Wacom pad thing Dad got me for Christmas—"

"Have you drawn me any otters yet?" Dad asks from the front.

"I've drawn blobs that might be otters someday," I say. My dad insists that learning to draw will stave off Alzheimer's (no idea why this is relevant to me at thirty), so he bought me a tablet and digital pencil, and honestly, I'm too embarrassed to admit that wee Elsbeth draws better than I do.

Of course Elsbeth is a prodigy. I delivered her.

Another wind knocks into us.

"Fucking hell," I whisper, squeezing my eyes closed. I do *not* want to crash into this tentacle of the Pacific Ocean today.

Ryan wraps his good hand around my fingers clenched on his

thigh. "Speaking of Elsbeth, what's she been up to? Has she stopped talking about the raccoons yet?"

"Only because you sent her the stuffed one."

With the next bump of turbulence, my dad's phone slides between the seat and the center console onto the carpeted floor. I wait until we've for sure evened out before I reach for it to hand back to him.

As I lift it, the screen awakens and reveals a text message preview.

> Can't wait to see you again, Bobby. Thanks for the other night. 🩶

The sender's name—Lady Marmalade—has a cheesy heart in place of an actual profile picture.

Oh my god. (A), my dad has a girlfriend, and (b), she likes Moulin Rouge*?*

I thought he hated musicals.

Why hasn't he told me he's met someone? Who is she? How long has he been seeing her? Is she someone from work?

And what the hell did they do the other night?

"Hol?" Ryan squeezes my hand. "You OK?"

"What? Yeah." I slide free of Ryan's grasp to scoot forward in my seat. "Dad—" He's talking away. I tap his shoulder with his phone, the screen again dark. "You dropped this." I point toward the floor behind his seat. I don't think he hears me over the conversation in his headset, but he nods and mouths *thank you*.

I sit back and refasten my belt, leaning over to whisper in Ryan's ear.

"I saw something I probably wasn't supposed to see."

He hikes an eyebrow in question.

"My dad—he's got some action going on."

Ryan smirks.

"Gross! It's my *dad*."

"He's still human, babe. And he's healthy and—"

"Do *not* say virile or I will punch your bad arm."

"Ohhh, too soon, Hols."

I rest my lips right against his ear. "It's OK for me to do unholy things to your body, but I do NOT want to think about my dad and—"

Yet another bubble of turbulence rattles our cage, and I grab Ryan's cast-wrapped arm. He winces.

"Sorry! Sorry!" I lift my hands away from his person.

"It's fine . . . I'm good."

I heave forward and dig into the pocket on the back of the pilot's seat, beyond grateful to find a tiny dram of Bulleit Bourbon. I crack the lid and pour the burning amber ounce down my gullet, praying that Tanner gets this aircraft under control because I do *not* want my last thoughts in this world to be about my father having sex with some frisky coworker.

Oh my god, it's like Len and Troll Lady in the wheelchair-accessible bathroom all over again.

And lord knows a hospital is *filled* with wheelchair-accessible bathrooms.

5

We land. Safely. We do not die.

Tanner helps his brother from the plane and then along and up the dock to the main pathway that leads to the grand front doors. My dad and I follow, him *tsking* at me all the way about chugging two of the tiny bottles, reminding me that Lucy Collins, my biological mother, is an alcoholic and thus I am genetically susceptible to favoring the drink and "You are too old to be day-drinking, especially when your husband is in such rough shape."

I don't have the heart to tell him that I needed to sterilize my brain from seeing that text message, from envisioning whatever *Grey's Anatomy* scene he's been reenacting with Lady Marmalade.

"Dad, I hate flying and then landing on *water*. You know that."

"Mm-hmm."

I haven't had enough to eat today, so that bourbon went right to my head. I stub my toe on a paver, and the heavy bag over my shoulder full of Ryan's medical supplies tumbles forward, though I don't drop it.

"Are you seriously drunk, young lady?"

"DAD, I'm fine. This bag is heavy."

He leans in and sniffs at me. I stop walking. "If you're going to be a jerk, I will have Tanner fly you back to Portland."

He snorts and keeps going up the slight incline. "You wish."

"Helloooooooo! My baby boy is home!" Our spat is summarily squashed when Miss Betty hurries out the front door, her arms aloft as she approaches her sons. She's careful about hugging Ryan, though he leans to kiss her cheek.

"Daddyyyyyyy!" In Betty's wake, Elsbeth flies out the front door, clomping toward us in her favorite rain boots. (They're printed with sea otters. I bought them for her. Because I'm basically the most awesome auntie in the whole world.) Els throws her arms around Tanner's legs right as Dad and I catch up.

"Auntie and Grampa Bob! Are we having a party?" Elsbeth launches herself toward my dad; he drops his overnight bag and scoops her up. She gives him a tight hug, but when she turns around, preparing to hop into Ryan's embrace, she freezes.

"Unca, what *happened*?" She stares at Ryan's bandaged arm, the bruise and sutured cut above his left eyebrow. "Did you get in another fight with a cougar?"

"Something like that, kiddo."

"You really gotta be more careful," she says, pointing a scolding finger at him.

"That's what I told him too," I say.

Elsbeth leans toward me, indicating it's Auntie's turn, even though she's growing so fast, by dinner, she might be ready to borrow my clothes. Only she'll flip through my closet and tell me I have terrible fashion sense and declare that she'd rather wear Gramma Betty's hand-me-downs.

She wraps me in a tight hug and announces, "Hollie Cat, Acorn pooped by the fireplace, but I smelled it before the Roomba drove through it again." Then she wiggles free, giggling like mad when one of her rain boots slips off in the process. "Unca, when can you skate with me? I've been practicing."

Els gently takes Ryan's good hand and walks with him into the lodge, talking the whole time about what she's been up to in the weeks since he was last home. The last third of Ryan's coaching season is always hectic, especially when they're doing so well. What am I saying . . . the beginning of the season is hectic, too, as new players acclimate and the coaches figure out who fits where.

It's a lot of hectic, and even when he's here, he's not always *here.*

He loves what he does. Coaching has reinvigorated him. I would never ask him to give it up.

But I miss the shit out of him when we're apart.

At Christmas, we talked about me maybe relocating to the mainland, maybe look for some new adventures there. We both know my job is flexible—I can maintain the resort's website and social media accounts and advertising campaigns and newsletters and all that from anywhere I have an internet connection. Ryan agreed. Seemed excited, even.

But then he went back to Langley, his guys were playing great hockey, and the conversation stalled.

Perhaps while he's convalescing, we can revisit. Firm up our plans. Talk about things like fixed vs. variable rate mortgages and built-in bookshelves and the kind of bathtub where you can fit two *and* submerge all the important parts at the same time. And I'm not averse to sliding into one of my most recent Valentine's Day-themed acquisitions to hasten negotiations. Does it matter if it's barely enough lace to cover my belly button?

I am nothing if not a master debater.

6

As much as everyone wants to say hello and see how Ryan's doing, he's exhausted. I record a quick video of us in our small kitchen, waving and sharing that "Ryan will catch up with everyone over the next few days" and then send it via the resort's private group chat. That should keep the wolves at bay. I mean, yeah, there are worse problems to have than staff who love their fearless leader.

It's so cheesy and almost red flaggy to say "we're a family operation," but we kind of are. Not like everyone is related, but it's a close-knit group. If you're a dick, you don't last long. We get those every once in a while, someone who blows in and thinks they're gonna take charge or be the funny fun guy who complains about having to work when they thought they were getting a paid summer vacation at an exclusive resort owned by famous ex-NHL'ers. They don't usually collect more than a single pay period's wages.

It's a good group. Sometimes I pinch myself to make sure it's all real, that Ryan is my husband, that I get to live this life.

All because my dad bought me a sweethearts spa & stay gift certificate package all those years ago that I treated my newly single self to.

I kind of have the world's best dad, if I hadn't mentioned it yet today.

Need more proof? He's elbow-deep in the bag of drugs and gauze on the kitchen island, sorting and organizing the loot, stowing antibiotics in the fridge, and counting out pain meds into a rectangular pill sorter old people use to remember their daily multivitamins and heart medication. I won't tease my husband that he requires a pill sorter because as soon as I do, a fresh calamity will befall me and we will have to sleep with the pill sorter on its own cushion between us so we can take turns swallowing assorted analgesia.

"Hollie, let's get him set up in the bedroom—"

"Nah, it's too early for bed. I can hang out with you guys."

My dad ignores my husband and points me toward the bedroom. "Pillows, lots of pillows. You have a TV in there?" Nurse Bob then fills two Blender Bottles, one with fresh water, the other with Ryan's trusty green vitamin drink (*shudder*) and counts out the next dose of medication. He even has a chart in a folder to keep track of everything. Awwww . . .

I've stacked all the pillows against the headboard, cracked the window, and dragged the nightstand closer so Ryan has access to the remote, his beverages, the charging port for his phone. I open the nightstand drawer to see if there's a box of tissue—

Nope. Just a collection of multicolored vibrators and assorted bottles of lube, some flavored, some empty, and the red faux-fur handcuffs (wedding present) that Ryan rather fancies.

Do I have time to gather all this and dump it in my dresser? What if Dad opens it?

"Hollie, tell my father-in-law I'm fine to sit out here," Ryan protests as he shuffles into our bedroom.

"She can't help you. I bartered your release from the hospital contingent upon my promise that you'd get decent rest." Dad is right on Ryan's heels.

Shit.

I close the drawer of debauchery.

"Hollie, climb over from the other side and set up the pillows for that arm."

I follow orders and run around our king-size bed, careful not to jostle too much with my pillow arrangement as Ryan relents, sits, and allows my dad to remove his shoes, complaining about how he is not an invalid and this is ridiculous and we're making a big deal out of nothing.

I can't take my eyes off the nightstand.

Dad's got Ryan's shoes off, the two men still nattering at each other as Dad lifts my husband's legs one at a time onto the mattress, and then assists as Ryan melts against the plush landing pad of fiberfill and feathers. And as if on cue, Ryan sneezes, the action followed by a quick moan from the pain rippling through his body.

"Kleenex!" he says, cupping his good hand over his slightly crooked nose.

And in perfectly timed response, my dad, noting there is no tissue box on top of the nightstand, proceeds to open the drawer, eyes widening in slow motion as he stares at and registers the contents, closes the drawer, looks at his son-in-law whose hand is still cupped around his nasal cannon, and then to me. A smirk tugs at his lips as he pivots into the en suite and grabs the tissue off the back of the toilet.

"Not a word," I utter as Dad hands over the flower-printed box.

"I wouldn't dream of it." He swallows his laugh on a hiccup.

7

Because Valentine's Day is next Thursday, a workday, we took advantage and scheduled *two* weekends of posh pampering for lovebirds looking to get away—this weekend before and then next weekend closer to the actual Hallmark holiday. Hey, if people want to spend their hard-earned cash to come up here to drink our booze and gorge on Chef Joseph's culinary cunnilingus, I will gladly swipe their credit cards and hand over the goodie bag of sheet-sullying party favors.

Side note: I ordered extra gloves, surgical masks, and OxiClean for the housekeeping team. It maybe be Cupid's big day, but last time I checked, he's not keen on postcoital clean-up.

Rude little freak.

My dad has been gracious enough to only wink and waggle his eyebrows a couple times since discovering the treasure in our nightstand. When he's not following Ryan around with an extra pillow or a little white cup of drugs, he's outside playing with Elsbeth and Acorn or laughing it up astride a stool as Miss Betty bakes her heart out for the incoming king tide of horny houseguests.

I *love* having my dad here.

Even when I catch him giggling like a teenager in one of the wingback chairs near the massive fireplace, his phone cupped in his hand, thumbs flying across the screen. I consider interrupting, ask what's got him so giddy—but then I remember the text from Lady Marmalade and flash a smile and the *I love you* sign and divert into the back office in search of something to keep my mind off my dad doing *that*.

Jeez, grow up, Hollie.

Fine. Let's think about YOUR dad having sexy funtime.

Awkward, right?

Your honor, no further questions.

By dinner, the last of our expected guests have checked in, the dining room and lounge are hopping, and poor Tanner is dragging himself through the lobby, exhausted from three back-and-forth trips from Victoria and Vancouver to our island. For those who opted to take the watercraft shuttle to Revelation Cove, we have two certified sailors who've been taking turns with the runs from the mainland and Victoria Harbour, so at least they're getting a break in between.

But Tanner is the only pilot right now. When Ryan was still here full time, he and Tanner split the piloting duties. I'm worried we may need to bring on another full-time air jockey if business stays as brisk as it has been.

Again, these are good problems.

Once my portion of the day's duties are handled, I sneak into the kitchen and build a tray of food for my sweet husband who has *mostly* followed Nurse Bob's orders and slept as much as possible, other than when Dad has had Ryan on his feet, walking twice a day around the property, only possible because February continues to behave like May. If there were snow on the ground, no way we'd risk slippery steps or pathways.

Ryan is a tough guy—most hockey players are—so a broken humerus, now surgically repaired, is no big deal. I'm more worried about the headaches. He never whines, but he gets this twitch in his left eyelid when he's in pain. And his eyes are a bit droopy—Dad says it's just from the pain meds and the antibiotics wreaking havoc on his gut. "Rest, Hollie. That's what he needs. You have to convince him to slow down. Maybe take another few weeks before going back."

Yeah, that won't happen. Ryan's been on the phone with Nils and his coaching staff whenever he's not sleeping. They're live-streaming practice for his input. And he's watching game video, even though it's obviously aggravating his headaches.

But now it's Friday night, his team is at an away game in Saskatoon under the care and handling of Nils et al., and we have a resort full of amorous drunks. I will feed my man and do what I can to bring him comfort.

Starting with a proper bath.

Ryan emerges from our bedroom, his phone on speaker and held in front of his mouth, discussing switching up lines and reminding the defensemen of their positional play and aggressive forechecking. After all this time, I should be able to translate most of what he and Nils talk about—some I can, but mostly I turn it all into sexual innuendo because inside, I'm a prepubescent pervert.

"Hollie's here," Ryan says, leaning over for a kiss. He looks delicious in his gray sweatpants and robe draped around his naked torso.

"Hi, Hollie."

"Hey, Nils. Thanks for looking after things."

"Take care of our boy so we can get him back soon."

"Oh, I plan on it." I wink at Ryan and move past to let him finish his call. Even though we live at the resort, I only ask housekeeping to help me deep-clean once every couple months, not because I'm incapable but because I'm busy. Also, when Ryan isn't home, I am not proud of how I let things go.

Our tub is pristine, thanks to the diligent efforts of Elsie, one of my favorite staffers. (I'm not supposed to have favorites. Obviously I do.)

I open the bathtub tap, letting it run a little hot just in case Nils keeps Ryan on the phone and the water cools. While the tub fills, I grab a clear plastic recycling bag that I will wrap around Ryan's bandaged arm and shoulder to prevent it from taking on water. Because as smexy as he is in those gray sweatpants, they need to the thrown in the wash alongside the funky bedsheets, and my husband needs a good scrubbing.

"Is that for me?"

I almost jump out of my skin. "Shit, babe."

"Sorry. Didn't mean to scare you . . ." Ryan saunters into the bathroom as I stand from where I was kneeling tub side. He cradles a stem of luscious, round purple grapes from his dinner smorgasbord. With soft lips, he plucks one free, holding it between his teeth, and then leans over to kiss me, passing me the grape.

"You're good at that," I tease, the yummy juice bursting across my tongue. "I have a bag. For your arm. You stink."

He kisses me again, pulling me closer with his good arm. "I'm not getting into that tub without a chaperone. Doctor's orders."

"Whatever you say, Coach."

I help him out of the robe, out of his gray sweatpants and boxer briefs, and gingerly we tie the plastic bag around and under his arm, up over the shoulder. I use medical tape to adhere it to the skin along his upper shoulder, careful to avoid as many man hairs as I can. Maybe I should've shaved him first . . .

"Déjà vu," he mutters, watching me affix the plastic bag to his body.

I smile. He's referring to wrapping my arm cast, applied after a crow protecting its nest sent me sprawling and I inadvertently "rearranged" a couple of fingers on my left hand days before our wedding. Despite our efforts to keep my cast dry and clean, it was soaked with the byproducts of Elsbeth's unexpected entry into the world shortly after application. Yeah, that was a lot of gross. Let's not dwell.

"OK, you slide in first. Check to make sure it's not too hot." I help Ryan ease into the tub, keeping him upright so his bad arm's position remains stable.

He hums as he sinks into the water's warm embrace. "Damn, this is exactly what I needed."

"Not too hot?"

"Hot, but good hot."

I kneel next to him, checking to make sure the plastic bag is doing its job.

"Get naked," he rumbles. "I'm injured. I can't wash myself." He smirks like he knows the last number to a winning lottery ticket.

I make short work of my clothes—I contemplate another strip tease à la the failed Christmas attempt, but I'm not feeling particularly cute at the moment after a long day of work and catering to guests, plus the scandalous lacy number I alluded to earlier I'm saving for Valentine's Day. He will have to wait another six days for his own personal peep show.

No matter how blech I feel, Ryan always looks at me like I'm a goddess. At first I thought he was just being nice—his ex-fiancée could've been a bloody supermodel, for fuck's sake—but we've been together long enough now that I am confident the shimmer radiating from his eyes when he sees me unclothed (and clothed, for that matter) is beyond him wanting to be polite. He loves me. A lot.

And as I slide into the hot water, sucking air through my teeth to lessen the sting, he parts his thighs and bends his legs, steam rising from his exposed knees, so I can slide closer. Our face-to-face position looks like some mutant lotus—four knees jutting like islands from a tub-size ocean. I reach for the new bar of soap and lather up, starting with his shins to his feet, up the back of his calves to his thighs, down the incline to where his legs attach to his torso—

It's his turn to suck in a breath as my hand drifts over the forbidden fruit.

But then I move up his abdomen, still carved with athleticism, around his ribs, up his beautiful chest, under his good arm (I will let him wash under the damaged side), up and around his neck. He rests his head against the wall, eyes closed, that flirty grin twisting his lips that vibrate with the occasional moan of *Damn, that feels good.*

I remembered to grab a cup from the kitchen before disrobing. Slowly, gently, I scoop water to rinse away the soap, the tub clouding a bit, but not so much that I can't see the stimulating effects of my careful ministrations. Once Ryan is free of bubbles, I let the cup float, scooching myself ever closer, hands returning to my preferred target.

"How's your pain?" I ask, stroking with a light grip in case he's not into this.

"Getting better every second," he says, lifting his head from the wall, his eyes hooded. "What did I do right to deserve such excellent care?"

"You answered the phone when some crazy drunk girl from Portland needed a friend." I adjust my position so I'm sitting on my knees, not super comfortable thanks to the tub's textured anti-slip surface, and tighten my grip, speed up my cadence, watching Ryan's face for signs of anything but pleasure. Since water is not the best lube, I don't want to fumble a stroke and break his penis.

He lifts his good hand and cups my boob, tugging the nipple, kneading, uttering "I'm good, it's OK" upon the occasional wince from being jarred. "Damn, woman, I've missed you."

We've been together long enough that I know what he likes, and I have learned from the best how to be a full-service concierge.

Ryan's hand moves from my chest to my arm, and he pulls me in close for a hot kiss, though I don't interrupt my rhythm, balancing my weight on my knees, my left hand against the wall next to his head. His fingers find a hiding place of their own, and suddenly I'm in the game too.

He also possesses an encyclopedic knowledge of my erogenous anatomy, and right now—

Bzzzzz. Bzzzzz. Bzzzzz.

"I love you so much, Hols . . ."

Bzzzz. Bzzzz. Bzzzz.

My phone. On the quartz countertop in the kitchen.

I need to be louder so Ryan doesn't hear it and then maybe he will break through that finish-line tape and I can hop out and see who the hell won't stop calling when everyone *should* know that I'm off for the night, tending to my invalid spouse.

Any tingly shivers from Ryan's dexterous digits have fizzled to the beat of my buzzing phone. Alas, I moan louder so he will just—

He freezes for a three count, then disengages and cups my nape so he can kiss me hard. "Thank you . . . I love you, babe . . . Did you . . ."

I kiss him back. "I'm good. Let me help you rinse off. Do you want more hot water?"

The buzzing seizure restarts.

Ryan's eyes are closed as he pants, head back against the wall. "Is that one of our phones?"

"It's mine." Carefully, I ease back, stepping from the tub to wrap myself in a giant bath towel. "Don't move. I just need to see who it is."

"Can't someone else deal with . . ."

His voice fades as I hurry into the other room to see who the hell has *once again* interrupted us. If there ever comes a time when we decide to start a family, we will need to leave the country. Maybe the continent. ALWAYS interruptions.

"Hello?"

"Oh, hey, Hollie, it's Tabby. Sorry to bug you——"

"Is everything OK?"

"Well, Tanner was knackered, so he took Sarah and Els back to their cabin, and Miss Betty said she's feeling a little under the weather, and since Ryan is kind of out of commission——"

"Spit it out, Tabitha."

"Two guys just beat the shit out of each other in the lounge. One of them says he knows you. He's drunk and refusing to leave until he talks to you. Maybe if you come down, he'll finally go to his room."

"Does he not have a partner with him?" The weekend's guest register is all couples, given the themed package.

"A girlfriend, but she got pissed and won't answer their door."

"Who is this guy?" How would he know me? I don't remember seeing any familiar names on the reservations list.

"Can you just come downstairs? Oh, and we might also need some of your dad's Band-Aids."

8

The guy who "knows" me? His name is Joe Cirillo.

Mushroom Cap Joe.

He's a friend of Keith's, my long-ago ex, who is now happily married to a woman named Felicia (and father to a kid about the same age as Elsbeth), neither of whom I have heard from other than the occasional thumbs-up on superficial "look at my great life" Facebook posts. (Aren't most Facebook posts like that thin layer of pond ice? Not thick enough to walk on but if you look too deep, it's all murk and reality underneath.)

Mushroom Cap Joe, who allegedly earned his name because of his lack of endowment in the wiener department. I didn't give him that name—I never saw his wiener, thank the gods—but when I worked at 911 a million years ago, there were lots of jokes about EMT Joe and his teeny peeny, mostly because he fancied himself a ladies' man, was an absolute chauvinist among the ranks of first responders, and drove a growling, smoke-spewing truck with lots of Vs in its engine and tires taller than most Hondas. Oh, and he regularly referred to women as bitches and skanks, and not even in a playful, ironic way.

And while *yes*, it is not cool to make fun of people for their physical attributes, Joe has it coming. Super fun fella. A fungus on two legs.

Tonight, he's smashed out of his gourd, his likely broken nose bleeding on our lobby floor. And since his antics cheated me out of what could've been a satisfactory orgasm, I'm not super interested in his side of the story. The other dude, Lance something, wants to press charges, and while Bill, our facilities manager, and I agree that's not at all unreasonable, we don't have any RCMP on the island, and if we do summon a constable from the nearest detachment, both Joe and his sparring partner will probably end up arrested.

Tabby rejoins us in the lobby with a towel for Joe's nose and a crackable ice pack for Lance's swelling knuckles.

"I want a discount—no, a refund—on our room," Joe whines, shoving the corner of the towel up his nostril. "Keith said this place was above board, but you let assholes like this guy in—"

Said asshole moves like he's about to charge Joe again. Bill, Brad, and the two brawny maintenance/operations guys we call the Vikings (they're twin brothers who look like real-life Odins) form a human wall so no more fists can fly.

"Until we determine what happened and who started what, there will be no discounts or refunds or anything of the sort," I say, turning to Lance. "Please, if you're not in need of additional medical care, return to your suite and sleep this off."

Lance glares at Joe for another beat, shakes his head, and mutters "dick" under his breath.

Ha. If only he knew.

Brad and one of the Vikings (it's either Sven or Arne—I *still* cannot tell them apart) follow Lance out of the lobby, down the wide hall that leads to the guest quarters, and disappear around a corner.

"So, what, you're going to question your staff and then take that guy's side? I didn't throw the first punch. He was mouthing off about—"

My raised hand interrupts his sniveling. "Don't care, Joe. You've caused enough of a scene for tonight. If you are unwilling to go to your room, sleep it off, and start over tomorrow, I will have these handsome gentlemen escort you to the dock where you can wait in the cold for the RCMP boat to show up."

Joe snorts. "You don't have any Mounties on moose on your island?"

"Never heard that one before, Joe." I force a deep breath so other guests wandering past to head to their rooms don't see me losing my shit. "What's it gonna be?" Fake smile pasted on.

"You're still the same old bitch from before. Keith is so lucky he dodged that bullet."

I nod at Bill—*THE* nod—which means he will slip into the back office and radio the police, after all. The remaining Viking isn't touching Joe, but he's poised to grab him should he do anything stupid.

"And you're still the same old Mushroom Cap Joe everyone in dispatch made fun of for all those years. I'm surprised you're even here with a date. Does she know about . . ." I twirl my finger in front of his groin.

Thankfully, the Viking moves fast enough when Joe chooses to do something stupid.

He throws a drunken swing—and misses—but when the Viking tackles him, they knock me off my feet and I eat the front corner of the check-in desk.

Because of course I do.

9

"I didn't think he'd throw a punch." I suck in as my dad applies a Steri-Strip to the new cut along my cheekbone. When it heals, the scar will match the one under the other eye where the Christmas tree (or maybe the momma raccoon) left its mark back in December. The kitchen's first aid kit sits unzipped, its innards exposed to the world on the spotless silver prep table.

"You and your damn mouth," he mutters.

"What was I supposed to do? He called me a bitch."

"You were supposed to be quiet and ignore him because he's a drunken fool and you're a mature adult who knows better. It's a good thing Sven was there, or this could've been a lot worse." Nurse Bob, his hair askew since I obviously woke him from sleep, isn't gentle as he pushes an ice pack against my latest injury.

"Ow."

"You're a baby."

"Am not." My cheek throbs in time to my heartbeat. "How do you know it was Sven and not Arne?"

"You can't tell them apart?" Dad asks, shaking his head as if disappointed.

I stare at him for a second. "Why's your face so red and shiny?" He looks a bit like Santa in the off-season at the moment.

"Why are the RCMP here?" Ryan asks as he blows into the kitchen. He's managed to get a robe over his shoulders but his delicious chest is still bare underneath. "Hollie, what the—*why* didn't anyone call me?" He moves right up to me, a finger under my chin as he tilts my head to inspect my latest calamity. "What the fuck, Hollie . . ."

"I had it handled."

"Yeah, looks like it."

After we were so rudely interrupted during our bath time frolic, I helped Ryan out of the tub, into clean flannel pj pants, and then into bed where I dosed him with his evening medication allotment. I fibbed and said they were having issues with one of the credit/debit stations in the dining room lounge and that people were frustrated they couldn't pay and go to their rooms and that I'd be back in a jiffy, before his drugs sent him to Nigh'-Night Land.

What I didn't account for was the RCMP boat having its bloody blue spinning beacons cranked so that when they approached the island, the lights bounced off everything in the otherwise pitch-black night and flashed into the windows of our apartment that just happen to face east, looking over the water and docks and the whole shebang.

"What happened?"

"Mushroom Cap Joe."

"Who—do I want to know what that means?"

My dad hands me one of Elsbeth's yogurt popsicles, probably as a joke, but I take it and yank off the wrapper. Strawberry banana? *Fine.*

"This asshole from my former life is up this weekend. Old friend of Keith's. He picked a fight with some guy in the lounge and it got out of hand. Tabby called me, Bill and the Vikings were on it, but they needed Tanner or your mom or me to decide what to do."

"And you chose violence?"

"Yeah, I chose violence," I mock. Ryan steals my yogurt pop and takes a healthy bite.

"Where are the Vikings now?"

"With Bill, down at the dock talking to the cops."

"Do they know about this?" My husband points at my throbbing cheek and swelling eye with what's left of my frozen treat. Before I can answer him, the kitchen door opens and a Mountie in full winter gear strides through, notepad in hand.

"I guess they do now."

The constable—the patch on his left upper chest reads HARRIS—breaks into a smile when he spots Ryan. "Heyyyy, man, good to see you." He offers his hand for a shake and nods toward Ryan's bandaged arm. "Those hockey players just keep getting younger and meaner, don't they?"

The small talk lasts for a couple minutes so the constable and Ryan, clearly acquainted, can catch up. Then Constable Harris asks me questions about what happened, if we have security footage we'd be willing to download and share, the usual. I explain that Joe didn't physically connect with my face, that I fell as a result of the Viking stepping in, but Harris asks if I want to press charges anyway, and although Ryan answers yes when I say no, I reassure the friendly, chatty policeman that I'd just like Joe Cirillo to be removed and banned from our idyllic corner of the world.

"Freaking Americans coming up here all macho and shit," Harris says. "Good thing he didn't have his gun with him." He laughs at his unoriginal joke, clicks his pen, and after another round of handshakes, he's out the door.

Neither Ryan nor I comment on the fact that we're both American by birth, Canadian citizens by paperwork and the good grace of Her Late Majesty Queen Elizabeth (Canada is a British commonwealth). Also neither of us have guns. It is not a requirement of American citizenship to be armed, even if it appears that way to the rest of the world.

Whatever.

My cheek hurts.

And Ryan slobbered all over my yogurt pop. Very rude considering how I manhandled *his* yogurt pop not even an hour ago. Metaphorically speaking.

"Come on, Mohammed Ali. No more floating like a butterfly for you tonight." Ryan wraps his good arm around my shoulders, waves to my dad who's wiping crumbs off his shirt from another of Miss Betty's scones, and leads me back to our apartment. He's quiet the whole way, a smirk on his lips. I'm not sure if he's annoyed with yet another of my genius moves or if his painkillers have kicked in.

He opens our suite door and nods for me to enter first. "I have something for you," he says as I walk inside. "I was going to wait until Valentine's Day, but maybe you could use it now."

"If it's not an all-inclusive trip to somewhere with no other people and an endless dessert buffet, I'm not interested."

Ryan smiles. I wince with my return attempt since, as noted, my cheek hurts and my eye has swollen into a slit. "Sit."

I obey and sink into our very cozy couch.

"Close your eyes, or your eye, I guess. And no peeking."

Again, I do as I'm told. I hear a bit of one-handed maneuvering from across the room before Ryan sits beside me. I take a healthy sniff of his freshly bathed skin.

"Give me your hand."

"You're ready for that again?"

He snorts. "Smart-ass. I'm serious. Your hand, please."

I flatten my palm in the air between us and upon it he places what feels like an envelope.

"You can look now."

I do, and indeed it is a red envelope the size of a greeting card. Scrawled across the front in Ryan's signature chicken scratch: *OPEN ME FIRST.*

"What is it?"

He shrugs. "You gotta do what it says."

His face reveals nothing other than a satisfied smirk that a person gets when offering a present.

"Will I like it?" I tease my index finger under the seal, careful not to rip the paper (or my skin). Once open, I slide its contents free —a single flat card, nice quality card stock, like a Save the Date or RSVP card, its message printed in ornate script:

> *Where Oliver frolics without a care,*
> *And memories of Clara fill the air,*
> *See where otters play and roam,*
> *In your heart's collected home,*
> *'Neath Enhydra's gaze, find me there.*

"Wait—is this a clue? Did you hide a present for me?" I push up from the couch with the card in hand, and the red envelope tumbles onto the area rug. "It is! This is a clue!"

I read it again, slower. "OK, I might be too dumb for this."

"Hardly." He snorts. "It took three of us to write that limerick."

"OK, Oliver . . . my tattoo! And Clara, our baby sea otter who's now a big girl . . . *'In your heart's collected home.'* Oh! My curio cabinet!" I drop the card onto the coffee table and bound across the room to the charming glass and wood collectibles hutch Ryan made for me after we got together. Inside on the four shelves sit my ever-expanding treasure trove of sea otters in all shapes and sizes.

I open the narrow doors and peer inside. The bottom shelf otters have been scooted to accommodate a perfectly square box wrapped in shiny red paper with a simple pink bow. "How did I not notice this before? When did you hide it?"

"I am very sneaky."

"Indeed, you are." I pluck the box from the shelf carefully. My prized pieces are made from glass, sandstone, compressed and carved volcanic ash, as well as wood, bronze, and even a gaudy rhinestone-encrusted, painted pewter otter that opens up to reveal a matching necklace in its belly. If there's a sea otter trinket in this world, my beloveds will find it and send it to me.

"Come. Sit. Open it before I fall asleep."

"Your drugs kicking in?"

Ryan bobs his head once as I ease back onto the cushion beside him. "Maybe I should share my pill sorter with you." He scrutinizes my latest fleshy insult.

"As tempting as that is . . . I'll be fine because you gave me a present!"

"So, are you gonna . . . open it?"

"But Valentine's Day isn't until next week—and I don't have anything for you."

Ryan leans over and lightly kisses me. "You're my Valentine, babe. Always and forever and every single day." Another quick kiss. "Now hurry up. I am seriously fading here."

The wrapping is lovely—I don't want to tear it—but his lids are about to slam closed on our evening. Paper removed, I gently tease the lid off the white cube. It's too big to be a ring box, plus Ryan knows I'm not a jewelry girl. He bought me a sparkly Canadian diamond tennis bracelet for our first anniversary and I promptly lost it. (It turned up again . . . a year later, in the couch, located when I was looking for Elsbeth's binky. Funny how you find stuff when you're looking for *other* stuff.)

A pillow of cotton fluff conceals whatever is nestled within. I pluck it free, and inside on a little blue pillow is another gem for my collection. "Ryan . . ."

I pull it out—an exquisitely carved and painted northern sea otter, her face and head blond, a perfect little black nose, with bristly, three-dimensional, wheat-colored whiskers dangling from her tiny cheeks. "Where on earth did you find her? She's my favorite!"

Ryan grins. "I had Matthias make it for you."

I look up at him. "Matthias the hockey player? From your team? Isn't he, like, seventeen?"

"He's eighteen, and yes, he carved it. His dad is a professional carver, like a real artist, so Matthias has been doing this stuff since he was old enough to hold a knife."

"She's . . . incredible." I examine every centimeter of the figurine. "I cannot believe a kid made this."

"Sweden has long winters. Said if he wasn't on the ice, he was carving."

I set the newest member of my *Enhydra lutris* collection on the coffee table and lean close to this living embodiment of perfection, speaking against his soft lips. "Thank you. I absolutely adore her. You are the best husband ever, Ryan Fielding."

He kisses me back, slow and languid. When he pulls free, his eyes beg for respite. "Happy early Valentine's Day, wife."

"I love you."

"I love you too. And I would love you even more if you would help me to bed because I cannot feel my tongue anymore."

I laugh and then stand to help him up from the couch. "When you're awake and relatively pain-free, you must allow me to show my gratitude properly."

He drapes his uninjured arm over my shoulders and we shuffle across the living room to our bedroom. "There is nothing more I look forward to than your demonstration of gratification." He practically slurs the words. I pull the sheet back, gently remove his robe, and ease him onto the bed. He settles into the mountain of pillows, a playful smile tugging at his mouth. "Speaking of gratification, there's more to Valentine's Day than one little otter."

I settle the sheet and the quilt over his legs and torso, careful not to put too much weight on his buggered arm.

"Oh yeah?"

"Just you wait, Porter. Cupid ain't got nothin' on me." His grin remains, even as his eyes close. With a soft hand, I push his wavy brown hair off his forehead and caress his bristly cheek with the back of my fingers. One more gentle kiss to his lips because I can't help myself, although bending over him reminds me of the pulse pounding in my cheek.

Mushroom Cap Joe would never do something so sweet as to commission a tiny hand-carved otter sculpture for the object of his affection.

Then again, I think tonight, the only thing Joe will be carving are his initials in an RCMP holding cell.

I love it when shit works out.

10

So rarely are we all together in one location—yes, Miss Betty and I live here full time and Tanner, Sarah, and Elsbeth are a boat ride away in their cabin—but Ryan is on the mainland months out of the year, and Dad lives in Portland and works way too many hours at the hospital. Point is, when it is declared that we will be dining as a family tonight, I'm thrilled.

Growing up, it was just me and Dad. And then me and Dad and Aurora the *very* strange stepmother and her daughter Moonstar and that *fucking goat,* omigod.

Yes. Mangala is still alive. He is, like, seventeen years old or something unnatural. I fear his evil will make him seventeen forever and he will never die and eventually he will become the head of the Volturi and rule over all the vampires with his lethal twisted horns and then when I am an old woman, Mangala will still be as evil as ever and, in fact, alongside his coven of ageless Italian vampires and a few sparkly cuties from Washington State, they will have taken over the government.

Wait. On second thought . . .

Anyhoo, tonight we're doing dinner, a proper dinner, in Miss Betty's apartment instead of the dining room where everyone has access to us to ask their burning questions about Ryan's injury, how his team is doing this year, or even *Hollie someone just hurled in the lobby restroom can you come handle it.* We have a houseful of romantic revelers with a two-for-one special on Cupid's Cure (it's red and bubbly and potent). There will definitely be some hurling going on, but Hollie Porter is *out of office*, bitches!

It's a tight fit with eight people (I invited Tabby because I do believe she is my cosmic twin from another dimension), and it smells *so* good in here. Miss Betty has a full-size kitchen in her place, so she's able to make two pans of her famous lasagna and fresh Italian bread to go along with it and a giant bowl of salad that looks tasty enough, *I* might even scoop some onto my plate, even if said salad consists of green things best served to rabbits. And immortal goats.

Tanner and Unca Ryan make a fort out of the couch cushions for Elsbeth and Acorn (rather, Unca supervises from a comfy armchair), though Acorn would much rather attack the cushions than hide under them, so the feat is rather Sisyphean. Tabby and Sarah and I sit at the dining table sipping a yummy Pinot and watch my dad and Miss Betty in the kitchen behaving as the grown-ups in the room—Dad does dishes while Miss Betty whips up whatever she's doing for dessert, the two of them talking about I don't even know what, but Dad makes Betty laugh so hard, she has to stop her whisking and bend in half for a beat.

Miss Betty has birthed four children. She says when she laughs too hard, she pees a little because "everything is loosey-goosey down there," which is way more information than I needed to know about my mother-in-law but also continues to freak me out about having children because I rather like everything high and tight in my undercarriage. Maybe I should mention to Dad not to make her laugh so hard or she will pee her pants for real.

Although watching them is nice. Dad is smiling, his heavy brow usually creased with the weight of the world smoother than usual, and Miss Betty—well, she always seems happy, though I know that's not true. She's been a widow and single mother since her Ryan and Tanner's father died over twenty years ago. That's why living at Revelation Cove has been so good for her. She has a whole new flock of ducklings to look after, and all this activity and frenetic energy (and all the people looking out for her) will keep her young and spry for decades to come.

Tabs has been filling Sarah in on the latest spa gossip, though I've heard it already in our running chat thread. My ears tune in when their convo transitions to talk of real estate. I raise my hand.

"I'm sorry, I was spacing out. Back up—are you guys moving?" I ask Sarah.

She looks over her shoulder toward her husband and daughter and indicates that I should keep my voice down. "Elsbeth needs to start kindergarten. She needs to be around other kids or else she will grow up to be that weird genius no one knows how to talk to."

"Those are the types who change the world," I say.

"Yeah, and they're weird as hell and completely self-absorbed and a little sociopathic. I don't want her to grow up isolated from the bigger world."

"I do . . . I don't want anyone near Elsbeth. She's too perfect."

"Ha!" Sarah laughs and sips. "She's five going on thirty. The kid needs way more than I can give her and there are only so many nature walks we can go on. She can name pretty much every plant and animal on our island."

"Your kid is way smarter than I will ever be," Tabby says, topping up her glass.

"So, are you going to Vancouver or . . .? Is Tanner leaving, because seriously, Sarah, this place will implode without him."

"No, no, he's not leaving. Nothing like that. And not Vancouver. We're only thinking about maybe Salt Spring. It's a tight-knit community and they have good schools."

"If you want her to be a certified genius, you should go to the mainland. Put her in one of those posh rich-people schools in North Vancouver."

I widen my eyes at Tabby in an effort to telepathically scold her for giving Sarah any ideas.

Our conversation is interrupted by Elsbeth's shriek and Acorn's bark—the pillow castle has collapsed and tickle torture is underway and I lock eyes with my boy toy sitting across the room and he gives me that smirk that warms up all my tingly bits.

"OK, good people of the village, it's time to eat!" my dad announces as Miss Betty pulls the second bubbling pasta pan from the oven and slides it onto a bamboo cutting board.

"I want more intel," I say quietly to Sarah just before her daughter bounds into her arms.

"It will all work out, just as it always does." Sarah, the eternal optimist. Elsbeth crawls across her mom and into my lap, singing her latest musical composition that I think was probably borrowed from Our Lady Taylor Swift but includes original lyrics about Acorn and sea otters.

That's my girl.

The table is elbow to elbow, except Ryan who gets lots of space to avoid jarring his boo-boo. The confabulation barely slows, only to allow diners to take a bite, chew, moan about how good it is, and then inhale another forkful. Dad teases Miss Betty about how she should start a franchise with this lasagna recipe; Miss Betty counters about not wanting the headache of having to figure out what to do with the billion dollars that would flow in.

When we reach the part when we're mopping our plates with what's left of the bread so as not to waste a single drop of sauce or cheese, Dad taps the side of his wineglass with his spoon. The table silences, although Elsbeth is intrigued by Grampa Bob's attention-grabbing maneuver and lunges for the nearest utensil, only to give a searing glare at her dad when he moves her water glass out of her reach.

"So, this is a good time for my big announcement, since we're all together."

I stare at my father—a big announcement? He has said nothing prior to this moment about this, and we text back and forth daily. He smiles at me, revealing the bit of green stuck between two front teeth. I'm about to gesture when Miss Betty hands him a water glass and says, "Swish."

Nurse Bob obliges without skipping a beat. He smiles again for the whole table. "Better?"

We nod our approval.

"OK, so, as I was saying before I was so rudely interrupted by a rogue piece of basil, um, I am . . . retiring!"

The table erupts with cheers and congratulations. Elsbeth finally reaches a glass and bangs her spoon against it, the tinkling bordering on aggressive. She's gonna break—

Sarah smoothly relocates it.

"Retiring?" I ask. "Are you sick? Oh my god, are you having health issues and you just didn't know how to tell me?" My throat tightens. Ryan grips my shoulder and squeezes gently.

"No, no, honey, nothing like that. I'm just tired of the bureaucracy, the long hours, the canceled time off, and the young hires—I don't want to sound like a stereotype, but our new staff are a bunch of babies. They complain about everything."

"Oh, I hear that loud and clear," Miss Betty replies.

"Dad—" I intervene before the two of them spiral into a conversation about boomers and Gen X versus millennials and Gen Z because I require further elucidation on this truth bomb he's just dropped.

"So, wow, you're retiring. That's good," I say, my words probably meant to calm myself more than him. "You'll have more time for yourself, then, to do stuff you've always wanted to do but were too busy being Superdad."

"Hear! Hear!" Sarah says, lifting her wineglass. More tapping and tinkling of glassware. (This must be very confusing for Elsbeth.)

Dad sips and scans the attendees, pausing on the youngest member of our party. "I'm not retiring so I can sit in a La-Z-Boy and watch bowling. I'm actually starting a new business. My own business. Figured it's time to step into the twenty-first century and become a *solopreneur*."

More cheers and applause.

Except I'm worried—if he knows that word, he's probably been spending too much time on social media, maybe taking advice from slick-haired scammers who promise a million-dollar business is possible in just five days if you open an Etsy store or hawk some manner of essential oil or green health powder. The snake oil salesmen of yesteryear would be so envious of their modern-day brethren.

"I am still going to be working in healthcare. My new business will involve an outreach program where I will visit nursing homes, assisted living facilities, anywhere a senior member of our population would live after moving out of their primary residence. I'll be providing education and resources about sexual health for those of us later in life. From there, I will arrange sessions at community centers for seniors who do still live independently in the—"

"Wait." I interrupt. "What does that mean?"

"That means your dad is going to teach sex ed to horny old people," Tabby interprets. "I think that's an *awesome* idea, Nurse Bob. Just because you're wrinkly and slow doesn't mean you don't appreciate a visit to Jiffy Lube now and again."

Tabby's response is met with giggles, but before I can clarify, before I can wrap my head around the visual of my father standing in front of a group of septuagenarians, sliding a condom over a banana or narrating a slideshow about genital warts, Miss Betty chimes in.

Of course she does.

"I, for one, think this is a brilliant idea, Bob." She pats his hand where it rests on the table and then looks back at all of us. "Not all my 'kneads' can be met by baking alone." Except when she says *needs*, she mimes kneading bread, and the table groans and quickly moves into awkward chuckles. I am unsettled as images of sweet Miss Betty taking it from behind flashes on the screen in my brain.

"Who wants whisky?" I jar the table in my haste to stand.

"I do!" Elsbeth shouts.

11

"But why didn't he tell me ahead of time?"

"Probably because he was worried what you would think." Ryan leans back into pillow mountain. Due to his current condition, alcohol is a hard pass. I cannot say the same for myself, though I did stop after two—three?—to ensure his safe return to our marital bed.

With Ryan sorted, I move to my side and begin my own preslumber ritual. "He's my dad—he knows I would do anything for him, that I support whatever decisions he makes."

"That might be true, but you seemed a little freaked out after his big announcement."

"Forgive me for having a moment where I couldn't stop envisioning my dad talking about orgasms and syphilis in front of a group of old farts."

"If you're lucky, you will be an old fart one day."

"You know what I mean." I toss my bra across the padded bench at the end of our bed.

"Are you telling me that when we're dropping our teeth in a glass before bed that you're not going to let me touch those fun bags?"

I laugh. "Babe, when we're old, you aren't gonna wanna touch these fun bags. They'll be more like sad thrift-store Samsonites by then."

Ryan's turn to chuckle. "Hollie Porter, I will always want to touch your Samsonites. Even when I'm a toothless geezer."

"Well, you are considerably older than I am, so when you're ready for elder care, I will be, what, thirty-seven?" Carefully, I slide under the bedcovers and nudge as close to Ryan as I can without bumping his arm cradled across his chest. "Also, I plan on keeping my teeth."

"Is this where I insert a joke about dentures and blow jobs?"

"Oh my god, *stop*. Please. And do not make that joke to my dad —he probably has some statistic about dentures and blow jobs, which is why he's becoming a sex fairy to randy pensioners." I lean up on my elbow to look at his face. "How's your pain?"

"I'm good. Mild headache. Arm's fine. Blowing out my knee was way worse. This is just annoying." He nods at me. "How's the eye?"

I shrug. "It's a black eye. I'm more worried about the cut leaving yet another scar."

"Scars are hot. They make you look tough."

"Yeah, great, because tough is the look I was going for."

Ryan snickers and then nudges me to move down, pulling at the pillow under my head.

"What, you want service? Now?"

"No, perv. Scoot down a bit so I can play with your hair."

"Oh. Well. OK, then." I accommodate, positioning myself so he can run his fingers through hair that probably could use a wash. My husband knows how to relax me, his fingertips light against my forehead and temples.

"This is a good thing, Hols. Your dad looks happy. Relieved to be leaving a job that has been wearing him down for years. And if he thinks he can build a business around teaching safe sex to old folks, more power to him. I'd be interested in sitting in on one of his—"

"Nope. Nope. Nuh-uh. If you need instructions on how to use a penis pump, I have an iPad in the kitchen and a VPN. I will find you whatever you want."

Ryan flattens his warm hand against my cheek, the bed shaking with his laugh. "You're all the penis pump I need, Hollie Porter."

More romantic words have never been spoken.

❧

"Babe . . ."

"Mmm."

"Hollie." Soft fingertips tug on my earlobe. "Your alarm is going off."

My eyes resist opening but my eardrums engage and sure enough, my wake-up call chimes from my nightstand. I awaken in the same spot I dozed off, my limbs heavy from lack of movement.

"You snored last night."

"Did not." I push up and grab my phone to silence it before flopping back on my pillow.

"That's a good thing. Means you slept hard. Or it means you're developing sleep apnea, which isn't so good."

"Why are you awake?" I ask, cracking my eyelids to look over at him. "Wait—you're up already? Are you hurting? Is everything OK?"

"Everything is fine. I woke up at four and couldn't get back to sleep, so I've been watching game tape and answering emails."

"Answering emails."

"One-handed typing sucks."

"You could've just waited for me. If you dictate, I can type."

"Not necessary. Besides, you were out. You would've slept through an earthquake."

"Don't joke about earthquakes. You know how I feel about the island cracking in two and sliding into the ocean, taking us along with it."

Ryan smirks. "I made coffee. Get up."

I slide deeper under the blankets. "I don't wannnnnna."

121

Ryan's weight lifts off the mattress. "Then I guess I will just have to find someone else to give this next present to."

I throw the blankets back. "You got me another present?"

"Every day until Valentine's Day, my queen."

"Shut up. You did not."

He winks and walks away, pausing at the door threshold to wiggle his luscious ass in those sinfully tight gray sweatpants.

"Tease." But it works. I jump up, quickly shower and brush my teeth, and throw on my robe. It's just after six a.m. I've still got time to dress and paint my face to be at the front desk by seven when the breakfast buffet opens.

Ryan stands at the kitchen island, coffee cup in hand, eyes glued to his laptop.

"Is that yesterday's game?" I ask. They lost in overtime. Nils texted as we were finishing dessert. Tabby tried to act cool, but I always notice the sparkle in her eye whenever Nils's name comes up.

"Yeah." Ryan pauses the video and nods at the steaming cup he's poured for me, its contents the perfect shade of light brown. Gotta love a man who knows exactly how you like your morning caffeine injection. "Your next clue." From his back pocket, he pulls a red envelope, a twin to the one from last night, and slides it across the island.

It reads *OPEN ME SECOND*. I do, of course slicing open my flesh on the paper because why not. I suck on the line of blood so I don't smear it on the card as I release it from its crimson sheath. Again, the clue has been printed in ornate calligraphy on heavy card stock. I'm impressed. This took some serious planning.

Where the Salish whispers tales under the moon's soft glow,
In a vessel of escape from a storm long ago,
Spy-hopping orca need not appear,
Pressed sand creates a receptacle so clear,
To hold the murmurs of love's words so dear.

I read it a second time, aloud. "OK, so—this has something to do with the water, maybe the rowboat I stole that night?" Ryan grins and sips his coffee, watching me puzzle it out. I reread the last two lines again in a whisper.

"This is, like, a legit treasure hunt," I say, grinning.

"It is."

"I need to get dressed and go look!"

"That sounds like a fun idea."

I pop off my stool and *carefully* lean on tiptoes to kiss my beloved. "Come on, then. Let's get moving."

Ryan's goofy grin doesn't disappear as I help him dress—except when I stop to examine and apply soothing lotion to the fresh chafing around his neck from his arm sling. I tell him to ask my dad about it when they have their next PT session, which right now only involves *very* gentle range of motion so his shoulder doesn't seize up. Until the headaches subside and his arm bone has had a chance to graft, Ryan's on limited duty—and he's gonna get bitchy about what he's not allowed to do here soon.

I'm applying a final coat of mascara to my twelve eyelashes when my phone lights up on the bathroom vanity. A text from Dad:

> Maybe overindulged on too much good food and drink. Feeling a little shaky this morning. See you at lunch.

My dad rarely drinks, and I only saw him sip a single pour of the pricey Dalmore.

> Is it food poisoning? Can I bring you anything?

> Nothing like that. Don't fret.

Except I will fret a little because at Dad's last thorough physical, apparently his cholesterol is elevated (he blames too many staff birthday cakes), his blood pressure has been on the high side (he blames stress from staff who are always taking days off to celebrate said birthdays), and his sugars have been flirting with diabetes (refer to aforementioned cakes).

Ryan pauses in the bathroom doorway. "Ma'am, will you kindly lace up my boots?" Our eyes meet in the mirror. "Why are you biting your lip? What's wrong?"

"Nothing, it's fine." I drop my mascara into my makeup bag. "My dad says he's not feeling great." I show Ryan the text.

"He did eat two servings of the lasagna."

"Yeah, no, I know . . . I just worry. Now that he's announced his retirement to the universe, I'm worried a heart attack will try to take him out like a rogue wave. You hear about that happening all the time—"

Ryan steps behind me and wraps his arm around my chest, both of us facing the mirror. Every time I see us together in a reflection or photograph, I want to pinch myself. How did I get so lucky?

"Stop worrying. Nurse Bob is healthy as a horse and too stubborn to do anything but exactly what he wants to do—and that does not include heart attacks."

We stare at each other for a few beats until I'm distracted by the toothpaste spatter on the glass.

"If it would ease your worry, let's go down and make him a plate, grab some Tums or aspirin or whatever, then you can take it to his room before we resume your treasure hunt."

"You wouldn't mind?"

"Absolutely not." He kisses the top of my head. "Now please double-knot my shoes so I don't trip and break something else."

12

I don't know what medications my dad has been prescribed, but given his occupation, I'm sure he has a handle on whatever he's supposed to be taking. Although he is a guy—and men are notoriously stubborn about self-care until body parts gravely dysfunction or fall off.

I can't tell you how many times he's tried to go into work only to be diagnosed with pneumonia when he arrived for his shift, breathless and wheezing from the walk across the parking garage. All it would've taken is a single glance at his reflection to notice he looked on the brink of death. It's a good thing he's surrounded by so many professional women who don't put up with his nonsense. They've probably saved his life on more than one occasion.

I have a tray loaded with fresh tomato juice, a bottle of sugar-free Gatorade, peppermint-ginger tea, buttered white toast, a banana, two scrambled eggs, even a steaming bowl of chicken broth, just in case. Chef Joseph knows how to put together a rescue breakfast. In a small plastic cup, I have two each of Tums, Tylenol, and Advil. Bases = covered.

The second treasure hunt clue is burning a hole in my pocket, but Ryan and I agreed to meet up in half an hour to proceed with my adventure. Tray balanced on my arm—a skill that has only taken me the past five years to master—I greet resort guests in the wide halls on my way to Dad's room.

I stop at his door and raise my left hand to knock but then pause. What if he's asleep? I don't want to wake him. The meal is covered with a silver warming bonnet so everything will be edible for another hour at least. I could just leave it on the small dining table and he can eat when he wakes up. I put my ear against the door to listen for a TV or even him on his phone.

It's quiet.

From my keychain, I fumble with the master key card and gently ease open the door. The rooms are designed like most hotels—the bathroom on the right or left upon entry, the main sleeping chamber just after. We always try to give Dad one of the multiroom suites, but he insists on a regular guest room so we can save the suites for paying guests. Straight ahead upon entering, a rustic wood, two-person round table sits in the corner. I'll just leave the tray for him—

Except as the bed comes into view, I am witness to a scene no child should ever see their parent in.

Even worse, the scene involves my husband's parent too.

"Oh! Oh my god, I am so sorry—" I back up too abruptly and smack my elbow into the forty-five-degree angle where the walls join and Dad's breakfast topples with all the grace of a china cabinet in an aftershock, egg and juice and broth and tea flying everywhere and not at all in slow motion.

I drop to the floor, my head down, hurrying to gather the spilled tray contents, mumbling "Oh my god, oh my god, I am so sorry," over and over again while Miss Betty fumbles for the blanket to cover herself. My dad bounds off the bed and throws on what I hope are boxers but Jesus, I'm not about to look up. Seeing his white ass in the air like that—

No, no, no, no, no, LA LA LA LA LA.

"Hollie, leave the food. Just go on and we'll clean it up."

"Right. Sorry, Dad. So sorry, Miss Betty. I'm leaving now." On all fours, I pivot and crawl, head down, toward the door, fumbling with the handle to get it open so I can escape. Once I'm in the hall, breathless, my face on fire, I lean against the wall, hand over my galloping heart.

On the other side of the door, my father and Miss Betty burst into laughter.

$$\approx$$

"You're making a bigger deal out of this than it is," Ryan says, placing a glass of OJ in front of me.

"I am *not*. If you'd walked in on that—seeing our *parents* doing—"

"Stop. One replay is more than enough for this lifetime." Ryan rounds the island and sits on the neighboring stool. "I mean, yeah, it's embarrassing to walk in on anyone doing that, especially your dad—"

"And your *mom*."

Ryan brings his coffee cup to his lips.

"Wait—if they're a couple, does that mean you'll be my stepbrother? I think there are laws against that. We're *married*, Ryan. We cannot become stepsiblings."

"It was sex, Hollie, not a marriage proposal."

I stand from my stool, arms crossed over my chest. "You are not upset enough about this."

"What is there to be upset about? Is it a little weird that our parents are hooking up? Yeah. But isn't it also kind of cool that your dad, who is younger than my mother, is offering her something she has been without for years?"

My rebuttal withers on my tongue. Miss Betty has been a widow for a long time, and though she's told me on a number of occasions that she was so in love with Ryan's dad, that they were soul mates, she's confided that she was resentful after he died, that he didn't take better care of himself and stop the smoking and drinking so they could grow old together.

"Now you make me sound like a swamp-dwelling goblin who hates love."

Ryan laughs and gestures for me to drop my pout and step closer. I do, resting my cheek on his broad shoulder. "I cannot scrub the image from my brain. My dad's ass cheeks are *really* white."

"I doubt they see much sun. Maybe we should tell him about Wreck Beach."

"Oh sure, that's a great idea. Then he and your mom could go sunbathe nude *together*. 'Bob, can you help me with sunscreen right here—'"

"Got it. Thank you." He kisses the crown of my head. "I am sorry for the trauma you experienced this morning, my darling wife." He nudges me back and touches his nose tip to mine. "At least our parents have excellent taste. I mean, I can hardly keep my hands off you."

I kiss my mister, the taste of coffee on his lips. His signature scent, woodsy and clean with the spicy fragrance of a new beard oil he's been trying, revs my engine. "OK, yes, I will concede that point. I can see why they'd be attracted to each other."

Ryan feathers his lips over mine. "And no one is getting married."

Another kiss. "So we won't be stepsiblings."

He licks my upper lip. "I'd still want you, even if you were my stepsister."

"Ew," I say. "We are neither vampires nor the royal family."

He smirks. "Are you prepared to get back to this morning's first order of business?"

The treasure hunt! I'd forgotten about it in my desperation to bleach my brain after the breakfast delivery gone awry.

I pluck the card from my back pocket, glad it was not dislodged in my haste to escape, and read it once again.

"Follow me, sir."

13

The morning breeze is brisk, as one would expect just six weeks into a new year, but the air smells so fresh, I will never take it for granted. I grew up in Portland, so I'm more than familiar with big-city scents, but on our island, it's all trees and sea and birds all the time.

I am endlessly grateful to be allowed to live at Revelation Cove, and in Canada, for that matter, even if sometimes it is lonely with Ryan in Langley for the Giants' hockey season *and* if I still can't help giggling whenever a Canadian pronounces *Mazda* or *drama* or *llama* with that funny *a* (*draaa-muh* vs. American *draw-muh*). However, right now, my Prince Charming is home, and with my arm looped through his, we're moseying down the walkway toward the docks under a mostly cloudy but not menacing sky as if we have all the time in the world, and there isn't a Mazda with llama drama anywhere in sight.

When we passed through the lobby and bid good morning to our staff already situated at their battle stations, only two guests paused us to ask Ryan how he's feeling, about this year's playoff run for his team. And being the consummate professional both on and off the ice, Ryan responded with the charismatic charm that turns first-time guests into regulars.

Miss Betty wasn't at the front desk like she usually is this time of the morning, but we are not thinking about where Miss Betty is or what she's doing because she's a grown-ass woman, as am I, so if my mother-in-law wants to have a leisurely morning in the arms of her lover, so be it.

Shudder.

"Stop thinking about it," Ryan teases.

"I'm trying."

Ryan pauses where the concrete yields to the engineered-wood planking of the docks. "Lead the way, Mrs. Fielding."

"See, that doesn't help. Mrs. Fielding is your mother. And your mother is currently getting drilled into a mattress by my—"

"Hols, stop. Seriously." He shakes his head. "Shared trauma is great and all, but now you're being mean."

"Sorry. I'm just wondering if my dad will want to legally adopt you so that we're full siblings—oww!" I slap at his good hand pinching my muffin-shaped pooch currently defying the boundaries set by the waistband of my uniform cargo pants. What can I say—a good man, good food and drink, and unfettered access to the resort's pâtissier have filled out my pear shape nicely.

"Please lead on, my precious princess." As if to punctuate his request, his stomach growls loudly. He will require sustenance imminently.

With the clue card cupped in my palm, I read it through again and set off down the dock toward where the rowboats should be tied off. Except, duh—our dinghy fleet has been pulled from the strait for winter, stacked three high on the double-sided steel frame under a metal-roofed canopy.

"My rowboat has been decommissioned," I say.

Ryan simply bobs his head once.

"You're not going to give me anything else?"

He mimes zipping of his lips.

That night when I commandeered the small wooden boat, I'd been completely unprepared for the strength of the current and had no idea an impressive thunderstorm was en route. I was feeling sorry for myself thanks to a sprained ankle from ill-advised shoes, my newly single heart stinging from betrayal of that slimy businessman who showered me with attention and innuendo, at least until he showed up in the dining room with his perfect wife and children and I morphed into an invisible idiot with one pathetic smirk delivered from across the dining room as he pulled out her chair.

In hindsight? Thank the gods it all went down that way. Pretty sure Roger Dodger's moved on to another trophy wife and left the first one (and their two kids) fighting for alimony. I hope she sues for punitive damages too—Roger was way too tan for a man his age, in this climate.

But to the task at hand—if my dinghy is out of service, the next logical place to look would be the cabin cruiser Ryan rescued me in that fateful night. He remains quiet, his lips playfully twisted as I slowly step backward in the direction of the boat. *Yes*, I'm mindful of where the dock ends and the water begins so I will not be providing further entertainment in the way of a slapstick tumble into the strait. I've done that plenty of times already so it's not really funny anymore.

I pause alongside the Fielding family vessel and point. "Am I getting warmer?"

"Sweltering."

Carefully, I step onto the outboard deck and unzip the canvas cover protecting the stern seating area. Before stepping inside, I turn to Ryan. "You want help boarding?"

"I'll wait here. Go find your treasure."

Every time I set foot on this boat, I think of that night when Ryan rescued me, the nights we've spent in the forward cabin in various stages of undress, the many times we've gone to observe my beloved sea otters, even our wedding day when Ryan secretly arranged to have the ceremony on Otter Beach instead of at the resort . . .

I still get choked up thinking about that day, how incredibly kind and thoughtful he was, how, from the first moment I met him, Ryan

Fielding has always looked out for me. Especially when Lucy Collins, my long-lost mother, reappeared and tried her best to upstage every single thing. Looking around the interior of this boat that's been in the Fielding clan for years, it's nothing but good memories. The best.

"You OK in there?"

"Yup!" I should probably look around.

Cupboards, crannies, under couches, in the cozy privy, and lastly in the forward cabin.

I should've checked their first.

It's where we first revealed our compatible body parts to each other. That was a fun night.

Smack-dab in the middle of the bed sits a brown paper gift bag, its exterior decorated with what look to be hand-drawn hearts and flowers. I collect the red-ribbon handles and exit the cabin, not peeking into the bag until I rejoin my husband. "Found it!"

"About time. I was about to drop a crab pot to see about getting myself some breakfast."

"Har har." I rezip the canopy and step onto the dock. "Should I open it now?"

"I thought that's what you were doing inside."

"No, I wanted to give you the joy of watching me discover your creative generosity."

"I would love nothing more."

I stick my tongue out at him and kneel on the dock. From within the craft-paper bag, I extract a big jar, clear glass, a big red bow wrapped around its lid and mouth, the inside filled with tiny paper cranes in every color of the rainbow. I recall part of his clue: *Pressed sand creates a receptacle so clear*. "'Pressed sand'—you meant glass!"

"Indeed."

"Ryan, you are so damn smart."

"I did all right in eighth grade science." He nods at the jar as I stand. "So, this present has a rule."

"A rule?"

"Kind of." He taps its side. "There are three hundred and sixty-five birds in here. I tried to do origami otters, but they were too complicated." He twists off the lid and pulls out a single pink crane and hands it to me. "Unfold it."

"But . . . it's so cute. I don't wanna ruin it."

"It's OK. Go ahead."

I set the jar back into the paper bag to prevent any chance of catastrophe and then carefully unfold the origami. "I can't believe you folded all these . . . how long did it take?"

"It's not polite to ask how the sausage is made."

"Mmm, sausage." I waggle my brows suggestively and eye his crotch.

With the last fold undone, I stare at the perfect square of paper, upon which is a message:

Because you make me laugh every single day.

My eyes and nose sting. Ryan closes the distance between us and wraps his hand around my nape. "Three hundred and sixty-five reasons why I love you. So, the rule is, you can open all of them at once, or you can dole them out, one a day, like a Valentine's advent calendar."

"Ryan . . . are you serious?"

"Do you like it? Is it super dorky?"

"Dude, come on. This is genius. You're the best fucking husband in the entire world." I tuck the note into my vest pocket and gently hug my man as the happy tears carve tracks in the freshly applied foundation that's already doing a woeful job of concealing my black eye.

Worth it.

I tip my head and meet his lips. Even his peepers are a bit glazed with emotion.

"How is this real life?" I whisper.

"Happy early Valentine's Day, Porter."

As we reenter the lobby, a blast of heat skitters over our chilled cheeks and fills our noses with the sumptuous aroma of morning food. The space is busy—guests heading into the spa or down the hall to the heated outdoor pool and hot tub or lined up at the concierge desk to sign out a pair of binoculars to do some wildlife watching from various spots on our island. We don't offer day cruises until April, though our winter guests are sometimes treated to a passing pod of transient orca. We have plenty of birds of prey in the neighborhood, as well as great blue heron, owls, and deer. Lots of creatures for our photography enthusiasts to fill their memory cards.

We haven't had a cougar sighting up here since Chloe, but that doesn't mean the feisty felines aren't hiding in the forests of nearby islands. (Fun fact: Vancouver Island, south of us, has the highest concentration of cougars anywhere in the world. And those suckers can swim.)

My sea otters (they're not really mine although yes they are) north of here, we leave alone most of the time. As a critically endangered species, they don't need human looky-loos disrupting their days. I will occasionally sneak up the strait to check in and count them, but that's with the express permission of Fisheries Canada. I learned my lesson after rescuing baby Clara.

The stream of humanity parts, and Miss Betty comes into view behind the front desk, smiling as she chats up a guest.

"Act normal," Ryan whispers in my ear.

Easy for him to say.

As we approach, Miss Betty's eyes light up at seeing her baby boy. "Good morning!" she chirps. "How're you feeling?"

Ryan releases my hand and steps behind the counter to hug his mom and kiss her cheek. "I'm good. We're just about to have breakfast. Have you eaten yet?"

I choke on my spit and launch into a coughing fit.

She would've eaten breakfast had I not spilled it all over the carpet of my dad's room.

"Um—" Cough, sputter. "I'm gonna—" Suck in a squeaky

breath. "Put this away first—" Still coughing, I hoist the gift bag. "Meet you in the dining room."

I leave before either has a chance to protest, coughing into my sleeve so I don't freak out anyone standing too close. Only I would choke on my own saliva with enough spirit to make it sound as if I'm dying of TB.

Just as I'm passing the sitting area, I notice Acorn in front of the fireplace, his paws wrapped around whatever toy he's chewing apart. I've never seen a dog go through toys the way he does.

Except—this toy—it's bright pink and it seems he's tearing off small chunks, pausing to chew like it's bubble gum before tearing into it again, the floor around his big paws littered with mutilated pink nuggets.

I approach, whispering so I don't restart the coughing fit. "Hey, buddy, what you got there? Did Miss Betty order you more goodies?"

I set my gift bag down slowly—if Acorn suspects he's in trouble, he'll bolt and take his prize with him. That's fine if it's a chewie toy he's supposed to have but not so fine when it's the remote control to the nearest TV. We've gone through at least a dozen in the last two years.

Except our remotes aren't typically neon pink.

"Whatcha doin' there, Acorn—"

Ohhhh, shit.

It's not a chewie toy or a remote control.

He's currently disassembling a vibrator that I'm almost positive belongs to me.

14

Acorn misunderstands when I try to take his "toy"—his doggie brain thinks I'm inviting him to a rousing game of tug-of-war, even though I'm really just trying to get this thing away from him before anyone notices or before he somehow activates it and it drops to skitter across the floor.

"Hollie Cat!" Elsbeth shouts from across the lobby. "Goo' morning! I'm here!"

Yes, of course you are.

She runs toward us and I strong-arm the vibrator from Acorn's mouth and drop it into the paper bag with my jar of love-soaked paper cranes.

"What are you guys doing?" Elsbeth rests a hand on my shoulder as I feverishly gather the torn pink chunks from the area rug. "Acorn, did you eat another toy?"

"Yup, he did."

"I'll help."

"NO!" In unison, Acorn barks and Elsbeth startles, her eyes widening. I have to divert before we move to full-on lip-wobbling, followed by the first tear. "I mean, Auntie's gonna clean it up. Have you had breakfast yet?"

Elsbeth sniffs and wipes at her eye. I scared her.

But I'm picking up pieces of silicone likely coated with unnamed germs from unmentionable body parts and now dog slobber on top of that—

"I'm sorry, baby girl. I didn't mean to yell. I just don't want you to get your hands icky, especially before breakfast."

"That's OK, Auntie. Mommy told me on the boat that you're having a tough day so that I should give you a hug as soon as I found you. And I found you!" She throws her arms around my neck and nearly topples me. I hug back, though careful not to touch her adorable North Face coat with my hands.

And if Sarah has told her child that Auntie Hollie is having a tough day, that means Ryan texted his brother to share this morning's salacious breaking news.

"Never a dull moment with you around, Hollie," Tanner says as he walks up behind us.

"That's why you pay me the big bucks." I'm still kneeling, balanced on one bent leg, trying like hell to cover the silicone chunks with the heel of my boot, even as Acorn nips and paws at my hand.

Elsbeth lets go of me and leaps into Tanner's arms. "Food, please, Daddy."

He raises an eyebrow at me and smiles at his daughter. "Yes, ma'am." Tanner then notices that I'm grabbing at chunks of unknown origin. Acorn thinks we're playing. "Did he chew up something he wasn't supposed to?"

"Yes." That's all I'm gonna say. "I got it. You guys go grab some food before it's all gone."

"Come eat pamcakes with me, Hollie Cat!" Elsbeth's tiny voice bounces off the ceiling.

"You save me a seat and I will be right there, OK? I'm just gonna clean up this mess."

Finally, they walk away, Elsbeth telling her dad how I scared her with my big voice but that I didn't mean it and it's just because Acorn is being a bad boy again.

I roll this golden repeat offender onto his back, checking

underneath him—sure enough, he's hiding bigger pieces of pink silicone. "You really are the worst dog, you know that?"

He stands and barks right in my face, dropping into a front bow like he's about to pounce, his tail whipping so hard, I fear with a few steps to the left, he will knock over the small vase of flowers on the coffee table behind him. Since I don't have any dog treats in my pocket, I quickly scan the area for any other distraction—aha! An actual Bully Stick he's *supposed* to be tearing apart.

I lunge and grab it, giving it a light toss across the sitting area, hoping he will give chase.

He does not. Only barks again, spraying me with dog breath.

"You cannot eat any more of this silicone," I growl at him, dropping every little piece into the bag to keep it out of his reach. I have no idea if silicone is dangerous for dogs—I mean, it has to be, right? Even if the stuff used on sex toys is considered food grade?

I need to go back to the apartment and see how much pink skin is missing from the device, i.e., how much is in this dog's stomach and what the ratio is of dog to silicone before it necessitates a trip to the emergency vet.

I'll need to tell someone. Miss Betty mostly cares for Acorn, so I should mention it—except then I have to explain what the dog ate, and I've already had one awkward encounter with my mother-in-law this morning.

Ugh.

Acorn finally loses interest when he realizes I'm not in the mood to roughhouse. Once I'm confident every pink shred has been plucked from the rug and surrounding area, I stand, my knees popping as I straighten and reach for my wonderful gift bag that is now filled with the remnants of—

"Hols."

I spin. "Dad."

He smiles. "Good morning."

"Hi. Hello. Good morning."

"Don't make this weird," he says, straightening his shirt.

"I'm not. It's not—it's fine. Everything's fine."

"We are consenting adults."

"Oh my god, Dad, you just said not to make it weird." I move to push past him but he gently grabs my arm.

"Betty is a wonderful woman. You know that."

"Yes, of course. That's great. I'm glad you're happy, that you're both happy."

Dad smiles again, and although he's trying to stay frosty, I can see the hint of embarrassment in his eyes.

"I just didn't need to see that part of your person"—I gulp and look at the ceiling for a beat—"first thing in the morning. Or ever, on any morning."

"It was very sweet of you to bring me breakfast."

"I thought you were sick. I was worried."

"Fit as a fiddle," Dad says, lifting his arms to showcase his hale and hearty self. He then notices the bag in my hand. "What's that?"

"Oh, it's just a Valentine's thing from Ryan."

"He's a good man. Apple doesn't fall far from the tree."

"Got it. OK, thanks." I can't make eye contact or keep the grin off my face as I step away. "Wait—" I pause. "Since I don't know that I could be any more traumatized than I already am this morning, how much do you know about dogs and silicone?"

My dad takes the lead on explaining to Miss Betty what Acorn did —she blushes almost as hard as I did after stumbling into their love den—and then he examines Acorn the best he can, considering he's a nurse for people and not canines. He suggests we call Acorn's vet, which Miss Betty does, delicately explaining that the dog ingested food-grade silicone without explaining in full where said silicone originated (or what it's likely seen in its lifetime).

The three of us are in the back office as she "Mm-hmms" and "Yes, sure, that makes sense" into her phone. Behind her, our wall of video monitors show a resort full of happy people. I understand that I am an adult, that my father and Miss Betty are both adults, but I don't know if this situation could get any more bizarre.

"OK, thank you so much, Dr. Welton. Say hello to Chris for us."

She slides her finger across her phone screen. "So, she said we are to watch his poops, see if the silicone passes. If he vomits or stops eating, then we need to take him in for scans. He could develop an intestinal blockage, depending how much he ate before you found him."

"Wonderful." A spike of pain pings up the side of my head—I'm clenching my teeth again.

"Do you not have the offending item in your bag there, Hols?" Dad points at the gift bag hanging from my fingertips. "We could try to put it back together—"

"Great idea. I will do that. You guys just watch his crap, yeah?"

Dad snorts and shakes his head; Miss Betty hides her smile behind her hand.

"Right then, good seeing you both. Busy day ahead. Make sure to eat!" With that, I'm out of the back office, practically sprinting down the hall so no one else attempts to stop me for idle chitchat about my dad's sex life.

Once in our apartment, I hoist my precious jar of origami birds from the bag, pluck an antibacterial wipe from the tub on the counter, and give the exterior glass surface a thorough wipe-down. I want to be able to touch it without being grossed out that it was in the bag with my dead vibrator.

From under the sink, I pull out a pair of nitrile cleaning gloves. Another double layer of paper towel spread on the kitchen island will serve as my operating table as I attempt to reconstruct the sex toy to estimate how much silicone is gurgling in Acorn's gut right now.

Dumb dog.

A sea otter would never eat a vibrator.

Acorn successfully degloved the main shaft and little rabbit head so that the mechanism itself is almost completely exposed. And there is no way I'll put this puzzle back together, not when many of the pieces are no bigger than my thumbnail. I stare at it for a few minutes, google the brand to see if that might help visualize, and then realize I could waste all day unraveling the mystery of the murdered vibrator.

I have a million other things to do. Cupid's Cove Ball is scheduled to start in mere hours.

I roll the deceased device into its paper towel shroud and deposit securely in our garbage can. I know we have a bin for recyclable electronics, but I don't know if this qualifies and I'm sure as shit not going to ask Bill, our facilities manager, or any of his crew. The Vikings would never let me live it down. I'm still finding paper cutouts of angry raccoons hidden here and there—and the Vikings weren't even present at Christmas to watch Momma Raccoon's assault happen in real time.

Hands washed, I make a quick cup of coffee and (try to) fix my face so I can get to work. The jar of winged love notes winks at me from the kitchen island—it's very tempting to pop the lid free and unfurl all the other reasons my incredibly thoughtful husband loves me—but patience is a virtue. Good things come to those who wait. Rome wasn't built in a day.

OK, no idea what Rome has to do with anything.

Before rejoining the troops, I pause to tidy the bedding and rearrange pillow mountain. The sun brightens the room but also highlights dust on everything. Maybe I should see if Elsie wants to earn an extra hundred bucks and clean for me this week. I open the drawer to the nightstand to put away my eyedrops and ChapStick—

And freeze.

My vibrator, the hot pink one with the long bit and the titillating bunny ears is sitting in its spot, intact, unmolested, unchewed by dog teeth.

Which means the one Acorn eviscerated belongs to someone else.

15

Acorn pooped.

A lot.

I still don't know whose vibrator he ate. I'm afraid to ask.

And I scrubbed a layer of skin off my hands once I realized it was not, in fact, my intimate instrument of ecstasy.

Last Saturday's Cupid's Cove Ball was a hit—just as we expected, lots of drunk people, loads of fun, great music provided by our staff band, the Garden Gnomes, who have been practicing every available moment since our Christmas fete (and it shows). Also, the addition of the Vikings, one twin on keyboards, the other on lead vocals, has helped tremendously.

Our first weekend of Valentine's revelers have returned to their lives and the next wave, many of whom are here for the "Galentine's Day" package, is arriving as we speak. Tabby is freaking out about accommodating all the mani-pedis, facials, makeovers, and massages; I told her worst-case scenario, we'll send the Vikings in to help.

The Galentines would *love* that.

Tomorrow is February 14, and *I'm* trying not to panic because Ryan, as he promised, has presented me with clues that have led to unbelievably cool gifts every day since the first one last week. I now have a gift certificate for a tattoo session with this insanely talented artist in Victoria who is impossible to get time with (its envelope was taped to the underside of the table in the main dining room where Ryan soothed my ego after Roger humiliated me); an excursion package from another Discovery Islands company that includes a sea otter viewing trip and photography lesson over an eight-hour day (hidden in a fake book on a bookshelf in the sitting area near the lobby fireplace); a huge "Gardener's Delight" gift box of seeds so I can start my own respectable vegetable and flower garden this year in a square of the land that used to be golf course (cleverly stashed in the—what else—garden shed); and last night—OMG— the hint took us down to our seasonal fake-ice rink, to center ice, where, sitting on a box of brand-new, fancy white figure skates was the puck from Ryan's first-ever NHL goal.

Isn't that the *sweetest* thing you've ever heard?

It made us both cry. The puck, not the skates. Although the skates are cool too. (It's more of an inside joke about how I suck at skating and always use the excuse that I'm wearing borrowed hockey skates so now, evidently, I don't have anything standing in my way of Olympic stardom.)

And then, after I thanked my husband *thoroughly* for his unrivaled kindness, I placed the puck—its edge wrapped in athletic tape with the game and date written in Sharpie—in the otters-only curio cabinet because it is very special and I cannot believe he gave it to me.

I mist up just thinking about it.

Hence why I am currently fluttering about like a one-winged moth because I have done nothing nearly as awesome for Valentine's Day for my hunky heartthrob. Sure, the lingerie I ordered is spicy, but how lame am I that I ordered a strip of lace and silk when he has given me *so* much?

I have totally blown it this year.

And now the lobby is filling with fit women in red-soled, four-inch heels who spend more on their nightly moisturizer than I do on my annual clothing budget. We get a lot of attractive, monied people staying here, and usually I can quiet the bitchy voice in my brain who whispers how I should try harder if I want to keep my man, but today, the head harpy is yelling like she's a *Titanic* survivor trying to summon a lifeboat.

It doesn't help that the fleshy insult from Mushroom Cap Joe's tantrum last week got a tiny bit infected, likely from me using my unwashed makeup brush to try to cover it, and so my dad has had to squeeze antibiotic goo into the pink-edged wound and now I look practically pubescent and my period is imminent so I have other spots to make my face resemble a dot-to-dot.

And yet, Ryan Fielding continues to profess his undying love.

If his farts weren't so rank and he didn't snore so loudly from that misaligned nose, I'd say he's too good to be true.

Alas, one of these days, I will defeat this insecurity monster who shares my skin.

But in the words of Aragorn in Peter Jackson's highly celebrated film, *Return of the King*, just before the good guys engage in the Battle of the Black Gate, "[I]t is not this day!"

Perfect, considering the guest who just walked in, surrounded by her posse. Nicolette Meyer. Gorgeous, blond, rich, mean like a feral barn cat.

We hosted her wedding a few years back, but a day or two before the ceremony, she "accidentally" speared her fiancé in the calf with an arrow during an archery outing, and then at the part of the nuptials when the pastor asks for objections—usually a rhetorical question—one of the groomsmen declared his loudly, so a huge fight broke out. Ryan used the airhorn we keep on hand for wildlife deterrence, the bride and groom did not get married, and we had enough leftovers from disappointed guests who skipped the non-reception to treat the whole Revelation Cove team to a decadent meal.

That was actually kinda fun.

What was *not* fun was how she treated my staff.

Even now, several years post incident when one would hope maturity might have calmed the poor dear, Nicolette Meyer aggressively taps a manicured fingertip on the polished surface of the front counter. I am standing at my laptop beside young Hannah, who slides into action.

"Welcome to Revelation Cove! Can I get your names?" Hannah didn't work here when Nicolette Meyer made her first impression on our team, but that doesn't stop Ms. Meyer from sighing and rolling her eyes, as if we should *all* know who she is.

I step in. "How are you, Nicolette? Good to see you again."

"We have a two o'clock with your spa," she says, gesturing to her four friends. "We need to get to our suites and settle in so we're not rushed."

A quick glance at the clock on the computer screen shows it's only 12:18, so plenty of time to "settle in," though I don't dare say anything. Whenever I experience the urge to snark back at someone, I hear Miss Betty in my head: *They are paying guests, even if sometimes you'd pay them to leave.*

Hannah and I make quick business of handing out key cards and Valentine's gift bags. I summon Cam, our very handsome concierge, to assist Nicolette and her party since everyone else who doubles as a bellhop is otherwise occupied. Nicolette's face lights up when she sees Cam approach—he has that effect on sentient humans of all ages. I must remember to warn him about her retractable fangs.

As if she's read my mind, Hannah leans close and whispers, "She looks like Rosalie Cullen."

I laugh, earning myself an over-the-shoulder glare from Nicolette that would scare Nosferatu.

By dinner, I consider googling the penalty for murder in British Columbia.

Three goals by a single player in a hockey game equal a hat trick, and obviously, that means the player is having a good game. However, I know the saying goes that bad luck *also* comes in threes. And I've had my three for this week: walking in on my dad and Miss Betty, the dog eating the vibrator and pooping all over the place, and Nicolette Meyer stepping back into her role as pampered, spoiled diva, as if those shoes were awaiting her return by our front door.

Granted, if she did have shoes waiting by our front door, Acorn would've decorated them with danger biscuits.

Whatever. I've dealt with my share of prickly guests during my time here at the Cove. But Nicolette makes problematic into an art form. In the salon, she didn't like her mani-pedi and said our tech was too rough on her cuticles and the shade of pink wasn't the one she chose, so the poor girl had to redo all twenty nails with nary a gratuity in sight. (In fact, Nicolette insisted we comp the service, refusing to pay for "shoddy work.") Then in the spa, the sauna allegedly smelled "weird," the towels weren't soft enough, she was mad Tabby ran out of lavender mask and refused to use anything with cucumber or mint and then lectured the spa staff about how superior the Korean skincare products are and that we should really be sourcing from overseas instead of local Canadian products that just aren't as good. In the dining room, she harassed the waitstaff about not enough Aperol in her spritz, about how the butter in her scallops tasted like margarine, how we really should have a gluten-free option for the baguettes (we do and even offered her one), and she made sure everyone around her knew she's American and her dad is a *very* important man in Portland and Los Angeles and how they really should've gone to Palm Springs instead of coming all the way up here to freeze to death with a bunch of lumberjacks.

Thou shalt not harm your guests.

Thou shalt not harm your guests.

Thou shalt not harm your guests.

If I close my eyes and tap my heels together three times, will Nicolette Meyer disappear?

The Garden Gnomes are halfway through a closed rehearsal in the ballroom for tomorrow night's Valentine's Day dance, though given the proximity to the lobby and front desk area, their jam session is still loud—just muffled. I offered to hold down the fort so Hannah could practice with the band (turns out she's handy with a tambourine), which means I am hanging out in the back office scheduling social media for next week on my laptop while watching *Schitt's Creek* on my iPad, in between helping guests who ding the desk bell with their random requests.

Speaking of *shits*, Acorn is mostly back to normal, other than fouling up the joint from the antibiotics and stool softeners the vet gave him. He's eating and drinking and running around like a raver on Molly, plus his poops are no longer pink-sprinkled. He will live to see another day.

Miss Betty and my dad are entertaining some Cove regulars in the lounge, and every now and again, I hear Dad's laugh above the din. I'm glad he's having a good time, and I've never seen Miss Betty's eyes sparkle so much. It's fine. It's just a Valentine's fling. I mean, Dad can't actually *move* here, can he? Because I don't think Miss Betty has any plans to head south. She loves living on the island.

Right?

Ryan keeps telling me not to worry about it so much, that it's healthy and good for our parents to have "alone time," even if it is still weird that *his* mother and *my* father are having "alone time" and we don't even live in Alabama so I'm not sure what the protocol is. Rather than fretting over it as much as I am, my insouciant husband is in our apartment live-streaming his team's game, coaching via FaceTime, despite the doctor's orders that he's not supposed to be watching screens or elevating his blood pressure.

As sweet as he's been this last week, and as much as I've *adored* having him home, he's counting down the seconds until he gets back to his team. And we've had a few more conversations about what it would look like if I were to leave Revelation Cove and join him in Langley, at least for the rest of the hockey season. I'm not totally ready to return to civilization full time, and Ryan has no interest in selling his stake in the resort, so we're trying to have our cake and eat it too.

"Excuse me, hello . . ."

Ugh. I know that voice. I pause my show right as Alexis Rose is about to launch into her spirited vocal audition for *Cabaret*.

"Hello!"

"I'm right here. Sorry, just doing a little work. How can I help you, Nicolette?"

She flattens her palms on the front desk counter and leans into it. I don't need to see her eyes to know she's hammered—her breath confirms it. "Why isn't the ballroom open? We can hear the music. My friends and I want to dance."

"They're rehearsing for tomorrow night, for the Valentine's Day party."

"Fine, but tonight is for *Gal*entines, and my *gals* and I want to go in and let loose."

"That's why tonight we arranged for the romantic comedy movie marathon in our smaller ballroom. We have a popcorn machine and open bar and tons of bean bags and comfy pillows to cozy up with."

"We're not fourteen"—she squints at my name tag pinned above my left boob—"Hollie."

Wow. I'm not even important enough for her to remember my name, despite the *many* phone and email hours I spent helping her plan her (failed) wedding?

"The lounge is open until one a.m., the outdoor pool is heated, and as you know, your suites have hot tubs. If you're interested in our special Galentine's Day dessert, I can grab a menu—"

"I've had enough sugar and carbs to last a lifetime." She drops a hand over her perfectly flat stomach. "I am so bloated from the food your chef made. Is he even a real chef?"

My fingernails carve crescents in my palms. "Nicolette, is there anything I can do for you tonight? You sound like maybe you're having a rough time."

She glares at me, and I give her the smile I would give a bear before it charged. And then, out of nowhere, Nicolette Meyer starts sobbing.

16

She cries so loud and so hard, I don't know what to do other than pull her into the back office so she doesn't attract a crowd.

"Where did your friends go? Can I call or text someone for you?"

She slumps into one of Miss Betty's floral wingback chairs. "No, don't call any of them. They're not even my real friends. They're just people who hang out with me because I'm rich."

I pull one of the wheeled office chairs from the desk under the wall of monitors. "Would you like some coffee or tea?" I gesture to our small caffeine station.

"Do you have any vodka?"

"Not back here, sorry." I grab a box of tissues and hand it over. She stares at it for a beat, as if trying to figure out what it is, and then takes it.

"Do you have any idea how hard it is to be me?"

"Um, no, I don't. I'm sorry you're struggling. Are you sure you don't want to talk to a friend about this?"

"No! I don't have any friends. Jesus, don't you listen?" She slurs and attempts to straighten in the chair as she wipes at a dainty blob of clear snot running from one nostril. Even her nasal mucus is pretty. "Those women are only here because I'm paying for everything. They're the girlfriends and mistresses of Daddy's friends. He thought it would be good for me to get away with some *gals* instead of sitting in my penthouse, feeling sorry for myself that my fiancé is fucking his secretary."

Yikes.

Hold up—which fiancé are talking about?

Nicolette Meyer carries on through the remainder of the Garden Gnomes set list. Apparently, after her matrimonial mayhem a few years ago, she and Edwin (the groomsman who declared his objection) immediately shacked up together and got engaged, the whole nine yards. They've been planning a destination wedding (another one? You'd think her parents would spring for a taxi to the courthouse at this point) in the Maldives, but then a couple weeks ago, Nicolette arrived home early from a Paris shopping trip and found Edwin and his barely legal secretary tangled in Nicolette's Egyptian-cotton penthouse sheets.

"Am I cursed when it comes to men? Like, what the hell is wrong with them? I'm hot, I've got my own money, I don't mind anal—like, I'm the full package. I just don't get it."

"Yeah, wow, I don't know. That sounds like you're dealing with a lot." Every ninety or so seconds, I glance at the security camera feed, hoping I will spot Nicolette's posse stumbling out of the lounge to come collect their sloppy leader.

"Sometimes I wish I could just be a normal person. Someone like you. A boring job, you don't have to worry about fashion because you're always wearing this uniform, you don't care about the gray hairs growing in or that your eyebrows look like sickly caterpillars."

Wait—what? Gray hair? And what's wrong with my eyebrows?

"You can eat whatever you want and you don't care what it does to your skin or your ass because you're not going to charity galas and red-carpet events all the time, so it doesn't matter if you have to ask your stylist to have the designer send over the size 4 instead of the 2."

"Mm-hmm, I hate it when that happens." She's insulted me

enough now that my flirtation with compassion has devolved into a date with sarcasm.

Nicolette plucks another tissue from the box and blows her nose.

I am so pleased to hear it honk like a Canada goose.

"I just want to be in love, ya know? My parents have a terrible marriage. They both cheat all the time and they both know it, and then Daddy will bring home the chlam and Mother gets angry and calls her private doctor for another round of doxy and then they fight about who gave it to who. Constant fighting."

Oh god, her tears are restarting.

"Do you know who my favorite person in our house staff is? The gardener. Luis. I mean, we have a lot of gardeners, but he's in charge. He's my favorite because he's always smiling, even though his job is dirty and sweaty and he works all the time, no matter the season, because he has a big family and lots of kids and they're all grown up now, so he has grandkids. He had a hip and knee replacement last year and still came back to work for us, not because he loves gardening but because he needed the insurance coverage for his wife. She's got breast cancer." Nicolette sobs harder. "It's the only time I've ever seen Luis not smile—when he told me about his dying wife."

This conversation has taken an unexpected turn.

"Like, I look at those people and they have so little. They live in an old subdivision with a bunch of crappy old cookie-cutter houses and the only reason Luis drives a nice truck is because Mother was embarrassed about him driving his piece of shit to our house every day, so she leased him a pickup."

"Luis sounds like a good man."

She nods. "I want that. I want a good man. I want someone to take care of, someone who will take care of me too. I don't want to fight every single day over stupid shit. I don't want my man to screw other women. I don't think human beings are supposed to go through life alone. Do you?"

"I think a person has to spend a little time finding out who they really are in order to find success in a relationship."

"What, like, go to therapy? I have a therapist. He always stares at my boobs."

"Well, *that's* inappropriate. Maybe it's time to find a new therapist."

"Maybe." She *hmmphs* back in the chair, grabs a perfect curled end of her hair, and feathers it over her lips. For a moment, she looks like a little girl. "I might be single forever."

"I doubt that very much. If you're open to finding a relationship, it will happen, but it has to be with the right guy—not just some hottie who's after your money. Do some work on yourself, figure out what you like, what makes you happy. Don't settle for abs and a pretty face. You never know—the love of your life could be about to bump into you around the next corner."

She honks into a Kleenex wad again. I pull the round garbage can from under the desk for her to throw away her snot rags. "Are you still married to that hockey player?"

Ha, so she *does* know who I am. "Yes, I am still married to Ryan Fielding."

"Is he a good man? Like, are you guys in love?"

I grin. "He is a very good man. And we are ridiculously in love."

"You're lucky. I don't think I've ever been in love for real. After Rob and I broke up and Edwin moved in, I needed some space, you know? So I took a month and tried my own version of that movie with Julia Roberts—*Eat, Pray, Love* or whatever. Totally overrated. I ate so much in Italy, I had to custom order a new wardrobe while I was there. The praying part was dumb—totally humid and there were bugs and we weren't allowed to talk. And the love, oh my god, what a joke." She hiccups on a sob.

The front desk bell rings.

"I'm so sorry—one sec, Nicolette. I just need to see who that is."

She snorts and nods. Maybe I should get her some Gatorade. And Advil.

I round the corner to the desk and find my dad standing at the counter. "Sorry for the bell. I texted you." He smiles that dad smile that makes me feel warm and safe.

"Yeah—no, I'm just . . ." I throw a thumb over my shoulder toward the back office. "Did you have a nice evening?"

"We did. So much fun. I forget how great it is to hang out with normal people." He chuckles. "Is Ryan in your apartment? I was going to check on him, make sure he's keeping up with his medications."

"Dad, you are not on duty tonight. You're supposed to relax."

"I know, but I would sleep better if I checked real quick." His phone buzzes from what sounds like the pocket of his blazer. I told him he didn't need a jacket for dinner, but knowing what I know now, I think he's dressing to impress.

Sure enough, he plucks the phone free, reads the screen, and his dopey smile widens.

I will guess it's from Lady Marmalade—

Ding! Ding! Ding!

Marmalade? Like, jam? Miss Betty makes the world's *best* jam? How did I not put two and two together?

"I'm off, then. See you at breakfast . . . in the dining room?" He winks and hurries down the hall.

"Hollie? You should come here," Nicolette calls.

What now? Oh god, she's gonna barf.

I step across the threshold into the quaint back office to find Nicolette standing in front of the wall of security screens. "What is that?"

She points at one of the monitors.

It's the camera down at the seasonal fake-ice rink.

Shit, shit, *shit* . . .

"That, my dear Nicolette, is a cougar."

17

I'd call it an unfortunate coincidence that we have a mountain lion on the island after what happened with Chloe, but this *is* British Columbia, and as I mentioned before, we have a significant concentration of the tawny, long-tailed pussycats in this part of the world. And given my and Ryan's prior bitey interlude with *Puma concolor vancouverensis* at Tanner and Sarah's cabin, we definitely have wildlife procedures for Revelation Cove.

First thing, I alert Bill and his crew, which initiates the lockdown of all exterior doors and requires anyone in the pool or hot tub to come inside. I then quickly record a warning message in our phone system; that message is subsequently sent to the landlines in every room and suite, followed by a text message to all our guests' cell phones and a banner warning across the guests' messaging system. This all happens in under five minutes.

All while I try to calm the PTSD pirouetting through my nervous system as I caress the scarring on my left forearm from Chloe's handiwork.

Both the private staff and open guest chats catch fire. Everyone wants to see the cougar, which is fine, as long as they do it from within the safety of our four walls.

Nicolette Meyer sits transfixed in the back office, watching the screens and sipping the Gatorade I fetched for her from the kitchen. "Will it come up here to the lodge?"

"I don't know. It's probably just looking for a place to snooze before resuming the hunt."

"Didn't you get bitten by a cougar or something? Was that you or am I thinking of someone else . . ."

"Yeah, it was me." I don't want to go into details. I, too, am watching the camera feed from the rink where the cat is now sprawled on the fake ice, leisurely bathing itself. If I didn't know firsthand how lethal these animals are, I'd think it hilarious that it grooms itself like a house cat.

"Hey, babe. You good?" Ryan breezes into the back office, pausing for a sec when he notices Nicolette in front of the surveillance wall.

"There's a cougar!" she announces.

"You notified Bill and all?"

"Of course."

He kisses the side of my head. "Well, as long as everyone stays inside, we'll be fine. The cat will get bored soon enough when it realizes we don't have anything delicious to eat."

One of the Vikings—still no idea if it's Sven or Arne—walks in.

"I'd say there's plenty delicious to eat," Nicolette purrs, her attention transferred from the cougar to the Norse warrior in our midst. "My god, you are a huge man."

Sven/Arne hikes his bushy brow at her and then looks back to me. "Patio and deck are cleared. Only a few people were in the hot tub and they're inside now. What else do you need me to do?"

Before I can answer: "You know what, Hollie, I am feeling a little woozy from all those cocktails, and now that you have a *cougar* on the premises, I'm scared for my safety," Nicolette says, leaning against the desk dramatically. "Do you think this—"

"Arne," the Viking answers.

"Do you think this *Arne* could escort me to my room, just in case that big kitty has found a way into the lodge? I'd hate for anything to happen that could lead to a lawsuit."

I look at the Viking—Arne. He shrugs.

"Come on, then," he says.

"Ohhhh, and he's bossy." Nicolette collects her long blond hair over one shoulder as she crosses the space that feels very small all of a sudden. Arne steps over the threshold, and Nicolette pauses before me, seemingly freed from her existential crisis. "Thanks for the girl talk. Also, whatever foundation you're using, it's the wrong shade. Your cheek looks green on one side."

She sashays out, hips engaged, as if the last hour of her sobbing through an entire box of tissue didn't happen.

"What was that . . ." Ryan looks through the doorway and then back at me.

"I'll tell you later." From the desk drawer, I grab my powder compact and pop it open to examine my skin. She's not wrong. My cheek and under-eye are still healing.

I wonder if that cougar would be interested in a little Nicolette au Vin. Maybe Nicolette à l'Orange. Soufflé au Nicolette?

Nah, that's mean. I'd never do that to the poor cat.

18

Our newest resident—Congratulations! It's a boy!—spent the evening scent-marking the property. The closest he got to the building was the walkway outside the front doors. We've been watching the camera feeds closely all night, and though we've not seen him in the last two hours, we're not a hundred percent sure he's moved on.

So, this Valentine's Day morning, instead of lying naked and satiated alongside my groom, I am in the back office on the phone with the Conservation Officer Service. It's an absolute last resort in my books—if they can't encourage the cat to leave, they may have to shoot it.

Wildlife murder is not great for business.

Except Conservation can't arrive until this afternoon, and there's no way our guests will be happy about being stuck inside the lodge on a day that has dawned as stunning as this one.

My dad raps on the open door and enters the back office while I'm still on the phone. Nurse Bob has brought me a breakfast tray this time, although he manages to keep it upright as he slides it onto the desk.

Finally, I hang up and practically dive into the steaming coffee. "You're the best."

"Any updates?"

"Our facilities manager is waiting for Tanner to arrive and then they will do a circle of the island in one of the boats, then on foot if they don't spot him."

"That seems dangerous if the cat is still here."

"They have rifles. And cougars are usually afraid of people."

"Let's hope you're right. I'm supposed to be on vacation."

From the tray he plucks a second mug, the tea string for Earl Grey draped over the rim. "How's Ryan this morning?"

"He seems good. No pain, at least not that he's telling me about. When I came down here, he was on the phone with Nils already, so yeah."

"No taking the hockey out of that boy." Dad smiles and gestures to one of the wingback chairs. I nod; he sits. "You've been avoiding me. I want to talk about—"

"Dad, it's fine. Whatever. We don't need to talk about anything." I pop my head out of the office to make sure Hannah is at the desk to help our guests and then click the door closed. I don't want anyone overhearing this conversation.

"I know it's been a bit odd for you to see Miss Betty and me flirting and hanging out this last week."

I close my eyes for the count of three, instantly regretting it as the image of my dad's white ass flashes against my eyelids. "Dad, seriously—"

"Hollie Cat, sit down for a second."

Please don't tell me you're getting married.

"We're not getting married," he says. Uncanny how he does that. "But it's more than just a Valentine's fling. We are dating. Long distance. Betty has been an amazing friend over the last few years. It's like she breathed new life into my world. I'd gotten a little stuck, I think, after Aurora took forever with the divorce and everything at work with budgetary restrictions and staffing issues—I think I was in burnout and didn't even realize it because I'd been running on autopilot for so long."

I finally do take a seat. This sounds more serious than I thought.

"Betty and I started texting last year after I came up for Canada Day weekend, and it's grown from there. She's an incredible woman. She cares so deeply for everyone in her life, and she makes me laugh every time we talk."

My throat tightens as I think of the first folded crane I opened from the love jar. Ryan wrote the same thing about me on that square of origami paper.

"Anyway, she's the one who encouraged me to think outside the box, to question why I'm giving so much of myself to the hospital. Yes, I love my coworkers—most of them—and helping people brings me so much joy, but the administration side of things . . . Hospitals are a for-profit business. They don't care that they're cycling through staff and burning people out. All they care about is making money."

A telltale red brightens my dad's cheeks—he's about to wind himself up. And as much as I don't want to dive into the best-kept-private details of my father's love life, I also don't want him to launch into a diatribe about the injustices of the American medical system.

"Dad, again, I am so sorry I walked in on you guys. I know I'm an adult and I should be able to just brush it off, and I will—it was just a little . . . unsettling." Nicolette Meyer's words from last night echo in my head: *I don't think human beings are supposed to go through life alone.* "So, if being with Miss Betty makes you happy, then you should go for it. Life is short and all that jazz, right?"

He snickers. "You have no idea how short it is, kid." He sets his tea aside and stands, pulling me from my chair for a hug. "I love you, Hollie Cat. You are the best human I know."

I laugh into his shoulder. "You're just saying that so I'll comp your breakfast."

"Nah, Betty already took care of that." His laugh bounces off the walls of this tiny office as he pushes back to chuck my chin with the side of his finger. "I promise we will try to make this as not weird as possible."

"Ryan and I want you guys to be happy. But it will get totally weird if you decide to tie the knot because then Ryan and I will be stepsiblings. That seems illegal to me."

"Well, at least you know Betty can't get pregnant."

"Aaaaaand you went there," I say, backing up and opening the door. "Have a pleasant day, Mr. Porter. Please remain indoors until we are certain the cougar has been relocated otherwise."

My dad collects his mug from the side table and pauses before me just as he's exiting.

"It's all right. I have a cougar of my own."

19

Apparently, it's good to know people in positions of influence. Constable Harris, the responding officer when Mushroom Cap Joe misbehaved, really likes Ryan. So Ryan called to ask if Harris had any pull with Conservation to get someone to come to the island sooner than this afternoon since our furry feline friend seemed uninterested in paddling across the Salish Sea to partake of the well-stocked black-tail deer buffet on nearby shores.

Lo and behold, Harris's brother-in-law, Joey Dunmore, is the head Conservation officer assigned to our neck of the woods.

So Harris called Joey and the cavalry arrived, and instead of lead, they shot our cougar with a tranquilizer, obtained blood samples and affixed a tracking collar, and then whisked him off our island via boat for relocation farther north. Many of the guests whined about why they couldn't go out and watch; Constable Harris made a general announcement in the lobby about the legal repercussions of interfering with law enforcement and Conservation officers in the performance of their duties.

Being the smart-ass I am, I unnecessarily added that I'd be happy to show pictures of Ryan's destroyed arm after our prior run in with Chloe. That shut people up. (Except for this one lady who actually did want to see photos and I told her I was only kidding and that maybe she'd enjoy a complimentary mimosa instead.)

With the Adventures of Cagey Cougar concluded, the Valentine's dance is once again front and center. As part of the staff, I'm expected to greet everyone as they join the party, and though my face will ache at evening's end from the permasmile and polite head-bobbing, it is fun to see everyone in their Valentine's finery, a fashion palette that includes everything from sequined, ball-worthy gowns to leather pants, from playful sparkly tights to fuzzy red and pink sweaters paired with iridescent angel wings.

I'm in a hot red satin number, tighter than is safe for work, but it's not meant to stay on my person all night. Not if I have my way.

The ballroom sparkles as if Chef Joseph has used a cannon to blast the whole place with lusty—ahem, *luster*—dust. In addition to her duties as the spa and salon manager, Tabby took on the role of chairperson for the special events planning committee, and not a moment too soon. I was running out of clever ways to use streamers and that annoying glitter confetti you can buy in bulk from Amazon.

Ryan stands with his good arm draped casually over my shoulders as we make the rounds. Tabby bounds onstage and welcomes everyone, telling a few jokes to warm up the crowd, promising a good time with the open bar serving Cupid's Cure all night and urging partygoers to eat as much as possible so that she's not left with the temptation of leftover pastries once everyone goes home.

And then, as if they choreographed the timing of their entrance —which they must have done since the lights dim and a spotlight shines at the doors and *oh my god*, the Garden Gnomes launch into a version of "Lady Marmalade"—my dad and Miss Betty saunter in. In front of a captive, whooping, applauding audience, they stroll to the center of the dance floor and take their bows. It's like this is prom, the votes have been counted, and they are crowned queen and king.

Dad is dressed in a three-piece suit, the shimmery, off-white fabric printed with red and pink hearts of varying sizes and shapes. And Miss Betty looks glorious in a fifties-style swing dress with an off-the-shoulder, cinched-waist bodice and a crinoline underneath to volumize the skirt.

They *match*.

I clap until my palms sting and holler until my throat aches. Ryan laughs so hard, he's crying, although I do wonder if the moisture seeping from the corner of his eye is inspired by how gorgeous—and *happy*—his mom looks.

The Garden Gnomes wrap "Marmalade" and slide into the next song of the evening, a slow oldie that must mean something to Miss Betty and Nurse Bob, since they've only got eyes for each other.

All right, yeah, it's still a little weird, but *oh my god,* they look so cute.

With each successive number, the crowd forms a pretty even split between romantic and raucous. The couples here to celebrate their undying love sway in tight hugs on the dance floor, no matter the tempo of the song, while the Galentines keep the bartenders busy and the beats pounding. They get especially excited when the Gnomes drop into a Shania Twain cover, the volume deafening as Gals of all ages yell along with the chorus about how they feel like a woman.

And Nicolette Meyer? She eyes Viking Arne, the microphone clutched in his hand as he croons through the set list, like she's going to devour him before night's end.

Ryan and I don't risk the commotion of the dance floor. He takes my hand and leads me to a darkened corner where no one can bump into him with a misdirected Cupid Shuffle. With his good arm wrapped around my waist, he presses his forehead to mine.

"Hi."

"Hi yourself."

"You look beautiful tonight. This dress…" He growls through a kiss.

"I figured you'd like it."

"I'll like it better when it's off."

"You always say that."

"I can't help it if my wife is the hottest thing since Mount Vesuvius."

"Nerd." I kiss him back. Since the cast and sling dictate his wardrobe for now, he's in a fitted black T-shirt with slacks—still ten-out-of-ten delectable. "They look pretty incredible, hey?"

We turn toward the dance floor where our parents are busting all sorts of moves.

"I've never seen her smile like that," Ryan says. "Did your dad come talk to you today?"

"He did. And you talked with your mom?"

"Mm-hmm."

"It seems our parents are *in lurve.*"

"Do you blame them? We are kind of awesome," he says. "Makes sense they'd be attracted to each other." Ryan slowly spins me so his back is to the crowd and I am shadowed by his height.

"I just want them to be happy. And as long as they don't break each other's hearts, holidays will be simpler with everyone gathering in one place instead of us having to split time down in Portland or whatever."

"True." He again fuses our mouths, tongue and all, before pulling back for a breath. "Any chance you wanna get out of here?"

"And what? Are you going to take me to your room? I don't know—maybe I should check with my dad first to see if he'll extend my curfew."

Ryan laughs and pushes into me, revealing that he is very much interested in breaking my curfew this evening.

"Come on, then." He hooks his pinkie around mine and I follow him out of the ballroom, my ears instantly grateful. He hums along as the Garden Gnomes fade the farther we get from the party.

We reach our front door and I open it, but Ryan stops me before I'm allowed to enter.

"Your last present awaits."

"Ryan, no . . . babe, you've done too much. *You* are enough."

"Entrez vous, madame."

I walk in, pausing only to kick off my heels, and on the kitchen island sits a huge bouquet of red roses in a sparkling crystal vase.

Propped against it is yet another red envelope that reads *OPEN ME LAST*, accompanied by a rectangular, red-wrapped box. Ryan moves in right behind me and kisses the top of my head. "Happy Valentine's Day, Hollie Porter."

I turn and stand on tiptoes to lock lips with my ravishing husband. "Thank you. I can't believe you did so much. I only bought a couple of crotchless teddies to prance around in."

A low rumble rises in his throat as he nudges his nose against mine. "Hurry up and open this, woman."

"Seriously, though, you went way overboard."

"Did not." He pecks my forehead and slides onto a barstool, nodding at the vase. "Card first, present second."

"Yes, sir." I unseal and pull another note free, only this one isn't printed in ornate calligraphy. It's in Ryan's handwriting:

> **A key made of sweetness, not brass or**
> **   steel,**
> **A token of our future, both hopeful and**
> **   real,**
> **It unlocks a dream, a nest for us to**
> **   dwell,**
> **Beyond the Cove's charm where our love**
> **   stories swell,**
> **A step to new chapters, with joy to**
> **   reveal.**

I look at him, a bit confused.

"Now the box." He smiles like his team has just made the Stanley Cup Finals.

I free the flat rectangle from its red paper. Inside is a chocolate key the length of my forearm. "What is this?"

"We've been talking about maybe picking out a real house. I would never just go and buy one without you there to help choose. So, this is me, your devoted husband, sitting before you, my favorite Hollie Porter, asking if you would like to go house shopping."

"Are you serious?" I'm shaking.

"Everything's arranged with the bank. We just have to pick out what we want."

I squeal and bounce into him, throwing my arms around his neck before remembering that my knight in shining hockey gear is medically fragile. "Sorry, sorry." I kiss the back of his hand and then cup his bristled cheeks. "Can we find one with locking doors so that when our parents come to visit, we don't accidentally walk in on them?"

Ryan howls. "Yes. We will absolutely get a house with doors that lock." He runs his hand through his hair. "Speaking of our parents and awkward moments—I meant to tell you this earlier . . ."

"Oh god, what?" I move my hands from his cheeks to mine. "I don't think I can handle anything else weird."

"My mom was really worried about Acorn."

"He's fine. He passed all the silicone."

"Yeah, but, uh, she . . . offered to pay for the vet visits."

We lock eyes for a count of three.

"*Oh my god*, Ryan, that was your MOM'S vibrator?"

The end . . . for now.

February 14, 1994
Just a quick TRUE story from your author friend (that would be me)

My (then) husband arrived home from his shift and did the tired-man shuffle into a kitchen desperately in need of renovation. We'd purchased this very old house last fall, and days before moving in, folks in the area told us it was haunted. I didn't necessarily believe it, but my subconscious got hold of that whisper and ran with it. I struggled with settling in, making it feel like home. No matter how many hours I spent scrubbing and repainting and then decorating the nursery around a rubber ducky theme (everything matched—it was perfect), something wasn't *right*.

That night, my husband found me hurriedly opening windows and fanning the smoke detector, not because of any ghosts but because, for a special Valentine's Day treat, I'd attempted to make his favorite meal: chicken-fried steak.

However, I had zero idea what I was doing, and this was long before Google, so I singlehandedly transformed a halfway decent piece of beef into an inedible charred brick.

I silently begged the decades'-old smoke detector to remain quiet. Our three-month-old was *finally* dozing in her Moses basket on the kitchen table, and this was the first reprieve I'd had all day.

Valentine's Day 1994 landed on a Monday, and my husband had walked into that smoky kitchen empty-handed. I knew our budget was tight; he reminded me daily, scolded me about remembering to sort and use the coupons when I did the shopping, was furious when I secretly saved $60 to fix the gold chain of his beloved crucifix necklace he'd snagged and snapped at work. Said that saving the money behind his back showed I had the ability to sneak and keep secrets.

He'd probably be pissed that I fucked up the ten-dollar steak.

I knew better than to be disappointed about no flowers or chocolate. Me "feeling sorry for myself" would just put him in a bad mood. Doesn't mean I hadn't hoped for *something* to show he'd thought about me just once during his workday.

Surprisingly, he didn't get mad or make fun of me about the ruined meat. Just looked at it and said, "Thanks, but I'm not eating that." Followed by, he hoped I wasn't disappointed that he forgot what day it was, that he was wiped out after too many days on and not sleeping well because of the new baby. He again mentioned our tight budget (even though he earned a municipal salary and co-owned two other properties nearby). I knew we wouldn't do something as extravagant as go out for dinner, especially not when our daughter's colicky fits started around eight o'clock every night.

I scooped his wrecked dinner into the garbage and the scorched pan into the sink to soak. "Let me make you something different. I have pasta."

"Can you come sit first?" He nodded toward one of our ugly kitchen chairs. They were secondhand from some friend or family member; I'd planned on painting and recovering the seats once I could afford the supplies. I grew up with parents who never stopped renovating and renewing and remodeling; I wasn't afraid of a little sweat equity.

I sat, carefully pulling the baby's basket closer so we could gaze at her.

Well, I gazed at her.

My husband sat forward and intertwined his fingers on the

scuffed tabletop. He didn't look into the Moses basket at all. Instead, he stared right at me sitting a mere three feet away from him, and said, "I'm in love with someone else, and I need you to move out."

It was the worst Valentine's Day ever.

But it was also the best.

Thirty years later, I'm happily married to a kind, thoughtful, artistic, supportive, hilarious GareBear. This October, we'll clink our beer mugs to celebrate twenty-four years. And that three-month-old baby girl? She's a journalist and photographer and the proud parent of Pippin Took, a miniature longhaired Dachshund who fancies himself an opera singer around dinnertime every night. Just like his mother did all those years ago.

This Valentine's Day, you may not have yet found your Ryan Fielding. Your Hollie Porter.

You may despise Valentine's Day as much as I did (for *years*).

Maybe you hate it because it's just another hyped-up, hollowed-out holiday designed to line those capitalist pockets and make everyone believe that without someone, they are no one. A flesh sack of unlovable garbage.

But your flesh sack is lovely, and you are absolutely the furthest thing from unlovable garbage, no matter how loudly the capitalists shriek that, to be a fulfilled, actualized person this (or any) Valentine's Day, you must give or receive responsibly sourced diamonds or heart-shaped boxes of Belgian chocolates or overpriced foie gras and Prosecco.

Love is out there.

Sometimes you just have to battle through the dense, suffocating fog a broken heart ushers in. You must learn to take care of yourself until the wounds seal closed and you get some distance to look back and say, "Thank fuck *that* ended."

I can't even imagine where I'd be today if Valentine's Day 1994 hadn't happened.

And I never did learn to make chicken-fried steak.
Chin up, cutie. Every single story, at its core, is about love.
That includes your story too.
XOXO,

Eliza

One more thing about cougars

...

My beta reader (and earnest fact-checker) Katie did a deep dive on the veracity of Hollie's wildlife tidbit about how Vancouver Island has the highest concentration of cougars in the world.

It's true. There are an estimated 4000 cougars in British Columbia, and 600 to 800 of them live on Vancouver Island. *And they will swim to nearby islands to hunt.* If you don't believe me (or Hollie), visit:

- https://www.vancouverisawesome.com/bc-news/cougars-bc-vancouver-island-population-1946304
- https://vancouverguardian.com/vancougar-island-cougar/
- https://news.mongabay.com/2023/03/island-hopping-cougars-redraw-boundaries-of-big-cats-potential-range/
- https://www.discovervancouverisland.com/blog/cougar-swimming-story/
- https://linnet.geog.ubc.ca/efauna/Atlas/Atlas.aspx?sciname=Puma%20concolor
- https://www.inaturalist.org/guide_taxa/340264

- https://bigcatswildcats.com/cougar/
- https://www.theglobeandmail.com/canada/british-columbia/article-cougar-disquiets-small-southern-bc-island/

For more on cougar safety:

- https://wildsafebc.com/species/cougar
- https://www.victoriabuzz.com/2023/03/heres-what-to-do-when-you-encounter-a-cougar-on-vancouver-island/
- https://vancouverisland.com/about/facts-and-information/safety-guide-to-cougars/

It wouldn't be an Eliza Gordon project if I didn't feed you info about my favorite creatures, now, would it? Hey, nerds gotta nerd, my friend.

You're welcome.

P.S. While we're on the topic of wildlife, the big gray and black and white goose with murder in its eyes is called a **Canada goose, _not_** a Canadian goose. They also respond to **cobra chicken**. (Another hat tip to Katie for that one because I laughed for a solid ten minutes).

Hollie Porter
Saves the Planet

ELIZA GORDON

To my acquired sister Toni whose enthusiasm for world preservation fueled the Planet Lara series and spurred me to tackle this fun little project. Thanks, sis.

1

This time when the latest emergency buzzes our phones across the kitchen island, we've at least *finished* with the evening's entertainment. And no one has knocked on our apartment door (yet)—if they were to do so, they'd find me in only a NSFW faux leather skirt hiked around my waist and Ryan in nothing but a necktie. (You guys . . . he looks really, *really* good in nothing but a necktie.)

"I'll get it," Ryan offers. We're still out of breath, but my legs are jelly, so I'm not moving anywhere for another few minutes.

With good reason.

When my darling husband returned to coaching duties after Valentine's Day (with his still-broken arm, but try to keep him down for more than a week and see how *you* do), he found a bottle of expensive champagne and a book wrapped in cartoonish Cupid paper on his desk. At first he was a little concerned—it's not uncommon for Ryan to get fan mail in the form of lingerie and perfume-laden envelopes containing hotel room key cards, even all these years after his NHL career ended and he's obviously very married—but his fear was assuaged when he learned the gift was from Nils, his assistant coach, and that Nils had bought equally weird Valentine's presents for all the coaching staff.

It's a role-play, sexy funtime book. We thought it was a joke, but Nils is European, so we're never quite sure if he's being funny, ironic, or totally serious.

Regardless, it's proven fun. (Even if I'm still convinced Miss Betty might've made another joke about grandchildren in Nils's proximity, thus inspiring the gift.) Every chapter contains a cheesy but spicy story and then there's a tear-out envelope thing that contains role-play instructions for each partner.

And yes—I flipped through it when Ryan brought it home, just to see if Batman showed up on any pages. I still remember that poor guy. Died in the cowl and everything. Now *that* is dedication to maintaining the fun quotient of the marital bed.

If I were Catholic, I'd cross myself in Jerry's honor. *We'll do you proud, Batman Jerry.*

Tonight was Ryan's turn to choose a chapter, so we cracked the champagne, and he ended up dressed as the Titillating Tailor, and I, a beautiful young ingenue, in search of the perfect red-carpet outfit. Since neither of us had access to a cloth tape measure a proper tailor would use, Ryan found a beat-up Craftsman twenty-five-footer with sharp edges in the kitchen junk drawer. It wasn't nearly as intimate or elegant as a cloth tape might have been, and the metal was cold against my inner thigh, but I trust he got a good enough inseam measurement with his fingers and his—

"It was Hannah. There's something wrong with the GreenMuncher again."

I moan and flop over onto my back. "That is the dumbest name." Ryan laughs. "Why can't Bill handle it?" I whine as I watch my husband remove the necktie and slide into a pair of work jeans. "Are you going commando, sir?"

"Fewer layers to remove when I get back. You have the second half of your dress fitting to get through this evening, little starlet." He slowly pulls on a T-shirt—that left arm, though out of the cast, is still messed up—and then leans to meet me halfway for a kiss so

French, I feel like throwing up a blockade and screaming about revolution.

"And you know why Bill can't handle it. Tough to do that when he's off island."

"Shit. Right." Bill is our head of maintenance, and he's on the mainland for a few weeks to take care of doctors' appointments and visit with his grandkids. "Did Hannah say what's wrong?"

"Just that it stinks again."

Hannah is our front desk agent, always ready with a smile and an offer to help, but she's not super resourceful when it comes to problem-solving. Then again, she's all of twenty, in her second "gap year" until she decides what to do with her life. I sure as shit didn't know what I was doing at twenty. I still don't know much more at thirty.

"Do you need my help?" I ask, fully hoping he says no.

"Do you have specialized knowledge in the inner workings of high-tech composters?"

"Only this one." I slap my bare belly.

Ryan sits to tie his boots. "I know we're supposed to be going green, but this thing is a pain in the ass, and it's only been here a couple weeks."

"Ask Lara Clarke about it tomorrow when she gets off her fancy yacht."

Ryan leans on his right arm, hovering over me. "Are you nervous?"

"Why would you ask me that?"

"Because you sounded bitchy when you said her name."

"You've seen pictures of her, right?"

He presses his lips to mine. "You are the only starlet for me, babe. Stop being neurotic and insecure." He grabs my bare left breast and gently bites the nipple. Electricity shoots to my toes. "I'll be back after I figure out why the kitchen and lobby smell like farts."

"Bring me back a surprise," I say as he saunters out of our bedroom.

He pauses at the threshold and turns around, his face uplit by the lamp just on the other side of the doorway. "Don't fall asleep. I have more measurements to take to finish my masterpiece."

"I am a very demanding customer and expect nothing but the best!" My sentence is punctuated by the *click-close* of our front door. With Ryan's warmth gone, I realize I'm actually freezing and this skirt around my waist is far from couture and I have to pee and I should grab my phone in case he needs my help or in case another pre-sunrise calamity befalls our wondrous oasis in the middle of the Salish Sea.

Feet to the floor (and so glad I bought area rugs because, despite it being April, we've had a few weeks of unseasonably cold weather), I have recovered enough postcoital muscle control to shuffle into the bathroom. Even though Ryan instructed I remain as is, I look ridiculous with this crappy skirt hiked so high.

Once I've used the potty, I shimmy out of it and find myself standing naked in front of the bathroom mirror.

Lara Clarke, a stunning, fit, billionaire heiress and eco-warrior, will be arriving on our island tomorrow morning with her equally gorgeous husband and their eco-friendly entourage.

I stand sideways, examining myself from every angle. Yeah, marriage has padded me a little, but I think I've still got it. I mean, Ryan seems happy, right? My boobs are definitely bigger than they were when we got married, but so are my hips and ass—side effect of having a full-time chef and patisserie on staff.

I turn to the other side and push out my gut, trying to imagine my body pregnant. I do this once in a while, testing the look, still not sure if I even want kids, worried I will ruin a kid with my mommy issues, worried that the economy will fall apart and our child will have no future or that nuclear holocaust is around the corner with all the wars going on or worse, what if everything Lara Clarke's environmental nerd friends are saying is true—will our future child(ren) even have a world to inherit?

This is far too much Grown-Up Thinking for one o'clock in the morning.

I just hope the surprise my Titillating Tailor returns with starts with *chocolate* and ends with *cake*.

2

I fall asleep awaiting my tailor's return and then am definitely awoken by the stench sticking to his person. "Grossssss. Shower, please."

The water's on before my sentence finishes.

When Ryan slides into bed ninety minutes after his original departure, skin damp and fresh smelling, it's obvious by his tired groan that Tailor Time is over. "I know the old composting system was too popular with local wildlife, but this GreenMonster 3000 or whatever the hell it's called—"

I interrupt him with my laughing. "Green*Muncher*. And I don't think it has the 3000 after it."

"Whatever." He cozies under the covers and nuzzles my neck with his crooked nose. "Sorry I woke you."

"Blame it on the Muncher. He stinks."

"Yeah, he certainly does." Ryan sighs and slowly extends his left arm above his head, performing the light stretches the physio recommended he do anytime it aches. "I understand that moving the compost system indoors means the local raccoon posse can't access it—"

"Rhonda."

"What?"

"The raccoon momma's name is Rhonda."

"Right. Rhonda. Silly me. Anyway, I think someone on Chef's staff is screwing with it. These damn things aren't supposed to stink."

"Maybe it's broken."

"Maybe . . ."

Within two minutes, Ryan's breathing evens out. I glance over at him—sure enough, he's zonked.

I, however, am now wide awake, brain whirring through mental checklists that would make even the most seasoned project planner weep, because in six and a half hours, Revelation Cove will be overrun by green nerds (their words, not mine) who know a lot more about Munchers than any of us do. And this is just the first wave of arrivals. Lara Clarke and the Clarke Innovations people are landing a couple days early to set up and finalize preparations for their big three-day event that culminates Sunday, April 21.

The day before Earth Day.

A week or so after Valentine's, I fielded a call from Lara Clarke. She runs Thalia Island, an "eco-utopia" located about ninety minutes south of here (by boat). Thalia Island and Lara Clarke have gotten a lot of press in the last few years, not only because of the island's ultramodern sustainability operations, but because Lara is basically Vancouver royalty, and when her grandfather died, he left her a mountain of money but also a mountain of problems that led to her boyfriend being kidnapped by some super bad guys and there was something else about a cult—I can't recall all the details. I just remember it was headline news for weeks that held Tabby's attention with the same vigor that she, until that point, had previously reserved for heated debates about the final season of *Buffy the Vampire Slayer*.

Lara's late grandfather's company—Clarke Innovations—has given us grant money in the past that we've used to rewild half of our (former) golf greens and purchase the biomass furnace that heats the resort. They also sent us the GreenMuncher to test out (so far, I am less than impressed). While I am by no means a green-blooded environmentalist, I want to do my part. And Clarke Innovations doesn't mess around when it comes to sucking up to Mother Nature.

Which is why the call on February 24 surprised me.

Every year around Earth Day, CI puts on an eco-summit where they invite loads of smart people—scientists, researchers, inventors, rich people who need tax breaks—to gather in Vancouver, BC, and brain-meld on all things environment: initiatives and technologies and developments and research stuff. Again, this is outside of my realm of expertise, so it's not like I've ever considered hanging out in the city on Earth Day to partake in a series of marches with dreadlocked humans who use dirt to bathe or to listen in on alarmist lectures about how we're all basically fucked.

As demonstrated earlier this evening, I panic if I spend too much time thinking about existential things such as our only planet dying, the fact that I won't live forever, and that in a hundred years, everyone I know and love will (probably) be dead, that with the planet warming, the permafrost is releasing some scary-ass viruses not seen in recorded history, that every single hour of every day, 7000 life stories die with people who shed their mortal coils and we have no way of recording the totality of their lived experiences, you know, like downloading their brains so we can preserve all the things they've learned—

Jesus, now I'm sweating.

I kick off the covers and click on the small fan on my nightstand.

I've always been a bit tightly wound, so me freaking out isn't new. It's been getting worse, though. Maybe it's because Ryan and I have been looking at *four*-bedroom houses on the mainland and my dad is retiring and starting a new business venture but his latest EKG was a bit wonky and Miss Betty has a nasty cough that won't let go and then there's drought and income disparity and plastic pollution and have you heard the rumor that the world is about to run out of chocolate and coffee? Can we even grow chocolate and coffee on Mars?

This is why I'm not allowed to watch the news unaccompanied anymore.

During hockey season, if I spiral into this vortex of doom and gloom, I have only Miss Betty and Tabby and Sarah to pull me out, and they all have a lot of other shit on their plates—new love, keeping abreast of gossip, and a five-year-old, respectively, plus their full-time jobs—which is the point of this whole rambling tale to begin with. I could call my dad, but I don't want to worry him that his only child is losing her marbles *plus* he'll probably be on the phone with Lady Marmalade, anyway, and I'd like to keep that long story, and related visuals, locked in the box in my head where they shall remain forever.

Or at least until some scientist downloads my brain and is secondarily traumatized.

Anyway, the aforementioned Clarke Innovations eco-summit means big money to the host hotel, and this year, instead of setting up shop in downtown Vancouver, they're focusing on coastal British Columbia businesses—everything from fishing expedition and whale watching companies, hotels, B&Bs, resorts, cafés, breweries, and restaurants, any business that offers hospitality and/or tourist-centric services. Owners and managers have been invited to the "Green It Up Eco-Summit" that includes workshops, seminars, and product demonstrations.

Three days of people learning how to reduce, reuse, recycle—and Revelation Cove is hosting. We're serving as the "test property" to show our coastal neighbors the newest tech that will help us all do our part to save the planet.

On the one hand, it's a huge honor to have been asked—and it will bring in six months' worth of revenue in a single weekend.

On the other hand, I don't want to cheer *too* loudly because the hotel where the eco-summit was *supposed* to happen (on another local island) burned down on Valentine's night. Something to do with an angry ex-wife and a pregnant mistress and a sex tape involving someone in a wolf costume and a significant cache of accelerant. I don't know—maybe it was actually a kitchen fire. Tabby was my source on that, and she's often more *National Inquirer* than BBC News. (Recall aforementioned note about how I'm not allowed to watch the real news at the moment.)

Saying yes to Clarke Innovations has both shaken *and* stirred our tiny Revelation Cove ecosystem. We, fortunately, weren't fully booked for Earth Week, since spring break for most schools and universities is in March and summer break is still a ways off, so the guests we did have coming in, we were able to rebook with the promise of steep discounts and free booze.

Bill and Tanner and I spent two days touring Thalia Island in March. The island's lead engineer, Finan Rowleigh (Lara Clarke's husband) showed us the incredible green-first stuff Clarke Innovations is doing there. The "downtown" area looks straight out of a Hallmark film, if Hallmark films had stores full of vegetables and handmade linens. They have a pub, a diner, a general store, a town hall, and a small school—even a seed depository and produce market on their Main Street called the Stalk Broker.

OK, that's damn clever.

Our time on Thalia was spent touring their vertical farms, the wind turbines, the solar array field, and seeing the systems they use for human and food waste management—it really is next level. When I asked Finan why they don't host the eco-summit on their island instead of in the city or at a nearby hotel, he noted they don't have accommodations for so many people and that they've avoided building a hotel since Thalia is a working but private residential community where residents must be vetted before they're granted access and is not an eco-tourist hangout.

Got it.

Since a large chunk of the eco-summit includes presentation and display of a number of Clarke Innovations' latest success stories, Revelation Cove has been treated to a few significant upgrades. Shipping containers converted into little solar-powered greenhouses for growing produce have been added along the southern end of the island, finished with rescued wood and landscaped to match their new surroundings; the GreenMuncher, installed in the renovated storage room off the kitchen, converts food waste (which, sadly, is significant given we're a resort and people like to loosen their belts) into nutrient-rich dirt we then use in our burgeoning agricultural practice; and an electric passenger transport vessel has been added to our fleet (on loan for now) to ferry guests back and forth to demonstrate how efficient it is compared to our usual gas-powered boats.

All that stuff is smart and cool, sure, but my team is most excited about the Clarke Innovations VIP, named NORA, arriving alongside Lara Clarke and her team in mere hours.

NORA is short for Nature-Oriented Robotic Assistant.

I wonder how she feels about sea otters.

3

"You'd think we were greeting the queen," Tabby whispers near my ear. "Wait—that would be weird. She died. Sorry. The king. You'd think we were waiting for the king."

She's not far off the mark. Revelation Cove staffers line the docks from the water's edge and up along the walkway, all of us in our khaki work pants and brand-new forest-green, bamboo-fiber Revelation Cove polos. Brad, our number-two maintenance guy, and his crew are in their Sunday best—a lot of Carhartt and relatively clean boots and those tight T-shirts on the Vikings that Tabby can't stop ogling—but yeah, we clean up pretty good.

As if she knew we were prepping a grand fete in her honor, Mother Nature is showing off—blue skies, no clouds, notably warmer today at 20°C/68°F, slight breeze, no chop on the strait. And all of our spring flowers stretch shamelessly toward the sun to show off their vibrant outfits. Ah, to have the confidence of a brand-new red tulip.

When the Clarke Innovations watercraft finally ties off (I am corrected that it is *not* actually a yacht), all eyes are glued to the youngish, uniformed deckhands who emerge to secure a railed gangplank. It really is like waiting for the king—I keep expecting the important-people music to start.

Instead, when the door finally opens, it's not the king of anywhere but rather a tall, dishwater-blond woman in a perfect, off-white suit and impossibly high heels.

"Jesus, is that Lara Clarke?" Tabby whispers.

Before I can answer, an equally tall, dark-haired man, trimmed but full beard, dressed more like one of our crew, steps out behind her—Finan, her husband. He is followed by an imposing dude with a lot of muscles and a high-and-tight haircut that makes him look like a marine or maybe a pro wrestler. Or He-Man.

"That one's her bodyguard," Tabby says. "Who is also her *dad.*"

I whip my head in my friend's direction. "What?"

"I told you about this!"

"OK, stop. Remind me later."

"Damn, Lara is gorgeous. I wish I had hair like that," Tabby whispers.

I nod in agreement, although the insecure fifteen-year-old in my head is looking for faults as this faultless woman approaches our spot in the line.

Lara Clarke and Finan the husband and He-Man are followed by a long stream of bright-eyed, healthy-looking humans, all dressed in the same coordinating colors, not unlike the Revelation Cove team—khaki or black pants, a few in denim, and shirts in various shades of green. As they make their way up the path, the otherwise serene setting is sprinkled with polite chatter and handshakes and "nice to meet you" on repeat.

Ryan sidles up next to me, a little out of breath.

"Cutting it close, Fielding."

He pinches my ass in response right as Lara Clarke finishes greeting Tabby, who takes longer than everyone else to say hello when she launches into questions about her hair regimen and what products she uses and how she would be "honored" to do a complimentary wash and blow-out while Lara is on the premises, "unless that's bad for the earth, of course." Tee hee hee.

I give Tabby the hairy *enough talking* eyeball.

"You must be Hollie and Ryan," Lara says, stepping away from Tabby to offer her professionally manicured hand to me, then my better half. "Lara Clarke. So glad to finally meet you in real life."

"You as well. We've talked on the phone so much, I feel like we're BFFs," I blurt. *Et tu, Brute?* What is it about this woman that reduces us mere mortals to babbling goobers?

Lara turns and gestures to the men beside her. "You've met my husband, Finan Rowleigh, of course. And this is my father, Len Emmerich."

Ryan clasps hands with the men.

"Hey, sorry to hear about your season," Finan says. "I'm a huge fan." He looks a little starstruck as he and Ryan slide into a quick conversation about the upcoming Stanley Cup Playoffs.

"Lara!" A shrill but loud voice cuts across the distance from the direction of their boat. "Is it time yet?" A kid who can't be more than twelve has hoisted herself up so she's standing on the boat's top railing. "Can I bring NORA out?"

Lara turns to me. "My apologies. That's Harmony."

"Your daughter?" I ask.

"Ha! No. Though, if I had a child, I'd hope she'd be as smart as Harmony."

"Maybe a little less smart," Len Emmerich adds under his breath.

Lara smiles and rests a hand on the big guy's beefy biceps (and I realize up close, he's not blond—his hair is completely white). "Harmony is the youngest intern Clarke Innovations has ever hired," Lara continues.

"She works for you? She's just a kid."

Ms. Clarke smiles and turns to wave at Harmony, throwing her a thumbs-up. "Her dad works for us—they live on Thalia Island. Harmony just happens to be smarter than pretty much everyone else, so we give her smart-people things to do so she doesn't spend her time writing code that will Robin Hood the bank accounts of evildoers."

I stare at Lara. "She could do that?"

"Harmony can do anything," Finan says. "It's both exhilarating and exhausting."

"Mostly exhausting," Emmerich says. I'm going to guess if he works as Lara's bodyguard that Harmony maybe falls under his umbrella of responsibility too.

"OK, LARA, we're READY!" Harmony shouts from the boat.

By now, the snake of humanity has reached the top, everyone gathered along the walkway and patches of neatly trimmed lawn near the resort's double front doors. (I know. Lawn is bad. But we can't go full hippie all at once.) The peaceful murmur of conversation is cut off by a shrieking PA system, loud enough to startle several trees' worth of birds. The feedback is quickly replaced by the upbeat, fast-paced tempo of a pop song.

I look at Lara, easily three inches taller than me in her heels, unsure of what's going on. She leans close. "We told her she could pick the entrance music. She's kind of on a Taylor Swift kick right now."

"God help us," Emmerich grumbles.

"Ladies and gentlemen and all those who identify as human but not on the predetermined gender spectrum, please put your hands together for NORAAAAAAAA!"

The Clarke Innovations crowd applauds with just enough enthusiasm that everyone from the RC gang follows suit as our attention is directed to the boat's side doors where Lara et al. exited just moments ago. However, instead of emerging with another human being, Harmony walks out holding hands with a robot.

White and black and silver with a humanlike face—similar to the robots Japan has been wowing us with for years—human shaped with four jointed appendages that articulate just like a person. Harmony's lips are moving, so I assume she's providing instructions to her robotic companion, though we still can't hear anything above the music.

Finan lifts his wrist and with a few taps on his smartwatch, the volume yelling at us from the boat's speaker system fades. It also allows us to better hear the mechanical *whish-whirr* of NORA's steps, the movement of her hips, knees, and feet, as well as her head as she looks from side to side, seemingly inspecting her surroundings. The morning sun paints sparkle spots on the robot's flawless surface. As Harmony and her very expensive science project traverse up the pathway, NORA doesn't misstep or struggle with the increasing angle or the pebbled terrain underfoot.

The Revelation Cove folks are captivated, everyone gathering around Ryan and me and Lara and Finan and the bodyguard as NORA and her tiny handler approach. When Harmony stops walking, so does NORA. The robot continues to assess the scene—she has eyes that blink and a mouth that moves as if she were breathing or smirking or about to say something.

Lara moves to NORA's other side, facing the crowd. "Hello, everyone. It is so fantastic to be here at the beautiful Revelation Cove ahead of this year's Green It Up Eco-Summit, co-sponsored by Clarke Innovations and the Archibald M. Clarke Foundation."

Pause for applause.

"I am so, so thrilled to present this year's very special guest. This, as you now know, thanks to Harmony's exuberant introduction, is NORA."

More applause.

"Harmony?" Lara gestures to the young girl who looks like she's about to jump out of her skin with excitement.

"Thank you, Lara. Hello, everyone! I'm Harmony Peck, and I'm super excited to introduce you to NORA, my Nature-Oriented Robotic Assistant! Right now, NORA is equipped to interact with guests, share fascinating environmental facts, and even lend a hand with gardening tasks like planting and harvesting vegetables." Harmony pauses to look down at the index card, what I'm assuming is her speech, cupped in her palm.

"But that's just the beginning! My vision for NORA will see her become a vital companion in protecting our planet. Imagine different versions of NORA used in agriculture to help plant and harvest in more sustainable ways. Imagine NORA venturing into our local forests to monitor wildlife and help scientists and researchers gather data to conserve endangered species. With advancements in artificial intelligence and robotics, NORA could revolutionize how we feed the planet *and* care for our environment.

"Together, we can unleash NORA's full potential to make our world a greener, more sustainable place for generations to come. Thank you for believing in our mission and joining us on this awesome journey!"

Damn. Wow. OK. I'm actually speechless.

Harmony beams with pride as the crowd again claps their approval and awe. She then says something to NORA and releases her hand, and the robot moves into action, walking directly toward me before stopping a polite distance away from my body.

NORA extends a hand. "Hello, Hollie Porter Fielding, marketing director and wildlife education provider for Revelation Cove. It is a pleasure to meet you."

Holy shit. I look at Ryan, his face a mixture of amazement and maybe fear, and then reach to shake NORA's hand, hoping she understands that I'm made of flesh and bone.

"It's very nice to meet you too, NORA." We shake hands, gently, and then she releases.

"I understand you are very knowledgeable about the northern sea otter, *Enhydra lutris*, and the North American river otter, *Lontra canadensis.* I do hope we have an opportunity to talk further about your fascination with these amazing animals. Perhaps we can work together to find solutions to safeguard the critically endangered sea otter populations along this northwestern coast."

I . . . literally do not know what to say.

"Umm, that would be terrific, NORA. Thank you. How did you know I like otters?"

"I have been programmed to learn a great deal about my friends and acquaintances simply by accessing the wealth of information available on the internet. I trust your father, Bob Porter, is doing well?"

My mouth is stuck open. "Umm . . ."

"So, shall we go inside and get everyone settled?" Ryan claps his hands once and then wraps an arm tightly around my shoulders.

The end of the world is here.

4

You know that feeling when you have a big test in a class you're not super strong in, like, history or chemistry or German (*why did I take German?*), and you cram and study and spend as much time shoving information into your brain in the hopes that it will stick to the gray matter long enough for you to barf it onto the test paper and thus pass the exam?

That is how this whole day has been.

We'd already installed all the eco-friendly stuff from CI's Green It Up checklist, thanks to the accompanying boxes of supplies that they sent when they booked our venue—LED light bulbs and fixtures, high-efficiency shower heads, low-flow toilets in most of the suites—and yet as we tour the property with Lara and her experts, Harmony and NORA included, it feels like we've hardly scratched the surface of things we can still do.

It's overwhelming, all this information, all at once. I know most of these things will fall under Bill's purview, but with him off the premises, today, I provided note-taking backup to Ryan and Tanner and Brad as the CI folks pointed out all the great ideas to get Revelation Cove up to environmental snuff. My aching hand and wrist from scratching notes onto a recycled-paper notebook (I forgot to charge my iPad—again) during our foray reminded me of days gone by when I actually *did* fail German and had to do summer school French to make up the foreign language credit. *Mein Deutsch ist schrecklich.*

My feet ache as I slide onto a barstool at our kitchen island and kick off my boots. Ryan is still playing host to our guests, and I will join them for dinner, but in the meantime, I've snuck back to our humble hideout to guzzle the dredges of last night's champagne and video-call my dad.

"Hey, Hollie Cat," he answers.

"Hi, Dad. Are you busy?"

"Busy? No. Look—" He turns the phone around to showcase his location.

"You're at the beach?"

"Hello, Hollie! Miss you!" Miss Betty says, leaning into frame.

Yup. She and my dad are dating. She luminesces with happiness. They both do.

"We're in Lincoln City. Thought it would be fun to grab a few days away before everything gets crazy in May."

My dad recently (and rather suddenly) retired from his long career as an ER nurse and is launching a new business next month. When he dropped this info during his February visit to the Cove, I panicked, worried something was wrong with him. But nope. He's just tired and ready to do something different.

"Good thinking. Are you having a nice time?"

"You can never go wrong on the Oregon Coast." The wind tousles my dad's thinning hair and I hear Miss Betty laugh in the background as the gauzy, floral scarf over her head takes flight. "One sec, kiddo. We're just going back to the house."

I wait as Dad and Miss Betty walk up the slight sand dune to a set of stairs. The gusty wind buffets the phone's mic as Dad hoists the camera overhead to give me a view of their surroundings. The sky is that misty blue common along the coast just before sunset, the tall grasses lining the beach bend with the persistent breeze coming off the ocean, and chattering seagulls catch updrafts while stalking beachgoers in hopes one among them will drop leftovers from their picnic baskets.

Revelation Cove is stunning, absolutely, as are the other parts of BC I've seen from both sea and air. But nothing pokes me in the heart quite like the Oregon Coast. Those frothy white waves kissing the beach, the violence of a summer storm, the water that, no matter what the scientists say about warming Pacific Ocean temps, always chills my toes and feet until they cramp. Growing up, Dad and I made a million good memories from Astoria to Brookings.

"OK, sorry about that," Dad says, closing the door of a tiny beachside house. "This place belongs to a friend from work, so we got a great deal."

"Nice. I'm glad you both could get away." I hear Miss Betty coughing in the background. "That still doesn't sound good."

"She has her inhaler. I'm keeping an eye on it." Dad sits, his phone wobbling as he props it against something; the angle gives him two chins. "Now. Talk to me. You have that line between your eyebrows."

I run my fingertip over the spot, as if I can smooth it out. "I'm fine. Just tired, I guess. The Clarke Innovations people arrived today to prepare for the big conference this weekend, so it's been a lot of talking and peopling already. And Dad, omigod, the robot. Did you get the video I sent?"

"Yeah, that's something else. What was its name again?"

"NORA. And the robot's handler is *twelve*. She's a child prodigy. But the weirdest thing is, when I met NORA, she asked about you."

My dad laughs. "I'll admit that's a little creepy, but it doesn't surprise me. The hospital has been bringing in all sorts of fun gadgets over the last few years. We have a few autonomous floor polishers that run twenty-four seven. And surgeons have been using the da Vinci robots for years now. They're the future, kid."

"Fine, but it's *weird*. She knew you were a nurse and everything."

"*Retired* nurse. Now I am a geriatric sexual health facilitator."

"Right. Yeah, I'm not telling NORA that. She can find that info all on her own."

Dad chuckles again and then leans on the table, closer to the phone camera. "OK, so what is really bothering you? It can't just be about a humanoid robot who has access to Facebook."

I spin so I can lean my back against the countertop edge. "I don't know. I guess I'm just overwhelmed with all the changes these people are making and the fact that we have a full house starting tomorrow afternoon and Ryan and I still haven't found a place in Langley that we both like and the hockey season will be here before you know it and what if we can't get settled before then and of course, all this planet-ending doomsday talk is kinda freaking me out and the summit hasn't even really started yet . . ."

"You're doing it again."

Catastrophizing.

"Are you pregnant?"

"Dad!"

"Well, are you? Pregnancy hormones wreak havoc on a woman's emotions."

"No. I'm not pregnant."

"What? She's pregnant?" my mother-in-law chirps from the background.

"Dad, you cannot make baby jokes in front of Betty. She's chomping at the bit for me to pop out a Ryan-shaped creature for her to spoil."

"Are you constipated?"

"Jesus, Dad, I didn't call you so you could take my medical history." I lower my phone for a beat in exasperation before returning to the call. "I'm pooping just fine. I'm getting plenty of exercise. I am not pregnant, and our sex life is robust and active."

My dad smiles from the other end, though I can tell I've made him squirm for once. *Good.* "Hollie Cat, I'm just looking out for you. You're my favorite daughter and all that."

"Har har." I'm his *only* daughter. Even though his ex-wife Aurora had an adopted daughter, Tanya/Moonstar hasn't stayed in contact with me or Dad since her cupcake company went viral and she became a confectionary bazillionaire. Just as well. It's not like we played the role of stepsisters for long.

And I called my dad so he could cheer me up, but maybe I'm

imposing on his mini getaway, and I should just suck it up and figure out my shit myself.

Knock knock knock.

"Dad, I gotta go. Someone's at the door."

"Call me tomorrow and check in so I don't worry about you."

"Say hi to my baby boy for me!" Miss Betty says, again scooting into the frame, her arm draped over my dad's shoulders.

Still weird.

"Love you both," I say, disconnecting just as the knock repeats.

"Coming." My calves are tight from all the walking. I open the door, fully expecting it to be Ryan without his keys or maybe even Tabby coming to gossip about the day's events.

"Oh! Hi, Harmony. Hello, NORA. Everything OK?"

"We brought you coffee," Harmony says, pointing to the evenly balanced tray in NORA's hands, upon which sits a French press, a Thalia Island-branded coffee cup, and a plate of what look like brownies. "Ryan told us your suite number. He said you really like coffee and sweet stuff. Also, we have a present for you." She lifts a craft-paper gift bag before her.

"Oh, wow. OK. Um, come on in." I step aside so they can enter. In the quiet confines of our apartment, the whirr of NORA's gears is more prominent.

"Shall I put the coffee in the kitchen?" NORA asks, scanning our space. I'm glad I tidied earlier.

"Sure. That would be great."

"Do you take your coffee with cream and sugar?" NORA asks, sliding the tray onto the kitchen island. "I would be happy to pour you a serving."

"Uh, sure. A teaspoon of both. Thank you." I switch between watching NORA and Harmony as she inspects our living space. While NORA pours, Harmony walks around the coffee table, cups her eyes to look out the picture window, runs her fingers along the book spines on one of the shelves, and then kneels in front of the curio cabinet that holds all my otter treasures just as NORA gently taps a teaspoon on the mug's lip.

"Here you are, Mrs. Porter-Fielding." The robot sets the perfectly lightened coffee in front of me on the island.

"Wow, thank you very much."

Harmony grins and hops to her feet, rushing toward me. She might be twelve, but she looks younger, her sun-kissed blond hair in a disheveled French braid. She has Band-Aids on three different fingers—I didn't notice that before—and her cheeks are bright with an enviable energy.

"NORA and I made these brownies with our own secret recipe *and*"—Harmony plucks the brown-paper gift bag off the counter and thrusts it toward me—"I made this for you too. Open it!"

"I'm the grown-up—aren't I supposed to be giving you presents?" I ask. Harmony grins widely, revealing some sort of orthodontia on her upper rear teeth. From inside the bag, I pull a tissue-wrapped gift, about eight-by-ten inches and flat, too thin to be a book. I tear the tissue free to reveal a painting of a northern sea otter.

"I painted it. In art class on the island. Do you like it?"

My eyes sting as I look up at the little phenom standing in front of me. "Harmony, this is the most amazing thing I've ever seen. I cannot believe you painted it."

"Harmony is very talented and improving her skills every day," NORA says. "I very much enjoy our nature walks and discussions about art history." The robot looks between me and Harmony as she speaks, much like a human would in natural conversation. "Would you like me to help you find a place to hang your new artwork?"

NORA moves past us and into the main living room. Our suite is on the small side, but when you live somewhere as beautiful as this resort, the apartment is really only for sleeping and downtime from work and guests.

The robot points at a spot on the wall above and left of the quiet gas fireplace hearth. "The painting should be at eye level for a human of average height to ensure maximum enjoyment." She turns toward me. "Do you have a hammer and small nail? I can install the artwork for you right now, if you'd like."

I'm pretty sure there's a tack hammer in the toolbox under the sink, but I don't love the idea of giving a chunk of molded steel to a robot I don't yet trust. Now I just hope she doesn't have X-ray vision. "Thank you for offering, NORA, but I would love to show off Harmony's work before hanging it in here."

NORA's lips pull into a smile that looks human *enough* but is still a tad unnerving.

"Harmony, seriously," I say, holding the painting before me. "I love it. Absolutely love it."

The kid beams and bounces on her toes before throwing her arms around me. "I'm so glad you like it! I read that story about you rescuing the baby sea otter, so I knew I just had to paint one for you."

Awkwardly, I return the hug. "Thank you again."

Harmony steps free and then plucks one of the brownies from the delivered plate, talking through a healthy bite. "I told Uncle Len I wouldn't bug you for too long, so we gotta go. We'll see you at dinner, yeah?"

"Yes." Not wanting to be rude, I choose my own brownie and bite into it. "Damn, this is good. You made these?"

NORA rejoins us. "It is a secret family recipe." She winks, albeit slowly. "We look forward to talking with you more at dinner, Mrs. Porter-Fielding."

"You can just call me Hollie." I smile at them both.

Harmony bounces to the front door, NORA fast on her heels. "Save me a seat by you at dinner! Bye, Hollie!"

And with that, the apartment is again quiet, nothing but me and my beautiful new art and this plate of the best damn brownies I've ever sunk my teeth into. I was insecure about meeting Lara Clarke, but I think this pint-size Einstein and her robot are going to make everyone feel inadequate this weekend.

I hear my dad's voice in my head: "The future is in good hands, kid."

As long as these brownies feature prominently in said future, he's probably right.

5

Since many of our guests are local, either from nearby islands or in villages and towns along the coast, our marina will be full of boats by day's end (yes, gas powered, but we have to start somewhere). Tanner is flying the keynote speakers, a handful of scientists and researchers, over from Vancouver, so arrivals should be a trickle versus the mad rush of a full passenger vessel all at once. As such, it's just Hannah and me at the front desk for now.

Chef Joseph and his crew have been up since before the sun, prepping and slicing and cooking all manner of deliciousness. I sense he's missing Miss Betty's hand with the baking, but Clarke Innovations brought three chefs with them to ease the catering burden on our team, despite Joseph's resistance to the idea. Last night in our employee-only chat thread, I saw Joseph grumbling about how they're getting in his way and how the GreenMuncher is already causing more problems than it's worth.

He's stressed out. He does not like strangers—or big changes to his process—in his kitchen. The CI chefs are spearheading an eco-friendly cooking challenge wherein guests will compete to create a tasty meal out of nature-first ingredients. (I do not know what that means. I thought all the food came from nature.) For that, they've

200

brought along with them huge coolers of stuff grown on and harvested from Thalia Island.

Thankfully, all of this food business is outside my scope of responsibility, so other than keeping Chef Joseph from going full Gordon Ramsay on the interlopers, my first concern this bright Thursday morning is finding places for everyone to rest their weary —and based on the number of Wandering Salamander lager kegs Finan rolled into the bar—likely alcohol-soaked heads tonight.

"Good morning, Hollie!" Harmony bounces to the front desk, NORA *whirr-clicking* at her side. I haven't had enough caffeine for this VERY exuberant child yet.

"Hey, Harmony. Hello, NORA." The duo stops before us. I glance at Hannah next to me and find her wide-eyed, mouth slack as she wearily watches the robot.

"Good morning, Mrs. Porter-Fielding. Although you did tell me to call you Hollie, is that correct?"

"Yes, NORA, you can call me Hollie."

"Thank you, Hollie." NORA looks at Hannah and shuffles a few feet closer. She lifts a hand. "Hello. I am NORA, the Nature-Oriented Robotic Assistant. And you are?"

Hannah reluctantly stretches to meet NORA's greeting. "I'm Hannah."

"Very nice to make your acquaintance, Hannah." NORA releases the young woman's hand and then slowly turns to take in her surroundings, including the group walking through the front door pulling suitcases behind them. "Please allow me to provide refreshments for your arriving guests."

"Oh, that's not necessary—"

"Yeah! We would love to! Come on, NORA." Harmony hurries toward the kitchen, NORA right behind.

Hannah leans close to me and whispers, "Robots freak me out."

"Did you not see her when they came off the boat yesterday?"

"I hid behind one of the Vikings."

"Not a bad view," I say, shrugging.

"And they do always smell so nice," Hannah whispers right as a couple approach the counter.

"What, no bell? It's always more fun to ring the bell." Smitty, owner of the general store south of us frequented by all the local island dwellers, leans an arm on the counter. His wife Audrey smiles at his side.

"Good to see you both." We make small talk about what's to come over the next couple days while Hannah types info and prepares room keys. I thumb through the Clarke Innovations-branded banker's box and find Smitty and Audrey's labeled conference packet and slide it across the desk, opening to show them the calendar of events.

"Clarke Innovations has been around forever," Smitty says. "In the days when I still wore a suit to work, I managed an equity firm that dealt with them quite a bit. Magnus Clarke was a good man. Honest, which is rare."

Audrey leans closer. "Is the granddaughter here this weekend?"

"Lara?" I ask.

Audrey nods.

"She's running the show."

"I just remember hearing about all that business with a drug cartel and some cult that had infiltrated Thalia Island." Audrey keeps her voice low and looks over her shoulder more than once as she speaks.

"You and Tabby should find each other and catch up on all the latest," I say. Hannah hands me their key cards and I push them across the polished wood surface. "You're in a suite, as requested. Private soaker tub on your deck, but remember that the door locks from the inside, so either prop it open or take a key card with you."

"Thanks, Hollie. Is that husband of yours around?"

"Somewhere."

"Sorry to hear about their playoff run."

I smile. "I'm not. I like having him home."

"I won't tell him you said that." Smitty laughs.

"Oh, he knows." I wink.

Just then, NORA and Harmony glide toward us. NORA carries a tray of coffee essentials while Harmony has yet another plate of those brownies, the dark chocolate squares of decadence circled by miniature muffins in a variety of flavors.

"Welcome to Revelation Cove. I am NORA. May I offer you coffee or tea? My friend Harmony has delicious, healthy snacks to start your day off right."

Smitty and Audrey look at me with the same awe and mildly afraid amusement we all experience upon first meeting NORA.

"Nice to meet you, NORA," Audrey says. "I would love a cup of coffee, thank you."

"Very well." NORA slides her tray onto the counter—and she's clever enough to look around, notice that more people have arrived behind Smitty and Audrey, and move to the quieter end of the check-in desk.

"That's new. You guys hiring robots now?" Smitty asks me under his breath as his wife follows NORA and a bouncing Harmony off to the side.

"She's just here for the weekend." I watch as NORA adds a splash of milk and a brown sugar cube to a Thalia Island-branded mug. Her hands move almost daintily as she lifts the insulated French press and pours a steaming cup. Audrey is entranced.

Hannah slides in behind my laptop and welcomes the next guest to the counter. Harmony talks a mile a minute as NORA prepares a second cup for Smitty. I'm about to welcome another guest forward and am stopped upon hearing, "Mr. Smith, how is your prostate?"

What the hell . . .

I rush to the end of the counter.

"Pardon me?" Smitty asks.

"I've learned much about you since our introduction, including that you have recently been diagnosed with benign prostatic hypertrophy and that your physician is referring you for further scans to rule out prostate cancer. Are you aware that prostate cancer is very treatable if caught early? According to the American Cancer Society—"

"NORA," I interrupt, loudly enough to catch the attention of bystanders. "Perhaps we can discuss something less personal than Mr. Smith's medical conditions."

Smitty's face is bright red, though I'm not quite sure if he's embarrassed or pissed.

"Smitty, I'm so sorry."

"How did you find this information, NORA?" Smitty asks. Audrey's trembling hand spills some of her coffee over the side of the cup.

"I am connected to all manner of digital records. I have your full name, address, and phone number from the guest list for this weekend's event. Your employment history and CV are available via social networking sites, so I am easily able to make sure you are Jonathan Richard Smith, a.k.a. Smitty, former investment banker and now owner of Smitty's General Store. Your general practitioner, Dr. Lawrence Rooney, works with a third-party vendor for billing and data analysis, and this vendor has very weak security protocols. I am therefore able to access your complete medical history during your time with Dr. Rooney. Do you have further questions for me, or may I offer you a baked treat?"

NORA turns to Harmony and gestures at the muffin and brownie plate.

Audrey slides the coffee onto the counter, staring into the mug as if she's worried it might be poisoned. Smitty then looks to me without accepting NORA's offer of food.

"I'm so sorry, Smitty," I say. "I had *no* idea she could do that."

"Did I offend you, sir?" NORA asks. "Please tell me so I can learn from our interaction."

Smitty looks right at me. "Did Clarke Innovations happen to invite any lawyers to this thing?"

Before I can answer him—pausing only because I'm not sure if he's serious and/or if I should be concerned and summon my husband's much keener legal mind—barking echoes through the lobby.

A guest in line struggles to hold the harness of her beefy yellow Labrador retriever wrapped in a school bus-yellow and white vest that reads *Working Dog in Training: Please do not pet.* "Luna, quiet. Behave yourself," the woman scolds.

Luna does the opposite of *quiet*, and then Acorn bolts onto the scene from whatever mischief he was causing, so we have two dogs barking, at each other but mostly at NORA. The service dog bares her teeth and growls, snapping as it resists its handler's tug and edges closer to the robot who stands, unfazed, watching.

Acorn seems to pick up that Luna is barking at the weird white thing that looks like a person but smells funny and then it's just a deafening chorus of barking and confusion until NORA lifts a pointed index finger and places it against her lips, as if shushing the furred, slobbery beasts.

Immediately, both dogs sit, whimpering, their eyes on NORA. Acorn paws at his left ear; Luna drops flat to the floor but watches the robot through wary, watery eyes.

"What just happened . . .," Hannah whispers next to me.

"I don't know."

"Should we be scared yet?"

"Maybe."

Which, of course, contradicts the voice in my head yelling *YES* at the top of her tiny lungs.

6

I text Lara Clarke to come to the lobby ASAP. Hannah resumes checking in guests as I pull Harmony and NORA into the back office. It's not my place to say anything to this brilliant but feral child, and yet I can't help myself.

"Did you know she could do that?"

"I mean, the possibility is always there, since she has real-time access to the internet, but we didn't specifically program her to be a nosy Nellie." Harmony gives NORA a dirty look, though I'm not sure if a sentient, non-human entity has the ability to interpret what that look actually means.

"I sense I have crossed a line in proper communication protocol. Is that correct, Harmony?"

"Yeah, NORA, you're not supposed to look up people's medical records and talk to them about it."

"I thought that would be considered polite conversation, to show Mr. Smith that I am concerned for his well-being and thus proving my mandate of providing help and service to my human friends."

"NORA, it's against all kinds of laws to delve into people's medical records," I add. "Polite conversation is usually about the weather or asking about people's kids or grandkids or pets or whatever. And I thought you were supposed to share nature facts with people, not talk about their . . . problems."

NORA's artificial stare is blank but when she hikes an eyebrow, it's creepy how real and yet how fake it looks, all at the same time.

"Lara said there's an issue here?" Len Emmerich's person fills the entire back-office doorway.

Harmony rolls her eyes. "NORA talked about some guy's cancer and now everyone's freaking out—"

"No, NORA accessed a guest's *confidential* medical records and asked very personal questions about information that should only be discussed between a patient and his doctor. Right, Harmony?"

"Fine. What she said." She throws herself into one of the wheeled office chairs and spins slowly, head back, expression annoyed.

"Mr. Emmerich, I meant no offense to Mr. Smith or his prostate. I appreciate the opportunity to learn more about acceptable interpersonal communication with humans."

Tanner's voice crackles via the radio on our communication and surveillance wall behind me. "One sec." I turn and pick up the mic. "Hey, Tanner, Hollie here."

"Yeah, hey, looks like I'm gonna need to fly one of the guests back. Something came up with his family, and he needs to go back right away. I didn't have a second trip planned today, but if you could log it and I'll file the flight note and radio Harbour Air that I'll be using their terminal again."

"Did something happen?"

"Not totally clear yet. I was just informed by one of the Clarke Innovations people that this guy has to go back to the city."

"Right. OK. Safe flying."

"Could you call Sarah and let her know? She's en route back to the Cove later today from Salt Spring. It would save me a step."

"Of course. Hollie out."

"Copy."

I pull the logbook from the shelf and make the appropriate notes and then text Ryan that his brother is heading back to the city —where is Ryan, anyway? Finished, I turn in my swivel chair to finish addressing the NORA situation and find myself alone in the back office.

"Oh. OK. Good. Now it's He-Man's problem."

Finally, a moment's reprieve.

As requested, I phone my sister-in-law and let her know Tanner is flying back to Vancouver but will be here for dinner. "Thanks, Hol. Here, talk to Elsbeth. I gotta untie so we can get underway. Love you." She then hands the phone to my niece.

"Hi, Hollie Cat. Mommy and me went to look at my new school, and it's SOOO big and nice, but I don't like the cabin we looked at because it's smelly, but Mom said it will be fine once we give it a good clean AND she said I can choose what color I want to paint the walls in my new bedroom."

"That sounds very exciting, Els! Tell me more about your school."

She launches into detail about the big windows looking out at the trees and the greenhouse where the kids are growing all sorts of things that they're even allowed to eat and that her new classroom has its own library and so many art supplies and how her new teacher, Ms. Dewey, was nice but she "talked to me like I was a baby and not five going on six" (I held my breath so Els wouldn't hear me chuckle) and how she hopes she's not the only kid in her class who knows how to read because she would love to have someone else to talk about books with.

Well, I don't know what's in the water here, but that's two child geniuses in the span of a hundred miles. Maybe between Elsbeth Fielding and Harmony Peck, we're not so fucked after all. Speaking of, "Elsbeth, when you get here later, I have a new friend for you to meet. Her name is Harmony. She's twelve, but she has a robot!"

Elsbeth squeals into the phone. She loves it when kids stay at the Cove. And I don't blame her—she's been mostly with her parents and us since she was born, her only interaction with other kids when they're here at the resort. She's super smart for her age, but like Sarah and Tanner have told us before, they're worried about her emotional and social development, that she won't know how to be "normal" around other kids. Hence, the repeated trips to Salt

Spring Island where they will be enrolling Elsbeth in a proper school and renting a place until they can sell their cabin an hour or so down the strait from here.

I'm sad we won't see Els and Sarah as often, but Elsbeth is so amazing, she will thrive no matter where she lands. Watching her befriend the youngest guests here at the resort always makes me nostalgic for those scab-kneed summers when Dad and I would set up our tent at a campground and within a half hour, I'd have four new friends, kids from surrounding campsites, and we'd find all kinds of adventure (and trouble) while our parents sipped beer and talked about boring crap like politics and the economy.

Hannah pops her head around the door, intruding on my happy thoughts.

"There's a reporter here, but he's not on the list. Can you come help me?"

I check the time. Still too early to start drinking.

Certainly enough, the journalist we eventually check in is not the one Lara Clarke had approved ahead of time. Apparently, *that* person got food poisoning from some dodgy sushi over Easter and still has not recovered, so this new guy—Trent Boullet—is filling in.

It's neither here nor there to me—we just swap out the other guy's room for Trent Boullet. Except Lara Clarke is very unhappy about this change, enough so that I find myself in the back office for an emergency huddle *again*, this time with Lara, Finan, and He-Man (Len—whatever) while the two men try valiantly to talk Lara off the fury ledge she's tiptoeing.

"He is an absolute *weasel!*" she whisper-yells. "That guy wouldn't know journalistic integrity if it bit him in the balls."

I bite my lip against a laugh. Hearing someone as refined and beautiful speak like a normal is kinda funny.

"You *know* what he wrote about Jacinta, that he's close, personal friends with Hale Watts. You know he's been looking for an angle to weave more of his lies, Finan." Lara then turns to her father. "You, of all people, know the damage Boullet can inflict. This weekend is supposed to be about positive change, about helping these local business owners. That dried-out foreskin will turn it into another of his gossip-fest 'exposés' where he'll drag out long-buried skeletons. And god, if Rupert finds out he's here—"

"Rupert probably already knows he's here." Len Emmerich places a hulking hand on his daughter's shoulder. "Boullet's been given the press packet everyone else has access to. The CI people know not to talk to him outside of the approved conference materials, on threat of termination and litigation."

Lara locks eyes with Len for a long beat, and he nods in reassurance. Not sure what has just transpired between the two of them—nor do I know who Rupert is or why him knowing about Boullet is problematic—but Lara's shoulders drop, and she shakes her head. "Fine. If that maggot so much as sneezes in my direction, he's out of here."

"Done." Len squeezes and then drops his hand.

Finan wraps an arm around Lara's shoulders and kisses the side of her head before turning to me. "So, obviously, we have some history with the so-called journalist. If maybe you could talk to your staff and let them know that we'd appreciate it if they'd stick to the talking points, that would be great. Boullet is known for his distaste for Clarke Innovations—long story—but we don't want to give this guy anything he can fester into a headline."

"Got it. No problem. I will let everyone know immediately."

"Thank you." Finan smiles, but it's tense, like he's worried, which naturally makes me think *I* should be worried too. He and Lara excuse themselves and exit the office, but before Len Emmerich leaves, I stop him.

"Did you get everything sorted with Harmony and NORA?"

He nods. "Sorry about that. I hope your guest isn't too pissed."

"Smitty's a good guy. It's just a little . . ."

"I know. Harmony is a lot. I'll keep an eye on her."

"Um, if it's any help, my niece is arriving tonight. She's only five and a half, but she's a smarty-pants like Harmony. Maybe if

Harmony and Elsbeth hit it off, it might encourage NORA to focus on the nature stuff, which is kind of the point of her being here?"

Len smirks. "Or maybe NORA's battery could accidentally go missing for a few hours and we'd all have some peace and quiet."

I think I like He-Man.

7

Whatever Len said to Harmony and her robot, it worked. We progressed through the rest of Thursday with no physical injuries, no distressed canines, and no further divulgence of anyone's confidential medical records. At dinner last night—a relaxed affair in the dining room where everyone mingled and drank their weight in ale and spirits—a mostly friendless Trent Boullet did approach NORA when she stood alone near the table where newly minted BFFs Harmony and Elsbeth, sugared out from the nondairy ice cream buffet, giggled like fiends.

The journalist was quickly steered toward the open bar by a CI staffer with the promise of a personal, pre-unboxing tour of the new LFC Biodigester first thing tomorrow. If that's not a lede to sell papers, I don't know what is.

And here I was worried my biggest task this weekend would be keeping people fed and entertained. I had no idea I would be conscripted to assist with dodging potential lawsuits and sordid tell-alls about the seedy underbelly of green nerddom.

He-he, get it … *seedy* underbelly? (Thank you for the courtesy chuckle.)

The glass shower door opens, startling me from my thoughts.

212

"You're not supposed to take such long showers. What if Lara Clarke finds out?" My beautiful husband steps under the almost-too-hot spray.

"I'd be more worried about her robot spying on us."

Ryan drenches his face and hair, and then I hand him the soap and offer him my back. He knows the drill.

"How'd you sleep?" I ask, practically purring under the ministrations of his lathered-up hands on my tight shoulders.

"I would've slept better if you hadn't been fighting someone all night."

"Yeah . . . sorry." I yawn. "My mother was center stage in dreamland. Again. She was here being all Lucy Collins with some sleazy new beau, and they were causing even more drama than we've already had and then her guy was pissed that we didn't have a runway big enough for his airplane."

Ryan snorts and returns the soap to the shower caddy and picks up the shampoo bottle. *Mmm, my favorite part.* "Well, she sure got you riled up. I was afraid you'd start throwing punches." He squirts a blob onto my scalp and digs his fingers in, scrubbing deep but not hard, washing the lengths and around my ears, relaxing me so much I could doze off right here.

"'K, head back." I follow his orders, and as soon as the shampoo is rinsed, he repeats the process with the conditioner. "Finan seems cool," he says.

"Mm-hmm."

"They're kind of an odd match . . . she's an heiress, he's an environmental engineer."

"Says the NHL star who fell for a lost cause at his posh resort."

Ryan pinches my butt cheek. "I was never a star, and *you* are not a lost cause."

"I was then."

He turns me around so our bodies are pressed together under the steaming stream. "Don't talk about my wife that way, please." He leans down and kisses me. "Did you call your dad yesterday?"

I fill him in, that our parents are canoodling on the Oregon Coast, and they look happy and relaxed. Our conversation transitions into our respective to-do lists as Ryan unfolds and then sits on the collapsible wooden tub stool so I can wash his hair and shoulders and back. (Yes. I bought him a shower stool. His bad knee has been acting up since the upper arm injury in February because why wouldn't it?) I will say, however, it was a good investment—*very* sturdy. Surprisingly so.

Once I have made sure my husband is well tended to, he's quicker out the door than I am so he can make sure everything's good to go for this morning's opening ceremony that begins in . . . ninety minutes. I cannot waltz into the ballroom looking like a drowned rat, so I pull my ancient hair dryer from under the sink. If Tabby weren't already booked solid in the salon, I would've begged her to make me look gorgeous, to quiet the insecurity harpy that catalogs every perfect detail of Lara Clarke and then runs a side-by-side comparison. And it's *so dumb*, I know, but my brain is mean, and whenever I spend an overnight REM cycle fighting with my mother and her terrible boyfriends, I'm a little off-kilter until about midday.

Ryan has left me a new Revelation Cove ~ Clarke Innovations Green It Up polo shirt folded on the bed. It's kind of a weird shade of green. But recalling some of Tabby's tricks from her many attempts to turn me into a proper girl, I choose an eyeshadow palette that I *hope* is complementary. I finally give up on trying to make my hair hold curl and pull it into a high ponytail. My growling stomach reminds me to hurry along or else I won't get food before the starting pistol goes off.

I avoid the elevators for expedience's sake and glide into the dining room to find it abuzz with happy guests eating and talking. Brilliant morning light pours in through the tall windows along the western wall—sky looks mostly clear, which is great since we have outdoor walking tours planned throughout the day. Everything in here smells so good—Chef, as usual, has outdone himself, so I beeline to the buffet table to grab a scrambled breakfast wrap and a cup of strong coffee.

Good mornings are exchanged with fellow staffers as I help myself to food. One of the dining room attendants sees me coming her way and pours a cup each of coffee and then OJ. "It's like you know me or something," I tease, thanking her as she follows me to a corner table where I can slide in and eat real quick before dashing off to be of use.

I've barely sunk my teeth into the whole-wheat tortilla stuffed with scrambled egg and cheese and veg when Tabby drops into the chair next to me. "Hi, good morning, I only have a second, but I have been dying to talk to you and it took you forever to get down here this morning."

I chew and swallow, chasing it with a sip of juice. "I thought you were booked to the gills."

"We are. I didn't think enviro-hippies cared so much about their hair, but the Clarke people brought *so much amazing product*, all-natural shit, I can hardly contain myself. We are going to have SO much fun next week playing beauty salon. Anyway"—she snipes a chunk of dropped scrambled egg from my plate—"that's not why I had to talk to you. Have you seen that reporter dude poking about?"

"Yeah. Trent something."

"Trent Boullet. Have you googled him?"

"No. Should I have?"

"He's one of the journalists who broke the story about that cult that was on Thalia Island, and apparently there was, like, a Mexican drug cartel involved." She lowers her voice and leans closer. "Lara Clarke's mother was a famous photographer, but she was also a *drug runner*. She died in a plane crash in some jungle when Lara was a kid, and then her *lover*, who is basically like Lara's aunt, was here hiding out in BC, on their island, but then she had to go on the run again and no one has seen her since."

"That would explain why Lara wasn't happy about Boullet sniffing around."

"I don't think he's here because he wants to learn about Earth Day." She steals another bite of fallen egg.

"Did you not eat, you little vulture?" I ask. "I sent out the memo to everyone based on Lara's request—don't talk to the reporter about anything other than what's on the summit agenda."

"I know, I saw it, but dude, come on . . . that is like next-level gossip, right?"

Before I can respond, a man's raised voice interrupts the room's conversational murmur. "Hey, I wasn't done with that."

I'm on my feet, programmed after five years of living and working here that unhappy guests are contagious. I freeze upon seeing that NORA has her left arm stacked dangerously high with dirty plates, most of which still appear to contain food. Diners look around the room at one another, expressions confused, many with silverware aloft in mid bite, as NORA stops at another table and picks up a plate from someone who is still very much engaged in eating.

"Shit," I mutter, scanning the room for Harmony, without luck. Someone needs to step in—I guess at this moment, I am Someone.

"Good morning, NORA," I announce as I approach, hoping not to startle her. (Do robots startle?)

She pivots, the plate pile haphazardly balanced but still upright. "Good morning, Hollie. How are you today?"

"Where is Harmony? It appears you are removing plates from people who aren't finished eating their meals. We have waitstaff who are happy to help our guests when their plates are ready to be cleared."

"Yes, I have noted that you have staff members whose job it is to clear plates and pour coffee. However, I am trained to observe and make common-sense decisions in real time based on where my help might be needed. Your waitstaff, while skilled and attentive, appear to be overburdened by the number of guests present in the dining area, so I thought I would step in to lend a hand." She turns her head and proceeds toward the next table.

Of course, I follow. "NORA, that's OK. Why don't we put those dishes in the bins and get you ready for this morning's opening ceremony?"

"I am ready for this morning's opening ceremony, just as I am prepared for the rest of the weekend's schedule of events." She picks up another diner's half-full plate, and I cringe when I see who it belongs to.

"Good morning, NORA. I'm Trent."

NORA pauses and gives the grizzled, greasy-gray-haired

reporter a once-over. The entire dining room is quiet, save the faint music playing through hidden overhead speakers. "Good morning, Trent. May I offer you fresh coffee or tea?"

Not sure how she'll manage that with an armload of plates. "I'll grab coffee for Mr. Boullet. Please, let's go to the kitchen and drop off these plates before they spill."

NORA's head swivels toward me. "Don't worry, Hollie. My body is configured to operate with safe, stable dynamics. I am perfectly able to balance this stack of plates." She then looks back to the guest who watches us, awestruck. "Trent Boullet. You are a reporter."

"That's correct. I am a journalist, NORA, and I'd love the opportunity to get to know you better over the next few days."

"No, thank you. I have been instructed to avoid conversation with all members of the press, unless you have specific questions about the flora and fauna of our local environs or should you care to discuss the benefits and drawbacks of general artificial intelligence systems or perhaps alternative energy systems."

"What if that's exactly what I want to talk about?"

"NORA, the plates—"

"NORA! What are you doing?" Harmony yells across the space, her tiny person standing on tiptoes at the dining room entry threshold, a grinning Elsbeth at her side.

And the robot who just assured me of her mad skills with object balancing *forgets* she has an arm full of plates and lifts her left hand to wave at Harmony, thereby dumping a dishwasher load of earthenware and half-finished breakfast foods all over Trent Boullet.

8

It's never a good look to have a guest drenched in food, especially when most of that food *should* have been consumed by the person who chose it from the buffet in the first place. It's an even worse look at a conference where one of the biggest topics of conversation is sustainable ways to deal with the huge amount of greenhouse gases caused by our global food production system. Or whatever Lara said last night over martinis. I complained about how gross green olives are; she popped two in her mouth and started talking about food waste.

From a customer service standpoint, I do everything I can to make sure Trent Boullet doesn't run to TripAdvisor and scratch out a scathing one-star review with his journalistic flair. On the flip side, when I offer to comp his food and drink for the remainder of his stay, I do feel a bit like I'm helping the enemy.

Boullet was pleasant enough, his jeans and light blue button-down drenched in maple syrup and Hollandaise and turkey bacon grease, though unrelenting when he again asked NORA for an exclusive. At that point, Harmony and Elsbeth had moved in and NORA easily ignored the reporter as the girls hurried her out. I think Harmony was even scolding the robot, but then when the threesome exited the dining room, the child prodigies erupted into laughter again, which then sent a wave of covert, hand-shielded chuckles across the tables.

A Clarke Innovations staffer swooped in to help, walking Trent Boullet out of the dining area, I presume to change clothes, and to fulfill the promise made last night to show Trent the new food digester thing.

Maybe Trent should've just gone out to the behemoth machine and fed it his yolk-soaked clothes and saved himself a step. (If he'd done that, he'd have to streak through the resort—and that is a privilege reserved only for me.)

I stayed behind to help staff tidy up the broken dishes and then made sure the last of the attendees was herded into the main ballroom for the Green It Up Eco-Summit opening ceremony. I had planned on attending, but Ryan is in there, so I'm sure he can fill my brain with whatever factoids he deems necessary. (I love it when he fills me with factoids. *wink wink*)

Once the opening remarks have concluded, I'll help escort the first group to tour our new modified shipping container greenhouses. Before, however, I require caffeination and maybe a banana to keep my mostly empty stomach from souring, since I know my abandoned breakfast has long since been cleared away.

I quickly check on Hannah at the front desk to make sure she's all good and am rewarded with a blueberry oat bar from a plate of deliciousness hidden from view under the counter. "Is this Chef's recipe?" I ask. Hannah's usually bright eyes are dull and a little bloodshot this morning. Me thinks she had too much fun at that open bar last night.

"Dunno. The plate was already here when I came down. I think the CI people made 'em."

"Have you tried these oat bars?" I moan on another bite. "Maybe hide the rest in the mini fridge so we don't have to share."

The unmistakable sound of crashing cookware startles us both. I look toward the closed kitchen doors.

"That didn't sound good."

"What now . . ." I shove the last of the bar into my face, hoping I don't choke to death between here and there.

"Good luck, boss."

I'm no more than a few feet away from the front desk when the smell hits me.

I push through the double doors leading into the kitchen and throw my hand over my mouth and nose. The kitchen, though never a hundred percent quiet when we have a big event going on, is in utter chaos. Chef Joseph is yelling and throwing utensils, staff are running around like their asses are on fire—

And the GreenMuncher is burping and belching smelly gas and undigested goo out of its bouncing lid.

It looks like a horror film where the machinery comes to life and eats all the people.

But I don't have to worry about trying to get everyone's attention.

The fire alarm does it for me.

Thankfully, the sprinklers do not kick on. *That* would have been a disaster too huge to overcome. As it is, the opening ceremony is unceremoniously interrupted, and as the guests file out and then gather outside (thank you, Mrs. Golden Sun, for showing us your face today), NORA and Harmony and Elsbeth take it upon themselves to walk around and ask if anyone needs anything.

Lara and her team work through the crowd, the CI people outfitted with little communication earpieces. Maybe we should have those too.

Ryan, Brad, Chef Joseph, and the Vikings follow our standard operating fire protocol and inspect the entire kitchen to make sure there is no active flame. Once it's cleared, the Vikings and Brad and a few other maintenance guys follow up with a thorough inspection of the main building to check if the alarm was triggered elsewhere. Tanner mans the radio and surveillance wall in the back office, communicating with the

Coast Guard and nearest fire station about whether we need assistance.

Ryan, me, Chef, and three dining room staffers stand in front of the GreenMuncher, now unplugged and quiet, but still as rank as ever. We take turns gagging and holding our breath until Chef passes out clean towels to cover the holes in our faces so we can keep our breakfasts in our bellies.

"This has to go. NOW," Chef declares. "I cannot even begin to count the number of health and safety violations with this thing in here. You guys are asking for a lawsuit, keeping it in the building when it's obviously severely defective."

He's not wrong.

With the rest of the building cleared of imminent threat, we meet with Brad in the dining room and quickly devise a plan for the maintenance crew to suit up in Tyvek coveralls and respirators, unload the contents of the GreenMuncher, and disassemble it for removal out of doors. In the meantime, housekeeping will come in and do a stem-to-stern cleaning, windows will be thrown open and fans set up, and Chef et al. will return to our former composting system, at least until the LFC Food Biodigester can be properly installed, which will be next week at the earliest.

While they're handling all that, I hurry back outside to find that Lara and her colleagues have successfully finished their welcome speeches and the guests are gathering in separate groups, ready to attend their first sessions upon the all-clear. I inform Lara that it is safe to go back inside, as long as everyone understands that the main floor will be a bit stinky for the next hour or so.

Three of the morning sessions are set up on the second floor, one each in our smaller ballroom and then in two suites we cleared of most furniture to make space for humans in bamboo folding chairs. A fourth group is heading to our huge, newly tilled garden that sits on former golf course land. Group five, who I am joining, is heading to the greenhouses that *I hope* smell better than the kitchen.

The expert in charge of group five is a forty-something woman named Dr. Toni Aiken. She's chipper and smiley and not at all put out by the unexpected derailment of the morning's events. As our group sets out along the pebbled path toward our destination, she makes easy conversation with the guests.

"This event is keeping you and Ryan on your toes, hey?" Smitty asks as he sidles up next to me.

"Seriously. At least it's not raining," I say, hoping I haven't just jinxed us. "Are you and Audrey having a nice time so far?"

"It's always fun to hang out here, even if it smells like fertilizer and a robot is telling everyone's deepest, darkest secrets." Smitty chuckles.

"Again, I am so sorry about that."

"Nah, don't be. It's fine."

Gravel crunches under our hiking boots. "Are . . . you OK, though? Like, is that weird for me to ask?"

"It's nice that you ask. That's what friends do." He smiles and pats my shoulder. "And I'll be fine."

"OK, cool. That's good."

"How's your dad doing?" Smitty, thankfully, pivots. He and my dad met the first year I lived here at the Cove and instantly hit it off. Then again, everyone hits it off with Bob Porter.

I tell him about how Dad and Miss Betty are now a "thing" and that it's kinda weird since Ryan and I are married and now our parents are dating, and Smitty cracks a couple jokes about how, if they get married, we'll have a family *stick* instead of a family tree, which inevitably leads to a jab about when Ryan and I are going to start building a hockey team of our own. I guess it's fair that he asks since I asked about the condition of the gland under his wiener that brews swimmer juice.

Gratefully, we reach the greenhouses before I can make excuses about why we're not parents yet, five-plus years after we married.

Dr. Toni Aiken thanks everyone for joining her session and begins her talk about controlled environment agriculture and how it is the most responsible, sustainable way to provide green, leafy produce for the planet. Though I did a cursory walk-through before the container gardens were set up with seed trays and everything, it's inspiring to listen to Dr. Aiken's obvious joy about the work she does.

"Let's go on in and visit some baby plants!" Dr. Aiken leads the way. The greenhouse is actually two rectangular shipping containers welded together down the middle to form a square structure. We have two complete greenhouse structures connected by a covered walkway in between. Inside are six vertical rows of young plants grown aeroponically—which means the plants aren't buried in dirt but rather their roots are exposed to the air and sprayed with nutrient-rich solution to encourage quicker growth.

Dr. Aiken demonstrates how the system works, explains how much better this system is for the environment, how the lighting and cooling systems are powered by the roof solar cells . . . I'm listening, lightly resting the newborn leaves of what I think might be cabbage over my fingertip, when a wave of nausea hits me.

It's likely because I didn't get enough to eat after the NORA dining room debacle, and I am woefully undercaffeinated, almost guaranteeing that a headache is en route. I take a few deep breaths with my eyes closed, hoping this gross feeling will pass, telling myself that in a few minutes, I will be outside in the fresh air and I can run in and grab a banana and some juice and see if any of those blueberry oat bars are left at the front desk.

I reopen my eyes, confident I can get through the remainder of Dr. Aiken's presentation.

Except with another few breaths, the nausea intensifies, and with it comes dizziness, severe enough that I tilt, almost losing my balance.

My dad's voice—again—echoes in my head: *Are you pregnant?*

No . . . I'm not. Right?

"Hollie, you OK?" Smitty grabs my upper arm. Before I can respond, however, one woman raises her hand, interrupting Dr. Aiken, and asks if there are chemicals or pesticides in here because she's feeling "woozy."

Her sentiment echoes around the space with a few head shakes and furrowed brows, more than a handful of people looking awfully pale and peaked all of a sudden.

"Why don't we finish this outside?" Dr. Aiken says, concern on her face.

Though I wait my turn to get through the exit door, I gulp the air like I've been under water for too long. The woman who complained of feeling woozy actually vomits into a bush while several other people ease themselves onto the manicured lawn to tuck their heads between their knees.

"Dr. Aiken, what is going on?" I ask, hoping to hell she doesn't tell me we have just poisoned these people. First the GreenMuncher fills the resort with toxic farts, and now this?

Dr. Aiken looks around nervously, pulling her cell phone from the pocket of her hoodie. "Well, uh, the greenhouses use pink-spectrum lights. And sometimes they can cause people to . . . feel unwell."

Another wave of dizziness hits me, like a proper spin of vertigo, and I reach out to grab her arm so I don't fall over. "You don't say."

<h1 style="text-align:center">9</h1>

Dr. Aiken suggests we return to the lodge for water and maybe crackers or bananas to make sure those affected recover quickly. We're halfway along the path when Harmony runs toward us, NORA trailing behind at a slower pace.

"Are you guys sick? I heard on one of the comms that somebody barfed," she asks, maybe a little too excited about the prospect of vomit. "NORA and I can help. We'll get ginger ale and ginger tea and whatever anyone needs!" She announces it loudly enough that group five members readily hear her, even those who still look a little green around the gills.

"That would be great, Harmony. Thanks," I say as she runs off. I then pull out my phone and text Ryan. I really think we should look into those fancy earpiece comms the CI folks have.

> Should probably get someone down to the
> greenhouses to check the air quality. A
> bunch of us feel sick. The presenter said it's
> the lighting, but just in case.

I can't watch my phone for his response and walk at the same time—looking down intensifies the lingering nausea. In under a minute, though, it buzzes in my hand.

RYAN

Shit. I'll send Brad down. Everyone OK?

I step off the path so I don't impede traffic and type a quick response.

I think we're fine. Going back inside for water and ginger ale. We shouldn't send any more tours through until it's checked, though.

RYAN

Right. OK, let me know if you need me.

I reply with the sign language *I love you* emoji and rejoin my group.

As soon as we walk back into the still stinky lodge, Dr. Aiken is joined by three CI staff members who, assisted by NORA and Harmony, pass out cups of ginger ale or tea to those who need it. Most everyone seems back to normal, except maybe the lady who hurled. And I'm not sure if it's because I didn't eat or what, but now I feel shaky and could use a minute of quiet.

Politely, I thank Dr. Aiken and excuse myself, considering for a second if I should check the back office for any leftover blueberry oat bars and then nixing the idea—if I don't skedaddle, someone will see me and need something. I do my best to look invisible as I head toward our apartment, keeping my eyes on the floor so no one makes visual contact and stops me. Thankfully, the halls are quiet. Guessing everyone is still engaged in their workshops and sessions.

I unlock our door and as soon as it closes behind me, I inhale a deep, steadying breath. In my old life as a 911 dispatcher, I dealt with some seriously messed-up stuff—heartbreaking loss and scary police situations and lovely old people trying to help their other half after a stroke or heart attack or diabetic incident. Not once have I missed those days; I'm not an adrenaline junkie. I only went into dispatching because I like helping people—my dad has always been a helper—plus it was a city job with good benefits. It was fine, for a while.

But after Ryan and I married and I started here full time, helping people took on a different shape. Initially, I worked as the wildlife experience educator, conducting walking tours around the island with guests and their kids to showcase our local creatures and plant life. Eventually, I learned I have a knack for marketing and social media, so my job morphed a bit, which has, in turn, helped Revelation Cove thrive.

I don't know if it's just this event or maybe that we've had a series of extra challenging situations over the last six months or that our future is in limbo, but I feel off. Tired. Irritated, even, from all the peopling. Like I'm a beat too late in the song and I can't catch up.

I should call my dad.

Except I know what he'll say.

I push off the front door, walk into the bathroom, and dig around in the under-sink cupboard for the box of pregnancy tests hidden back there.

At least I'll know, one way or another. And when it's negative and my dad teases me again, I can definitively tell him *no*.

I lock the bathroom door, just in case, and follow the instructions on the package.

While I wait for the pee-soaked stick to work its chemical magic, I count back to my last period. I'm not late, although my last period was lighter than usual. A careful grope of my boobs reveals tenderness, but nothing significant or out of the ordinary. I've only had the one episode of nausea—in the greenhouse—so why would I think that one stomachache automatically means I'm pregnant?

Because it's more than just a stomachache.

I stare at the stick, waiting for it to announce my future.

Except these are the hospital-brand tests that my dad snagged from the supply closet and secreted into my care last year when I was down in Portland visiting. (It's not like I want to talk about my love life with my dad, but he's a medical professional, plus he's excited about being a grandfather at some point, even though he *knows* I'm not sold on the idea of having children.) It doesn't have the fancy little window that says in plain English "pregnant" or "not pregnant," just colored lines—and I can't tell what the fuck that second line means. Sweat forms on my upper lip and the light-headed nausea returns.

I need backup, preferably someone who knows what she's talking about.

After a quick splash with cold water and a cool cloth on the back of my neck, I text my sister-in-law:

> Where are you at the moment?

Tick tock, tick tock … bubbles dance.

SARAH

> Elsbeth and I are in the garden session. You OK?

> Can you come to my apartment real quick? I have an urgent question.

SARAH

> Be right up.

I unlock the bathroom door and shuffle into the kitchen for a glass of water. Three bananas sitting in the fruit bowl are one brown spot away from being ready for bread, but I don't want to risk eating anything yet. Too nervous.

Oh my god, what if we're pregnant?

I've been on the same low-dose pill for years, mostly to manage my cycles and help with migraines, but maybe Ryan and I have had too much sex and his little spermies are just super aggressive and holy shit, I don't think I can do this—I'm not ready to be a mom.

Knock knock.

I rush over and crack the door to make sure it's Sarah and not

Ryan. "Come in," I say, yanking her by the wrist. "Where's Elsbeth?"

"She's with Tanner. Are you OK? You're white as a ghost."

I don't respond but instead pull her into the bathroom and point at the stick. "What does that mean?"

Sarah looks at the test stick and then back at me, eyes wide and mouth in an *O.* "Holy shit, Hols . . ."

"Sarah, what does it *mean*?"

She leans closer to the stick, grabs a wad of tissue paper to pick up the pee-free end, and then holds it up and moves so the lighting is better.

"Um, I think this means it's positive. But . . ."

I grab Ryan's shower stool and drop my ass onto it so I can tuck my head between my knees.

"I don't know, Hollie. This test is weird."

"It's from the hospital," I say, my voice muffled with my head upside down.

"Nurse Bob?"

"Yeah."

Sarah walks out of the bathroom with the stick—from my spot on the stool, I see her hurry across our bedroom and stand with the test by the window where bright sun pours in like a spotlight. "Yeah, I don't know . . . do you have any more tests?"

"I have one more. Do you have any of the store-bought kind?"

"Not here. I do at our cabin." She returns to the bathroom, places the test on the sink, and washes her hands. "What are your symptoms?"

I tell her about the nausea in the greenhouse but that it's more than that, especially since other members of group five felt sick and I can guarantee none of them have run back to their rooms to piss on a test strip.

"I think you should take the other test."

"Now?"

"Or wait until first thing tomorrow morning. That's when the hormone is most concentrated in the urine."

"But I don't want Ryan to know yet." My eyes suddenly sting. "I mean, if it's positive, he will be over the moon—but I don't know if *I* will be. And if it's negative, he might be bummed out, plus he might start talking about how we should think about trying, and again, I don't know if I want to do this yet."

Sarah kneels on the floor next to me. "Everything you've described could be stress too. One bout of nausea is not proof of anything, and like you said, all those other people were affected. I think you've just had a lot of shit going on with Ryan's injury, managing everything here, nonstop carnage the last few months, plus you guys are house-hunting and your dad and Miss Betty hooking up is still a little . . ."

"Weird. You can say it."

"I mean, it's great, and I'm definitely happy if they're happy, but yeah. It is a little weird."

We share a light laugh.

"You think it could be stress?"

"I do. Plus you're thirty now, kid. Things change with every new decade."

"Delightful."

She stands, groaning as her knees pop with the movement. "See? Nothing but fun times ahead, little sister." Sarah pulls me to standing and wraps me in a hug. I melt into her—Sarah's hugs are divine and heartfelt. She's not my sister by blood but by circumstance, and I could not have found a better one.

She releases and moves her hands to my shoulders. "If it were me, I'd take another test in the morning. This one is inconclusive. Either it's an old test and the chemicals have gone wonky, or it might be too early for the hCG to show up."

I nod—hCG. The preggers hormone.

"Either way, worrying about it is not going to help anything. Why don't you just hang out here a bit, maybe take a nap?"

"I can't. I have work to do."

Sarah shakes her head. "If you are feeling unwell, you need to take a minute. There are plenty of people here who can make sure things run smoothly. Think of it as Hollie o'clock."

I laugh. "Did you just make that up?"

"No, it's something Tanner and I do. When it's Sarah o'clock, he's on Elsbeth duty and handles everything so I can take a nap or a long hot bath or read a book or whatever else I want so I can unwind."

"I kinda love that."

"Me too."

I smile and hug her again. She's right. I could use a few minutes of no people. "I'll text Ryan and let him know," I say, pulling my phone from my back pocket. Sarah snatches it out of my hand.

"*You*, missy, are going to recline your body on that bed. I will find your charming husband and tell him you need a break and you are not to be disturbed."

"But I should be downstairs helping. Hannah cannot manage the front desk alone."

"Hannah won't manage the front desk alone. I will help, as will the other Revelation Cove employees who are paid good money to be here." Sarah herds me out of the en suite to my nicely made bed. Ryan's doing—he cannot leave the apartment without making sure the bed is made. "I will put your phone here, but you are not to pick it up when I leave to scroll social media or chat with Tabby or call your dad. You are to rest for one hour. Got it?"

"Yes, ma'am." I recline on the queen-size mattress and Sarah pulls a light blanket off the chair in the corner, draping it over my legs. Before she steps away, I reach up and grab her hand. "Thank you, Sarah." My throat tightens when I look at her and at once remember that she and Els will be living on Salt Spring Island soon, and our days like this will be farther and fewer between.

"One hour, mandatory rest, or no dessert." Sarah grins and squeezes my hand before walking from the room and closing the bedroom door behind her.

Out of nowhere, the first tear trickles out and soaks into my pillow.

10

I obey my sister-in-law. Mostly. I do rest for about an hour, though I don't fall completely asleep. I feel guilty napping in the middle of the day, during a very busy and important convention, when everyone else is working. But it's long enough that the nausea has abated and I feel stupid for freaking out and taking a pregnancy test *and* pulling Sarah into my self-created drama.

When I collect my phone from the nightstand, I am pleased to see only a few notifications instead of the deluge that usually happens if people can't get hold of me for more than ten minutes. A text message from my darling husband tells me to call him if I need anything, followed by two emails from our real estate agent in Langley with listings for houses that have just come on the market in our price range and preferred area. I see that she cc'd Ryan, so I won't worry about forwarding the emails. I *also* won't look at the houses because that is why I'm freaking out in the first place. Too much stuff going on for my tiny brain to handle.

I can't dally in here any longer, so with a quick freshen-up—and a thorough tidy of the bathroom *plus* hiding the pregnancy test in a wad of paper towels buried in the kitchen garbage because that's just nonsense, there's no way I'm knocked up—I'm ready to rejoin the world.

Except what if you are . . .

Quiet, harpy.

As I walk from our unit around the curve of the building toward the elevators, I come across a group of summit attendees gathered in front of a window that overlooks the northern expanse of lawn and the first few rows of our new garden area. Usually, we have bright orange temporary deer fencing around the plot, but it's been unstaked and put aside so people can watch as Clarke Innovations shows off a miniature prototype of one of their new agricultural robots that plants seeds. That's about all I know—it plants seeds.

But in the plot nearest the building, it's not the CI seed-planter bot carefully tucking unborn romaine lettuce into a nest of moist soil. It's NORA, and she seems to be planting tree seedlings, which are not at all what's supposed to go there.

"Wait—is she putting them in the ground upside down?" one of the guests asks.

I step right up to the window glass and squint to try to see better. Sure enough, NORA has a tray of fir tree seedlings, and she is planting them in the soil, pokey green end first, the tiny little root ball sticking out but due to its weight, bending the whole thing in half.

"I should probably tell someone." The small crowd chuckles and I hurry off in search of anyone who might have the controls for this mechanical knucklehead.

❧

I follow Len Emmerich, Lara Clarke, and two other CI staffers outside to the garden plot. One of the CI people who introduced herself as Meg, has an iPad balanced on one arm and is quickly swiping and mumbling under her breath as we walk.

"Does that control NORA?" I ask.

Meg smirks. "It's supposed to, but Harmony likes to express her creative side when it comes to writing code to train NORA."

"Does that mean you don't really control her?"

"Harmony or the robot?" Len asks, snorting. A look over my shoulder reveals that the people who were just upstairs watching out the window are now joining us. And a look ahead shows a small crowd has gathered, watching NORA work.

Lara, despite the high heels, steps right into the garden plot, the stiletto of her red-soled shoes disappearing into the soil with each step. The loamy, fertile ground has been shaped into mounded lines by the other smaller robot in preparation for planting seeds for food, not fir trees.

"Hi, NORA," Lara says, waving at the robot still about twenty feet from us. Between here and there, upside-down fir tree seedlings dangle sadly in the dirt row. The little things kinda remind me of a Charlie Brown Christmas tree—one branch and a tiny burlap-wrapped dirt ball, the baby tree bent in a curve from its own weight.

NORA pauses. "Hello, Lara. How are you today? Lovely weather we're having. I know you were concerned about rain, but the weather models show no chance of precipitation until the middle of next week." The robot bends and sticks another seedling into the dirt.

"NORA, do you mind pausing what you're doing?"

"Do you require my help elsewhere? I am happy to be of service." She plants another upside-down tree.

"NORA, my schedule says that you were meant to be assisting with the seminar on calculating the carbon footprints of our attendees' businesses."

"Yes. It was a very interesting discussion. One of the presenters talked about the importance of trees serving as a carbon sink to absorb the emissions human beings release with everything they do. When my part of the presentation concluded, I took it upon myself to be of use. These trees, when full grown, will participate in the process of absorbing carbon and creating oxygen, which is the point of your Green It Up Eco-Summit."

Lara interlaces her fingers and rests them against her chin. "Meg . . ."

The young woman with the frizzy hair and iPad steps beside her boss.

"Can you do something here, please?"

"I'm trying, but I can't get into Harmony's system without her password."

"Len, where is Harmony?"

"Last I saw her, she was with NORA." Len presses the little button that allows him to talk into his earpiece mic. "Does anyone have a twenty on the tiny tornado?"

I smile to myself. Perfect name for her.

"Hiiiii, Laraaaaaaaaaa!"

The adults freeze and look around.

"We're up here! Yoohooooooo!"

The *yoohoo* is echoed by a smaller, more familiar voice.

"Elsbeth, where are you guys?" I holler, slowly turning in a circle.

Then I see it. The flash of Elsbeth's favorite yellow sweatshirt, at least twenty feet up in a tree. Harmony is even higher.

"Aw, shit," Len growls.

11

Removing the girls from the tree consumes more resources than gassing up my dad's old farm truck to buy hay for the demon goat. Gathered are Sarah and Tanner, Ryan, the Viking twins Sven and Arne, Brad (who is annoyed because he's been looking forward to the Green Certifications 101 workshop for weeks), Finan, Len Emmerich and some of his guys, and now NORA, plus a very tall ladder that still doesn't reach high enough—and since the girls climbed a fir tree, a few lower branches have to be cut away to place the ladder.

By now, about half the people who were supposed to be in the afternoon seminars are outside watching what's going on, more than a few laughing about the nearly full garden plot of seedlings planted upside down. We kind of forgot about what NORA was doing when we realized the two youngest members of this weekend's island community decided to play Edward and Bella at the top of a Douglas fir. Except Harmony is not an immortal with superhuman strength who can transport a "spider monkey" on her back with vampiric grace and agility, and Elsbeth is not physically able to climb down the way she *somehow* managed to climb up. I'm sure the view is breathtaking, but unfortunately, we don't have a fire ladder company on hand to help with a rescue operation.

Lara and Finan, though not Harmony's parents, tag-team to cajole her down. They don't beat around the bush with bullshit sentiments, like the promise of ice cream or a trip to the toy store. Finan sternly reminds Harmony that she agreed to participate in the science of the weekend, not the mischief, and if she doesn't come down, her privileges afforded as part of the Clarke Innovations and Thalia Island team could be revoked.

She yells back that she's planning on coming down, but first they're waiting to see if any orca pass through the strait "because Elsbeth said orca are her favorite after sea otters." I bite my lip so I don't smile—that's my otter girl.

But soon, we're all rubbing our aching necks, tiring from looking up. NORA surveys the tree and surrounding area, offering her two cents on the best angle to set the ladder, but no one is really listening to her. She just planted a whole field of trees upside down—how can we trust that her math is solid?

The makeshift rescue squad moves the ladder a few more times, ignoring NORA's polite recommendations, and discuss the best way up. Once they've decided upon a route, one of the maintenance guys jogs around the lodge to the supply barn to retrieve the safety harnesses we use for tree trimming. Secondarily, they will affix ropes to the trunk and then around the girls' waists using a pulley system apparently borrowed from rock-climbing.

Then one among them—Finan volunteers—will climb up, secure each girl in the myriad straps and buckles, and then descend, first with Elsbeth, then with Harmony.

Ryan is under the tree, jaw tensing with frustration and likely fear as he keeps his eye on his niece. He would've climbed up there on his own already if his left arm wasn't still weak since February's injury.

Sarah is a nervous wreck, muttering harsh words about Harmony Peck goading her baby so high into the tree. Tanner wraps an arm around his wife and reminds her that he spent his childhood in trees with his siblings, and everyone turned out fine.

"Yeah? Should we call your mom and ask how much of your childhood was spent in an emergency room?"

Tanner snorts. "You know the likelihood of this arboreal adventure being Elsbeth's idea is probably better than fifty percent."

"No jokes until she's safe on the ground."

I nod in agreement at my brother-in-law. Although I, too, was a fearless kid, so it wasn't that long ago when a young me would've been up a tree looking for trouble. And seriously, how *cool* would it be to see orca from that vantage point? (Almost as cool as seeing them eye to eye in a rowboat during a storm.)

As Finan gets underway, he's only a few rungs up the tree when Tabby appears breathless at my side. "What the hell is going on? We were just doing a Zoom seminar with this kick-ass stylist from Los Angeles and I didn't want to cut it short."

"Harmony and Els climbed the tree. Now they're stuck."

"That kid, man . . . I hope they get them down before the fashion show. The Vikings are modeling, and I've been *so* looking forward to running my fingers through Arne's luscious locks."

"Haven't you run your hands through his luscious locks on *other* occasions?"

"That was Sven. But Arne? No. He's too traditional for me. Talks about babies and stuff." She shudders. And then I shudder, thinking about the dodgy, inconclusive pregnancy test hidden in the bottom of my kitchen garbage.

Hands on her hips, Tabby swivels and surveys the surroundings. "Um, what is planted in the garden?"

"Ask NORA."

Tabby's eyes widen in disbelief before she walks toward the symmetrically tilled plot. I watch her. She stops along the border that's usually blocked off by impermanent fencing and plucks one of the seedlings out of the ground. "Does she know they're upside down?"

I shrug. Clarke Innovations should've just given me the millions used to purchase and program NORA. I may not be an environmental warrior, but at least I know which end of the seedling goes into the dirt.

My phone buzzes in my ass pocket. First instinct is to ignore it—pretty much everyone who might need me is out here, so who could be texting? It buzzes a few more times. Shit, maybe it's Dad. Maybe something happened to him or Miss Betty and he needs me urgently and I'm already in the middle of something—

I yank it from my pocket. No text from Dad. Just a stack of Instagram notifications piling up in real time.

I click on the top one, opening the app. It's a picture of NORA's freshly planted field, posted in an account called Flat Earther. They've used that same picture as their profile image and the caption reads, "Clarke Innovations shines again with a robot who doesn't know which end is up. And Revelation Cove guests slurp the propaganda like kittens on a teat! #liberalagenda #greennewdealscam #solarminimum #poorstupidrichpeople."

I read it again. Then a few more times to make sure I understand what I'm seeing.

Someone *here*, on the island, has posted this, and within the last few minutes.

Despite the drama ongoing in the tree—which is less dramatic as Finan almost reaches the ground with Elsbeth strapped to his torso—I rush over to Len Emmerich.

"Uh, you might want to look at this." I hand him my phone. The likes on the post have increased in my short walk over.

Len's jaw clenches and crimson colors his cheeks and ears. Guessing that's what anger looks like. He pulls his own phone out, scrolls to the account, and then talks into that little mic thing again to alert his team that trouble is afoot.

"Thanks for showing me," he utters and then moves right in next to Lara and her two assistants under the tree. I'm just far enough away that I can't hear what he says, but he shows her the screen. I watch her face as it registers, and she looks up at her bodyguard slash dad.

It's not anger I see. It's fear.

<h1 style="text-align:center">12</h1>

Once the girls are back on terra firma and the spectacle is over, Sarah and Tanner disappear to Miss Betty's apartment with Elsbeth for what I assume will be a good talking-to and probably a bath. Given the amount of sap on her clothing, I think the tree was trying to hold on to her itself. Since Harmony is under the care of Lara, Finan, and Len, her lecture takes place as we walk into the building to deal with this latest insult. NORA follows behind us, quiet save the *whish-whirr* of her mechanical body.

Meg, one of Lara's assistants, agrees to escort Harmony and NORA back to their suite for a "rest," although pretty sure they just need her sequestered where she can't cause any mayhem for a bit. Life for Harmony must be very confusing—she's so damn smart, she doesn't know where she fits in society, and yet she's approaching that magical time when the hormones and attitude slowly take over reason. You can see she wants to snipe back at her keepers, but she's also wise enough to understand her position among the adults is at risk if she acts like a brat.

Either way, she's coaxed back to their room with the promise of preparing for the evening's fashion show since she and NORA will be walking the runway. As Harmony bounces away with NORA and poor Meg following, she questions if NORA will be the very first robot to walk in a fashion show in North America.

"To Google!" she yells as she takes off ahead of her cohorts.

"At least it will keep her busy for the next twelve minutes," Len grumbles.

We squeeze into the back office where Ryan and I offer whatever help we can to Lara and Len as we review our guest roster. I pick out and vouch for the local business owners who I know were excited to be a part of this weekend. The people I don't know, Ryan does—no red flags as far as he's concerned. I try not to get defensive when Len inquires about any staff who might be capable or interested in making waves. The people who work here are more like family than employees. But someone is causing trouble, and as Len so cynically puts it, "You think you know someone until you learn that you don't."

OK, He-Man, it was a snarky photograph, not a death threat.

Of course, Trent Boullet is number one on everyone's hit list, but he's been in sessions all day, plus his social media footprint is suspiciously small considering his line of work. And him, a flat earther? I doubt that. After NORA dressed him in breakfast foods, I asked the Clarke Innovations people to tread lightly around Mr. Boullet—he may be a rabble-rouser in their circles, but he's a guest in ours, and falsely accusing him of slanderous behaviour probably won't bode well for whatever article he's piecing together. I guarantee their PR department is much larger and better funded than ours, so unless they have evidence with which to poke the bear, let's not.

When it becomes obvious we will not solve the great mystery in this cramped space hunched over the hotel laptops, Ryan and Len excuse themselves to handle other pressing matters—Ryan, off to the kitchen to make sure the GreenMuncher has been fully dismantled and relocated out of doors (it certainly smells better in here), and Len Emmerich to gather his security team to triple-check that the ballroom for this evening's event is secure.

Finan pops in briefly to check on Lara, to make sure she's not upset or otherwise, and then disappears to finish the day's last session where he's supposed to be co-presenting with the shipping container greenhouse folks on the benefits of vertical and microfarms.

"You thirsty or hungry?" I ask Lara. "I think everything's mostly under control for the moment." More than anything, Lara Clarke looks tired. Her in-charge energy that usually radiates like static electricity is muted.

She looks up at me from the comfy but old, floral-printed wingback chair and then checks the smartwatch on her wrist. "Got any whiskey?" Her cheek pulls into a devilish half smile.

So that's how Lara Clarke and I spend the rest of the afternoon. I pour what remains in the Black Label bottle stashed in the back office into two coffee cups—I give Lara most of it, pouring a splash into my mug and then quietly diluting with water. I don't want to have to explain anything, but I am afraid to drink booze until I take that second test, just in case. I *feel* totally normal again, but yeah . . .

Just in case.

We then stroll around the resort to check on sessions in progress. Her worried face relaxes with each sip. She's probably used to top-shelf whiskey, but she doesn't complain and it's doing the trick. She explains that she's not usually so hands-on with these summits, so this year she's extra nervous since everyone has access to her, and that "it's been a weird few years."

During our walk, she asks about how I came to be part of Revelation Cove and then shares a bit about taking over Thalia Island after her grandfather's death. I'm *dying* to pick at the threads from the gossip Tabby shared, but I know better. If Lara wants to tell me more about whatever happened that has her so freaked out about that Instagram post or why she thinks Trent Boullet is such a menace, she will.

As the afternoon sessions are dismissed, the halls and dining area fill with people. The mood is high—I answer random questions while Lara, greased up from the whiskey, greets and chats with attendees as they mingle in the dining room lounge. Drinks flow and our guests seem excited and even antsy for dinner, the aromatic hints of which float from the very busy kitchen.

Vendors have small booths set up in the lobby and in the sitting area so our guests can pick up all sorts of freebies, everything from seed packets and countertop greenhouses to an Energy Saving Kit from BC Hydro that contains LED bulbs, weatherstripping for windows, and tap aerators. One table has the sign-up for the eco-friendly cooking challenge, inviting any novice cooks who want to participate using the home-grown ingredients the CI chefs brought as well as items foraged during tomorrow's boat excursion up the strait.

Honestly, before the weekend is over, as long as I get the recipe for those brownies Harmony made, I'll be a happy camper.

Lara is pulled away when her husband reappears, and I sneak into the kitchen to see what I can plate up to nibble on since I won't be joining the dining room crowd. I promised Tabby I'd help out with prepping the models for the fashion show; the catwalk will be populated with members of the Revelation Cove staff and some of the CI people.

When talking about the fashion show during our walk, Lara called herself a *shoe slut* and said she'd do just about anything to hang on to her Louboutin collection. After her grandfather passed away, she learned so much about the harm of fast fashion as well as which designers and fashion houses are working toward more sustainable practices. I joked about how *not* into fashion I am, relying instead on the same uniform day in and day out, and she declared that we need a girls' trip to Vancouver, her treat, so we can play makeover.

"I mean, yes, I love my life on Thalia, but sometimes a little retail therapy is the only thing that will keep me from poking people in the eye with a freshly grown carrot. You know what I mean?"

I do, in fact, know what she means.

When I walk into the salon with a platter of sustenance for myself and whoever else is in need of energy, it's already a hive of activity, Tabby at the middle of everything. The clothes for tonight hang labeled on rolling racks, and although I've seen pictures of the clothes in the slide decks the CI people sent ahead of time, it's fun to see them in real life.

These aren't outlandish or outrageous works of art fresh from some designer's Dali-esque brain. This stuff is practical fashion for every body size, every shape, manufactured in eco-first factories with alternative fibers derived from bamboo, orange peels, algae, mushrooms, pineapple leaves, cactus, grape skins and seeds, and abacá. In a word? Incredible.

I would wear these clothes. When I first read about this part of the event in Lara Clarke's proposal back in February, I'd expected to see weird outfits of cactus leaves, sans prickly bits, stitched together with, like, twine or something, maybe some burlap held together by snail slime—like Lady Gaga's meat dress, except with pineapple leaves.

These items are definitely way cooler than the meat dress. And free of *E. coli*. At least I hope. I have no idea how much Pepto we have on the island.

Maybe I should check.

13

A catwalk has been set up down the middle of the ballroom, flanked by rows of folding chairs. Attendees stream in, many double-fisting drinks from the open bar. And why wouldn't they? The bartenders were all too happy to come up with a menu of summit-specific drinks, including the Salish Sea Spritz (Empress 1908 or Fynbos Citrus gin, spruce tip syrup, and soda water), the Pollinator's Delight (a honey wine with lavender syrup, lemon juice, garnished with an edible nasturtium blossom), the Forest Floor (Shelter Point single malt whisky, edible dried mushroom, a dash of maple syrup, and a sprig of thyme), and the Zero-Waste Watermelon Margarita (Azuñia Tequila, watermelon juice made from leftover watermelon flesh, lime juice, Triple Sec, and sea salt on the rim).

The drinks are gorgeous enough that many guests abstain from sipping until they can snap a good picture to post to their socials. I'm dying to try every single one of them, but right now, I have to help direct traffic backstage and manage our "models," many of whom *have*, in fact, tested the cocktails already. Tabby and her helper flutter about with powder brushes and last-minute touch-ups, and it's clear she did get to put her hands in Arne's luscious locks. He looks as gorgeous as ever with a lustrous fishtail braid long enough that it drapes between his beefy shoulder blades.

Also? I can now tell the Viking twins apart: Sven cut off all his hair last month after he lost a bet with his brother, something involving a bench press. I don't know. They do have a lot of muscles.

I didn't realize this earlier, but among the outfits being modeled are those geared toward the hospitality industry specifically, from housekeeping uniforms to outdoor gear. Considering most of our guests operate hospitality and tourism-based businesses, it makes perfect sense to sell them on fabrics and products that are not only good for the planet but gentle to their bottom line—and they look way better than the usual stiff, itchy polyester crap.

So much for my burlap sack and snail slime idea.

As soon as I'm able, though, I'm gonna order one of the anoraks made of banana peel fiber. I wonder if they have anything strong enough to stand up to a cougar bite . . .

Lara Clarke is tonight's emcee, dressed to the nines in what must be an eco-friendly power suit complemented by another gorgeous pair of red-soled high heels—her trademark, I'm learning. She sips lemon tea backstage in the corner as one among her people fixes her hair and another one brushes powder over her cheekbones, Lara unbothered as she reviews a stack of notecards for the imminent presentation. Our very own band, the Garden Gnomes, have set up alongside the stage and play mellow covers of pop songs to serenade guests finding seats.

"Doesn't everyone look amazing?" Tabby says as she rushes up to me. A clear, cross-body plastic purse slash tool bag hangs from her front that holds all her beautifying instruments. "I didn't think this would be so much fun."

"Good evening, Hollie." I startle as NORA appears out of nowhere. There's just enough noise back here that I missed her telltale mechanical gait. "What do you think of my outfit? I've never worn human clothes before." NORA pinches her skirt and pulls it to the side to display the fabric. "This skirt and blouse combination is made of bamboo and orange peel silk. It hangs nicely on a person's body, don't you agree?"

"I do, NORA. It looks great."

"Thank you, Hollie. Also, I apologize for planting your fir seedlings incorrectly. Harmony informed me of my error, and I would be happy to rectify my mistake first thing tomorrow."

"It's all right, NORA. We'll get it sorted."

"Thank you for your understanding. Did you know this is my very first fashion show?"

"I figured it might be. You look terrific."

"I do look terrific. Thank you." NORA stares at me, I think—her artificial eyeballs are supposed to mimic that of natural human muscle movement, but her gaze is still blank, even with one eyebrow lifted, a few blinks, a partial smile. "Are you not participating in the fashion show this evening, Hollie?"

"It's enough for me to help backstage. I'll save the showing off for the beautiful people." Elsie, modeling one of the *very* cute housekeeping outfits, overhears me and twirls, her red curls fanning out around her.

"Do you not consider yourself a beautiful person, Hollie?" NORA asks.

"No . . . that's not what I meant." OK, so this robot doesn't understand humor or nuance.

"Hollie, is it because your mother, Lucy Collins, is incarcerated that you feel that you are not one of the beautiful people?"

I freeze. "NORA, how do you know about my mother?"

"I looked up your Facebook profile. With a few quick connections, I have learned that your mother was not present in your life when you were a child. After conducting a wide search of public records databases, I came upon a hit from the Oregon Department of Corrections via their offender search tool. Would you like me to provide the URL for my search results?"

"No. That's more than enough for tonight, NORA."

"I think you are a good deal more accomplished than your mother. You do not have a criminal record whatsoever and your physical attributes, while not perfectly symmetrical, are pleasing."

Oh my god. "Yes, wow, OK, thank you. Where is Harmony?" I look around us, hoping the wunderkind will appear so I can let her know her robot is doing that THING again.

"Harmony is changing into her outfit for the fashion show," NORA answers. "Would you like to know the recidivism rate of women your mother's age who commit crimes such as fraud, forgery, and petty theft?"

Now it's my turn to stare blankly at NORA. "Um, will you excuse me? I should go see how close Lara is to getting underway."

"I would be happy to send her a text message for you—"

"Nope, I'm good. I'll just walk over and ask. Thanks!" I hurry away before she looks up recidivism rates or my tax returns or Jesus, what if she finds my long-abandoned blog from high school on which I wrote bad poetry while under the influence of pubescent ennui and Red Bull?

Just what I need—NORA sharing it with Tabby and then I will never hear the end of sad Hollie who thinks "love is for losers." Hey —fifteen is hard when your history teacher is hot as sin and every day, instead of paying attention to lectures about the assassination that kicked off World War I, you are cursing fate for bringing you into the world a generation too late because a torrid romance à la Danielle Steel novels between you and Mr. Doty will never happen.

"Hollie!" Harmony waves as Tabby's assistant dusts her face with a light powder. "How do I look?" She does a quick 360, almost losing her balance.

"Amazing!" I offer. She does too—she's wearing a coordinating shorts and top outfit that looks straight out of a J.Crew summer catalog. I don't think the Converse are environmentally friendly, but like Lara has said multiple times this weekend, "baby steps."

"Hols!" Tabby whisper-yells at me from across the space. "T-minus two minutes!"

I give her a thumbs-up and pluck my own index card listing the model order from my back pocket and then make sure everyone's queued properly. While we don't have a proper stage in this ballroom, Clarke Innovations brought in an entire framework that includes lighting and a heavy, pulley-system curtain made out of repurposed billboard canvas. It's so cool—I should ask Ryan about buying it from them.

Quickly, I peek through a split in the curtain to see we have a full house, the conversation a light buzz above the live music. Usually the Garden Gnomes vibrate the windows in their panes with their shows, but tonight, they're channeling their inner Muzak.

I scan the crowd and then the backstage area for my husband—we've been like passing ships since this whole conference started. Was it only yesterday all these people arrived? Tabby tried like hell to get Ryan to model tonight, but he declined on account of wanting to support Len Emmerich and his team, just in case there's more funny business along the lines of the mean-spirited Instagram post.

Trent Boullet is front row, his black notebook resting on his thigh while he sips one of our signature cocktails. He's not dressed up for the evening, unlike many of the guests who've changed into fancier duds. I hope he doesn't write cruel stuff about the fashion show. The clothes are actually really nice, and the fact they're made of earth-friendly fabrics and manufacturing processes is icing on the cake.

Or maybe they're the cake itself.

The Garden Gnomes wind down their current selection (with apologies to Adele for what they just did to "Rolling in the Deep"), and the drummer picks up with a steady snare roll as the lights dim and the conversations hush. Instead of live music, the evening's soundtrack—a prerecorded EDM mix that vibrates through my molars—pulses through the speaker system. Lara Clarke, mic in hand, slides through the curtain, immediately warmed by a spotlight.

"Good evening, everyone, and welcome!"

Applause.

"We have an amazing show for you tonight . . ." She thanks everyone for attending, then launches into a list of the designers, the fabric manufacturers, and the innovators behind the tech. She also points out that the program for tonight's event, printed on one hundred percent consumer-grade recycled paper, has all the contact information for the presenting companies with three reps available on-site to talk about custom orders. "But I would rather let the clothes do the talking for me, so off we go!"

The spotlight darkens, the music changes, and the heavy curtains part wide enough for a human to sashay through. The music volume decreases enough as one at a time, the models strut their stuff down the catwalk accompanied by Lara's narration of fabric, designer, and product availability. This show does not have any professional models—everyone showing off the clothes are actual people with hips and thighs and tummies—which is great. We might be encouraging our attendees to find ways to reduce their carbon footprints, but an anemic runway model who looks like she's on the verge of fainting will not save any cows from the abattoir.

I'm still backstage, keeping the models in order and trying very hard to avoid additional interaction with NORA. She stands perfectly still next to Harmony, who bounces on tiptoes as she watches the people ahead slip through the curtain into the spotlight. She looks a little nervous. Can't say I blame her.

My phone buzzes against my butt. I pull it free to find a text from Ryan: *I'll bet none of these designers would be as skilled as the Titillating Tailor.*

I smile, warmed by the recall of the other night.

Oh, I guarantee none of them are. I miss you. I need some tailoring.

RYAN

Me too, babe. You feeling OK after this morning?

Yeah. I'm PMS'ing, so that didn't help matters.

I don't need to tell him about my weird mood swings or the erratic urge to take a pregnancy test. Around dinner, my usual lower backache settled in, and a headache hints it's about to make landfall —all signs of an imminent visit from my crimson cousin.

RYAN

Sounds like someone needs the Masterful Masseur to pay a visit and work out any KINKS.

Mmm, kinks. What page is that on?

RYAN

Page 69.

Ha ha ha ha ha … sounds about right. But will the Masterful Masseur be too tired to service his customer?

Our flirtatious banter comes to a screeching halt when the throbbing EDM and audience applause is overtopped by the angry yells of individuals very much not on our guest list.

14

The duo gets some good shouts in and unfurl signs above their heads before Len Emmerich and his crew escort them —not gently—from the stage. They continue to yell on their way out of the ballroom, through the lobby, and then out of doors. We don't have a brig or jail or anything here on the island, so I'm guessing Len and company will have to wait outside with the interlopers until the RCMP are summoned. Again. They were just here on Valentine's Day weekend when Mushroom Cap Joe, a fungus from my past, respawned and doused himself in liquor and bad choices.

The protesters yelled about how Lara Clarke is a hypocrite, that CI is among the rich polluters lying to consumers, that CI is "lining its pockets by raping Mother Nature." They continued screaming about corporate greed and planetary collapse as a result while being dragged outside.

The fucked-up thing? *We don't know who they are.*

Lara is visibly distressed by the intrusion, enough so that she hands off the mic to her assistant, Meg, who tries valiantly to corral interest back to the show and the handful of models remaining. Meg doesn't have Lara's charisma, however, so despite her excited efforts to describe the final few outfits and designers, guests are either hunched over their phones or huddled in wide-eyed conversation.

The guests at the Cove this weekend are business owners who live on small nearby islands or in remote coastal communities, each business catering to a specific demographic, which is almost diverse as the creatures that live in our expansive wilderness. To say they're not accustomed to protesters or those situations that might be considered "big-city problems" would be very accurate.

The show concludes with quiet applause, and the audience filters out of the ballroom. The reps from the clothiers showcased on stage mingle in the lobby and dining room lounge, offering seed-paper rack cards printed with their QR codes. The kitchen staff lay out the eco-friendly dessert buffet a bit earlier than planned, and bartenders work double-time to loosen the tight knot the protesters tied everyone in. It doesn't take long, thankfully. Sugar and gin have that effect on people.

Tanner gets hold of the local RCMP detachment while Ryan encourages the Garden Gnomes to restart—maybe get people dancing so they're not all rubbernecking to get a glimpse of the two protesters still yelling at the top of their lungs down on the dock. Len Emmerich and his team have it under control—the couple have been "helped" to the ground, their hands zip-tied behind their backs. And still, they yell. We can't hear what they're going on about anymore since they're far enough away from the lodge's front entry, but I'll make sure someone gets Len Emmerich an industrial-size dose of Advil before the night's end.

"What the fuck, dude?" Tabby slides around the counter, a cocktail in one hand, a plate of baked sweets in the other, to join me at the front desk. I retreated here to answer questions and maintain order when Hannah was summoned to resume her spot as the Gnomes' tambourine queen. "Who was that and how did they even get in here?" Tabby sips a purple-hued beverage from a highball.

"If they're not on the guest list, then they probably snuck in while we were all occupied with dinner and then the fashion show."

"Oh! Let's check the security footage." She starts to move toward the door to the back office.

"Leave it for now. I don't want to accidentally erase anything that could be evidence."

"Right. Smart." She picks up a powdered-sugar-dusted brownie, bites into it, and moans. "We *have* to get this recipe."

From stage left, Sarah hustles toward us, Elsbeth in pajamas and her otter slippers, wet hair combed back post-bath, her bright expression announcing her glee to be back at the party. After dinner, Sarah scuttled her daughter off to Grandma Betty's apartment for popcorn and movie night—young Elsbeth had spent enough time in the presence of trouble, a.k.a. Harmony Peck, for one day.

"What happened?" Sarah asks just as Elsbeth spots Harmony and yanks free of her mother's grip to rejoin her elder compatriot at the dessert table.

"Party crashers," Tabby says. "Here, try this." She slides her drink toward Sarah, who lifts a hand to refuse.

"Two people jumped onto the stage just before the end of the fashion show and started screaming about Lara Clarke and her company," I say.

"*How?* Where did they come from?"

"Don't know yet," Tabby answers. "I'll bet you a hundred bucks that reporter dude smuggled them in somehow."

I scan the mingling crowd in the lobby and sitting area, searching for Trent Boullet as Tabby and Sarah hypothesize how the protesters got here in the first place. I didn't get a good look at them, so I can't say for sure whether they're guests, although Len Emmerich made it very clear they vetted everyone invited ahead of time.

The couple could've easily landed a small boat along one of the beaches on the opposite side from where the lodge sits and then walked across. It only takes about fifteen minutes to walk from the most western side to here—far enough away to be hidden from view of the main resort area but small enough to still permit a quick getaway if needed.

Though our legit guests look like they've recovered and forgotten the disconcerting encounter, Lara is all business as she, Finan, and

Len Emmerich reenter the lodge. If they're finished at the dock, the police have picked up the trespassers.

Sure enough, right after, Ryan and Tanner walk in. My husband and I make eye contact and he nods, his sign that everything is handled.

Good. OK.

We just have to get through another hour or two without any major disasters and then I can retreat to my sanctuary and molest my husband and then we can all start a vibrant new day tomorrow and be one day closer to all these people going back to their lives far away from here.

Other than Acorn and the service dog going mental about NORA again, we made it to lights out without any further assault to our person or property. People danced, drank, and desserted until they were blue in the face.

"I thought service dogs were supposed to be chill." I'm naked, on my back in our bed, exhausted but satiated, as Ryan offers me a glass of water. He, too, is devoid of clothing, standing over me on my side of the bed, a sheen of sweat on his lightly haired chest.

"I just gave you the ride of a lifetime and you're thinking about the service dog?"

I sit up and accept the glass. "Thank you, my lord." I chug the clear, cool water and watch his fine buns as he circles the bed and reaches into the bathroom to turn off the switch. "I'm just saying … and I feel bad for Lara Clarke. It's like she's always lived under this microscope and now they keep having weird shit happen to them. Did you see her face when those protesters were screaming on the stage?"

Ryan slides under the sheet and as soon as I've set the empty glass down, he pulls me toward him, his long body the ladle to my spoon. "She's pretty freaked out, but her husband and Len are managing it."

"Did you know Len Emmerich is Lara's *father*?"

"Who told you that?" Ryan asks, trying to get comfortable.

"Tabby."

"And you believed her?"

"Oh, and when we were backstage getting ready, that stupid robot asked me about Lucy Collins."

Ryan lifts his head from his pillow to look at me. "They're just begging for a lawsuit with that thing prying into people's personal lives."

"NORA told me my mom's in jail—oh, and that I have an almost symmetrical face."

He drops his head again and takes a deep breath. "You already knew that."

"About the jail or my face?"

He pinches my ass under the cover in response. "I don't remember the last time we had an event with so many issues. Tomorrow will be better," he says against my bare shoulder. His beard whiskers tickle.

"Did you honestly just say that out loud?"

"I take it back." He kisses my nape.

"Too late. You just poked Fate right in the booby."

He bites me softly and wraps his skinny, scarred left arm around my front where he tucks his big hand between my scant cleavage. "No more talking, Porter. Time for sleeping. I want to surf this afterglow right into la-la-land."

I grab his hand and kiss his knuckles. "Good night, my sex god. Love you."

"Love you too, vixen enchantress."

Within a minute, Ryan's breathing slows. How does he do that? How does he fall asleep so fast? Like a milk-drunk kitten.

I should be out too. I could've fallen asleep on my feet an hour ago, but now? This is the time of night when my brain decides we should revisit all the bad choices and lost arguments we've had since my cells learned how to form memories.

Speaking of memories . . .

I give Ryan another couple minutes to really fall under and then carefully *streeeeeeetch* my arm to the nightstand to grab my phone. What the hell did I call that blog again . . . OH! The Bleeding Quill.

I google it.

And sure as shit, *The Bleeding Quill* is still alive and well on the interwebs, an untouched time capsule of terrible poetry, imagined conversations, and poorly composed black-and-white photographs taken when I was trying to be an *artiste*.

I cannot believe it.

I'm dying to show Ryan, and yet I might die if he sees it.

Aw, melodrama, my most steadfast compatriot.

I flip through, rereading the sappiest, gooiest shit I don't remember writing—cringing through most of it, giggling into my pillow more than once—and make a Note to Self to apologize to Nurse Bob for putting him through my adolescence. That poor man.

An hour lost to the scroll, my eyes burn and my lids keep dropping closed.

Enough for tonight.

I slide my phone face down on the nightstand, smiling about how maudlin, heartsick, fifteen-year-old Hollie thought she'd never find love, convinced she was destined to be alone forever, locked in the old farmhouse, and no knight would dare approach because Mangala the demon goat would spear them to death should they intrude upon his domain.

As I cozy under the blankets, my real-life sleeping knight wraps his arm around my midsection and pulls me close, nuzzling the back of my head as his soft snores fall into my ears.

I like thirty-year-old Hollie's story much better.

15

When Ryan's home, I don't have to set a wake-up alarm. He is still my concierge in all ways, so even though he's usually up and out before I am, he knows how much I love to wake to the aroma of freshly brewed java. As such, a full pot awaits my zombified shamble and haphazard pour into my lucky otter mug. Not a bad way to wake up, if a person were interested in doing such a thing.

Today, I am not that person.

Alas, I am a grown-up with grown-up responsibilities and if I don't throw off these blankets and face the day . . .

As if reading my mind, my phone buzzes on the nightstand.

"Leave me alone," I mutter to no one, yanking the bedcovers over my head. After a minute, the phone does its courtesy buzz to remind me an unread message awaits. Although the sun is up and shining through the sheers over our bedroom window, I keep my head under the blanket and thrust out a hand to search the top of the nightstand. Naturally, I search too aggressively and like a puck on an air hockey table, my phone slides off and wedges itself between the small cabinet and the wall. *Goal!*

"Fuuuuuuuuuuuuuuuh," I growl, striking out at the covers like it's their fault I have to get up. I then twist myself into a pretzel to find that effing device that allows everyone in the world way too much access to my personal time. Finally, I slide it free, noting I forgot to plug it in to charge so the little battery icon at the top glows a finger-wagging red. "This better not be a sign of the day ahead."

I roll onto my butt and sit crisscross applesauce against the side of our bed as I grab and insert the charger dangling from my nightstand drawer. The screen brightens with the message that just couldn't wait.

SARAH

Did you take the other test?

Shit. I totally forgot about it.

Not yet. I think my period is on its way. Explains why I was temporarily insane yesterday.

SARAH

Or . . . could be those early hormonal changes.

FINE. I will take the other test just to be sure. You just want me pregnant so you can laugh at MY swollen ankles this time.

SARAH

LOL, not true, but maybe it will get Miss Betty off my back for a while. She doesn't understand the concept of one-and-done. Are you coming down for breakfast?

Yeah. Will you see if the CI chefs have any of those blueberry oat bars left? Be there in 30.

I pull myself up, grab clean clothes for today, and then lock myself in the bathroom, hoping that when I emerge, I am still one person and not two.

§

I'm tying the laces of my second boot when someone knocks. Anxious thoughts blast at warp speed through my brain: *Did I bury the second NOT POSITIVE pregnancy test deep enough in the kitchen garbage? Did I drop any evidence on the bathroom floor? Are NORA and Harmony here to deliver a fresh batch of mayhem?*

"Hols, lemme in by the hair of my chinny-chin-chin." Tabby.

I pull open the door and pause as I take in my friend standing on the threshold. "OK, I do not like the look on your face," I say.

"You're gonna like it even less when you see this." She holds her phone in front of her, but I turn and retreat to the kitchen without taking the bait.

"Coffee first."

She follows me. "Have you talked to anyone other than Ryan this morning?"

I shake my head no.

"Well, it seems whoever made this latest shit post on Insta might be connected to the protesters last night, who, by the way, did land a small boat on the west side of the island and then snuck in. They weren't guests, but they must have someone on the inside helping because they were dressed like the rest of the crowd—they didn't stand out."

I add too much lightener to my coffee. "I guess that's both good and bad."

"Yeah, I don't think Lara's bodyguard dad got any sleep last night. He was in the back office keeping an eye on the surveillance wall when I went to bed, and he was there when I got up." Tabby darkens her phone, sets it on the island, and helps herself to the coffee cup cabinet. "You know what I was thinking? Maybe Len Emmerich isn't an actual person. Maybe *he's* the robot and NORA is just a decoy, you know, like a distraction so we don't see the truth. Maybe Len is Robocop or something."

"And maybe you've been drinking already this morning," I say, sliding onto a barstool.

"I'm just saying"—she pours herself a cup of Joe—"stranger things have happened."

Grudgingly, I retrieve my phone from my pocket, navigate to the settings, and turn on Instagram notifications. I silenced them after the first nasty post from Flat Earther—nothing can be done about it, unless we search the phones of every single person here (totally illegal, BTW), discover the agitator, and boot them out. Just because participants had to sign nondisclosure agreements for the weekend doesn't mean they'll adhere to them.

I scroll to IG, my empty gut knotting and growling at the same time. Sure enough, Revelation Cove and Clarke Innovations have been tagged in a series of images showcasing last night's protesters on our stage, them being dragged off stage, and then the two people zip-tied on their asses down at the dock. The captions include more of the same rhetoric from their prior post with a few new hashtags: #globalwarmingmyth and #CO2islife.

"This doesn't make sense. Is Flat Earther supporting the protesters yelling about rich hypocrisy and corporate greed or are they confused about their own cause? It doesn't line up."

Tabby leans on her elbows on the island, her mug cupped in her palms. "I think Flat Earther is probably looking for any and all angles to stir up shit."

"Obviously, but like—*who* could this be? Based on the positioning of the photos, they were obviously in the ballroom and then outside with a view of the dock."

"Or maybe someone here is just taking the photos and sending them to Flat Earther off island who is then posting them to cause trouble."

"Either way, it *is* causing trouble. Look at all these likes and comments." I hold up my phone.

Tabby slurps her coffee. "You know what they say—all publicity is good publicity."

"I'm gonna go out on a limb here and suggest that Lara Clarke probably doesn't see it that way."

"Which is why she has Robocop to keep her safe." Tabby checks her watch. "Shit, I gotta go. Excited to try out some of the new toys CI brought us. Demonic chin hairs will not get the best of me today!" She dumps the rest of her coffee in the sink, rinses her mug, and snatches her phone from the countertop. "You going on the cruise later?"

"Yeah."

"Take a raincoat." She slides her phone into her back pocket.

"It's supposed to be warm and clear for the rest of the weekend."

Tabby holds out her hands in front of her, fingers splayed. The pinky finger on the left is bent funny—a break as a kid that never properly healed. "My lucky finger aches. That means rain is coming."

"That's your professional meteorological opinion?"

"Absolutely. No charge." She heads toward the door. "Thanks for the coffee. I'll keep an eye out for Flat Earthers today."

And maybe kick them off the edge if you get a clear shot.

16

I will admit I've been looking forward to this part of the summit. Beyond showcasing the speed, silence, and zero emissions of this *very* nicely appointed electric passenger watercraft, the plan is to drop anchor about thirty kilometres north of here, take guests ashore via Zodiac, and then we will forage for ingredients for the big eco-friendly cooking challenge tonight. Because not everyone in our crowd is an experienced forager, Clarke Innovations has provided custom guidebooks with full-color pictures and very clear descriptions about safe food items one might find in our local wilderness.

My former stepmother used to forage for mushrooms, but I'd rather fight Mangala for a bucket of grass than eat anything Aurora cooked, *especially* if it included ingredients picked from the woods or fields near Dad's old house. (I still do not know what my father saw in her. Best leave that scab unpicked.)

And if the guidebooks don't do the trick, NORA is on board with explicit instructions to talk to the guests about nature-oriented topics *only*. I just hope no one relies on her "wisdom" when it comes time to harvest dinner ingredients.

Since this vessel belongs to Clarke Innovations, they have their own captain and skipper running the show, a lovely change from our usual excursions when Ryan pilots the boat and I provide all the safety instructions to our passengers. It's a welcome break—Ryan and I sit on a padded built-in bench on the bow's outer deck, my body nested against his, his left arm resting on the railing and his right wrapped around my midsection like my human seat belt. It's supposed to warm up later, but for now, our long-sleeve T-shirts and Revelation Cove vests are adequate. The sky is clear enough that I didn't think a raincoat was in order, contrary to Tabby's pinky-finger forecast.

I rest my head against Ryan's chest and take a very deep breath.

"This place never lets you forget why we live here." His lips close to my ear send a delicious shiver down my back.

"Kinda fun being the tourist for a few minutes."

Ryan kisses my temple. "Yeah, we need to get away for a bit."

I snort. "And go where?"

"I don't know . . . someplace warm where people can't text, call, or knock on our door."

"That would require an airplane ride." I grab his right hand from its resting place on my thigh and entwine my fingers with his. "Have you not been paying attention this weekend, sir? Planes are bad for the environment."

"No, *food waste* is bad for the environment. Planes aren't blameless, but they cough out way less bad stuff than the world's food production system."

I twist and look up at him. "Wow, I stand corrected. Maybe it is I who should be paying closer attention."

"You've been a little busy with rascals and robots."

I pinch my fingers together in front of me to indicate *a little* and quickly scan the deck for said robot. She must still be inside.

"Seriously, though . . . we should try to go somewhere. Take a minute off."

"We keep saying that and never plan anything. And is that before or after we buy a new house and before or after training camp starts?" I ask. Just because their hockey season ended in March, the next one is never far off.

Ryan is quiet for a few breaths. "Did you see the latest listings from Jill?"

"I saw the email, but I haven't had time to look closely. You?"

"Yeah, the winner isn't in that batch," he says, sighing. "I need to remind her that I don't want to commute from Abbotsford or Chilliwack."

I'm midsentence in my response about not being interested in (a) living so far from the ocean, and (b) being surrounded by cows and pickup trucks, when Trent Boullet seats himself on the end of our bench. He's wearing the same outfit as yesterday morning, only this one's not covered in food. Guessing the light blue button-down and Costco-brand jeans might be his standard uniform. Hey, I respect that. No fast fashion for this guy.

"Good morning, Mr. and Mrs. Fielding," he says, nodding at us and then leaning back, taking in the stunning vista of the strait. The boat is moving at a good clip, enough to stir up a soft breeze as we journey forward. Heading north from Revelation Cove, the channel widens quite a bit before narrowing again about ten kilometers up. We're not going as far as Otter Beach (though I would *love* to pop in and check on my girlies) but rather to a popular landing spot with a small dock and marked trails. Safety first!

The breeze is enough to lift Trent's wispy gray hairs from his freckled crown, pulling them loose from his scant ponytail. I think under the rimless, unwashed glasses and unfortunate hair, he's not a bad-looking man. I'd bet if Tabby could get him in her chair for an hour to divest him of that rat tail, he'd emerge reborn, freed of the ick factor.

"I had an interesting conversation with NORA this morning," Trent says, turning his body in our direction. "She noted that while Revelation Cove has had a few stellar years, the rewilding of half your golf course has put a dent in your month-to-month bookings. And apparently one of your owners wants to jump ship?" He smirks and looks around us. "Pardon the pun."

Ryan stiffens and releases my hand. I scoot forward so he can prepare for battle. I sit straight, my back against the boat's side, to watch how this will unfold.

"Seems NORA has a lot to say on my private business matters."

"Especially when a reporter needles her for confidential information," I add.

Trent reveals a wolfish, veneered smile. "I did nothing of the sort. I asked her how she was enjoying her time this weekend, and she took that to mean I needed a detailed history of Revelation Cove, its owners, and its financials."

"And you didn't stop or correct her," Ryan says, his usually lush lips in a flat line, the hand I'd been holding just moments ago now in a tight fist.

"I didn't come to this event in search of gossip about your precarious financial situation, Ryan."

"Mr. Fielding to you."

Trent bobs his head once in a non-apology.

"And our financial situation is not precarious. We are pivoting with the industry and looking for more sustainable ways to serve our clientele. Kind of the point of this entire weekend."

"Even if your corporate bookings are down as big names flock to the Interior for the hot weather—and eighteen-hole golf courses?"

Boullet's—or rather NORA's—information is technically accurate. Our corporate bookings have taken a hit over the last couple years since we halved the golf course, but we're more than making up for it with smaller groups and families, and our wedding bookings have almost tripled since I took over the marketing management position.

I look at Ryan to see if he's going to respond, but before he does, I stand and face the reporter, still seated. "Mr. Boullet, did you know that I, too, had a conversation with NORA? She had some very interesting things to say about your ex-wife and her involvement with that cult on Thalia Island."

Trent pales but then scratches at his patchy goatee. "She was my ex-wife a long time before she got involved with that cult."

"Didn't Revenue Canada think differently?"

His jaw clenches as he looks right through me.

"Yeah, that sounds like a problem you'd want to keep quiet." I shrug and turn to Ryan. "I think I've had enough fresh air. Shall we grab a coffee before we arrive at our destination?"

Ryan smiles, rises, and takes my hand. "Have fun finding your dinner today, Mr. Boullet," I say. "Be sure to stick to the pictures in the guidebook. You only get one liver, and it only takes one wrong mushroom to put you on a transplant list."

With that, I lead Ryan across the bow deck and through the door into the spacious main passenger cabin. He slides next to me, arm draped over my shoulders. "What the hell just happened? Did you really talk to NORA about him?"

I look behind to make sure Trent's not following us. "No. Tabby did."

Ryan snorts and shakes his head, leaning against the bar counter, behind which CI vessel staff offer beverages and light snacks. I ask for two coffees and then mimic my husband's stance. "Are we in a precarious financial situation?" I ask quietly.

"No." He casually scans the crowd, offering a wave to Smitty and Audrey seated in a couple of forest green barrel chairs across the bright, airy cabin. "We're fine. One of the original partners wants a buyout, so we've had a few meetings about possible restructuring—"

"Wait, what? How come you didn't tell me this?"

"I didn't want you to worry. It's not a big deal. And we're talking with Clarke Innovations about using the Cove as a test property for their flagship eco-hotel certification program, which would involve possible investment and more cool upgrades."

I stare at Ryan Fielding like I've never seen him before. "Um, *hi*. As a shareholder of Revelation Cove, I think I deserve to know this information."

"And you will, as soon as there's information to know. The lawyers and accountants are dealing with it—Tanner is more in the loop than I am."

And yet neither he nor Sarah have mentioned it to me. "Does Sarah know?"

Ryan turns to me, his hands on my shoulders. "Hols, come on— don't be mad. This just came up over the last few weeks. I didn't tell you because you've been a ball of nerves about this event, about house hunting, about your dad and my mom—I figured I'd just wait to tell you until I had all the details."

I back up, his hands dropping. "You should've told me if we're having financial problems. I'm a big girl."

Ryan opens his mouth to respond, but then the vessel shudders under our feet, glasses and mugs tinkling against each other on the shelves behind the beverage bar. The cabin lights blink off, on again . . . and then off. Although this passenger sitting area is well lit via the walls of wide, arched windows, the loss of the warm accent lighting drapes a blue filter over the space.

Forget about silence where you can hear a pin drop—in this silence, I hear myself blinking.

The vessel is still coasting along, but I know just enough about boats to understand that when there's no power, there's *probably* no steering.

"Ryan—"

"Ladies and gentlemen, good morning. This is Captain Dubus and I'm so sorry to interrupt your leisure time . . ."

17

This brand-new, multimillion-dollar electric passenger boat has mysteriously lost power. In the middle of the strait. In very deep water. Ryan and I immediately join the CI people on the bridge to decide upon and implement a contingency plan that will ensure everyone's safety.

As the vessel has lost propulsion power—and they don't yet know why—Captain Dubus is drifting us into shallower water so we can drop anchor. Since our original destination is just around the next rocky outcropping, our guests will be shuttled ashore via Zodiac to start the day's activity while the captain and crew figure out what's going on and hopefully make the necessary fixes to get everyone home before our freshly picked spoils *spoil*.

Ryan and I descend the bridge stairs with our marching orders —ensure everyone has a life jacket so when our guest lecturers are done with their opening remarks, we can get folks lined up to disembark. Ryan stops at the entry to the main cabin, his hand on my elbow. "Babe, please do not worry about what that asshole reporter said. Everything's fine, I promise."

Before he can land a kiss on my cheek, I turn and walk away. I'm pissed that he didn't tell me about the OG RevCove partner wanting out; I'm pissed that Sarah and Tanner know about the restructuring and eco-hotel certification stuff; and I'm pissed that he thinks I'm not strong enough to handle important news.

And while I'm at it, I'm pissed that he made the stupid comment last night about how this event has been nothing but trouble and that today would be better. THIS dead-boat business is all his fault.

Turd.

The Clarke Innovations people have calmly explained the situation to the guests, and no one seems riled. We're clearly not sinking, we haven't crashed into any rocks, and no mayday has been issued. "It's a faulty battery connection. Easy-peasy." Captain Dubus's words, not mine. And they actually don't know if it's a faulty battery connection yet, but I understand not wanting to incite panic.

Meanwhile, the two PhD presenters in charge of our walking/foraging tour—Dr. Toni Aiken from the container greenhouse tour yesterday and Dr. Lisanne Shalvis—have everyone's rapt attention in the main cabin as Dr. Aiken passes around a bowl containing small slips of folded paper. Each person draws from it while NORA assists Dr. Shalvis with distributing the colorful, coil-bound foraging guidebooks.

"Since we're unexpectedly short of electricity this morning, we will forgo the PowerPoint I spent hours sweating over and instead give you an A-B-C primer on how today's activity will go down," Dr. Aiken says, smiling as she pats her closed MacBook. She then asks everyone to open the folded squares of paper—they are numbered 1 through 4. "Find your fellow 1s, 2s, 3s, and 4s, and form your teams!"

Thankfully, everyone's in good spirits as they shuffle about in bulky life jackets and organize into their respective groups, offering friendly greetings to their new teammates. Once quiet returns, Dr. Shalvis explains the rules for today.

"Each group will be provided with a different recipe and are to find ingredients suitable to make it delicious. The protein portion will be provided for you at the resort, since we didn't bring crab pots, clam shovels, or fishing poles," she says. "For the cooking challenge, we have an amazing selection of BC seafood, fresh caught and delivered by your fellow guests, Rob and Randi Gilbert, from Chinook Hook Fishing Expeditions up in Port Hardy."

She pauses for the crowd to hoot and applaud as Rob and Randi offer polite waves. Dr. Shalvis also reassures the group that should their baskets be light by the end of our foraging adventure, no one is to fret as the Clarke Innovations culinary team has brought huge coolers of fresh, Thalia Island-grown ingredients for teams to select from to really "knock it out of the park."

With the expectations outlined, Dr. Shalvis hands it off to Dr. Aiken, who then moves into her modified presentation, holding up one of the guidebooks and flipping through to explain the basics of wilderness foraging and what folks can expect to find today.

She notes that since it's only April, finding berries is unlikely as native berry varieties won't have fruit until later in the summer, and even then, the bears will have dibs on whatever sprouts. She moves on to greens, such as dandelion, nettles, and fiddleheads, but my mind wanders . . .

Why didn't Ryan tell me about all that stuff? Does he seriously think I'm not able to handle it, or that I'm not as invested in the success of the resort? Who is the partner who wants out and why? How much will that cost us and the other stakeholders?

Should I be worried? Because other than my career as an emergency dispatcher and my years spent at the Cove—garnished by my unfinished university degree—it's not like I have a résumé hiring managers will fight over. If we're moving to the mainland so Ryan can continue coaching, *will* I actually be able to run the Cove's marketing department remotely? Who is going to put out the day-to-day fires if I'm not on-site all the time? Is Miss Betty planning on following my dad into retirement by hanging up her apron? Will they run his new sex-tips-for-old-people business together?

If I don't have a steady income, can Ryan and I even afford a house in Langley with interest rates where they are and a possible hit to our portfolio with the restructuring? The only reason *portfolio* is part of my vocabulary is because I married a former NHL'er who, despite being young when he made his first million, has always been smart minded about his moolah. (My "retirement" account is more suited to a squirrel than a human.)

Should I go back to school? Should I finish my degree or maybe train to do something else? But what would I do? And what if, one of these mornings, the pregnancy test *does* come back positive and then I'm dealing with nine months of feeling like molten garbage, followed by eighteen years of trying every day not to ruin my child —more, probably, if the world keeps setting a new bar for insanity every few weeks, never mind all the scary shit Lara Clarke and her friends have been talking about this weekend with fun activities for the whole family, like drought, famine, and +2.0° Celsius heat thresholds.

Hell, what if Ryan and I and our adult child have to fight off marauders trying to steal our canned provisions and fresh water when the suburban dream turns into a nuclear nightmare of formerly cute homes now dressed in salvaged metal plates to keep the zombies out—

"Hey, Porter, you in there?" Ryan gives my shoulder a shake.

"What? Yeah. Sorry."

"We're ready to head out. You good?"

"I'm fine." I nod at the group assigned to his care and follow the line downstairs to the still-silent vessel's stern where two Zodiacs sit —one huge with dual outboard motors, and another smaller vessel with a single motor. With my life jacket zipped up, I await my turn to board, glad that Ryan steps onto the smaller boat so I don't have to pretend like I'm not super mad at him.

18

The forage is a success, or at least it seems to be. Group one looks happy upon emerging from the forest trails, their faces pink with exertion, sweatshirts and coats tied around waists like we did as kids during lunch recess. Since the four groups arrived on shore at staggered times, so too will we return to the vessel. Once on board, Drs. Aiken and Shalvis will review the collected foodstuffs in each group's basket to make a hundred percent sure everything is safe to eat.

I did not follow Mr. Fielding into the woods with group two but rather stayed on the beach with a few CI staffers in case anyone needed anything. Again, it's probably best I avoid talking to my husband until I have an uninterrupted moment to collect my thoughts—and call my dad, of course. I checked my phone after we landed on the beach to see if I had enough bars to maybe barf my worries all over Nurse Bob, but we're too far from the nearest cell tower.

I mean, if it was bad, Ryan would've told me, right? We're not that couple where he controls all the finances and I'm just happy to be the oblivious wife who collects her monthly allowance. And yet I don't know the specifics . . . mostly because I haven't needed to.

Ryan takes very good care of me, he's responsible with his investments and the resort's financial affairs, and he has at least two accountants who take care of all our tax issues.

I'm not a spendthrift, I don't have any expensive vices or hobbies (other than spoiling Elsbeth), and the money I earn from my position at the Cove goes into our joint accounts. Maybe I've gotten too comfortable letting him take charge of our financial picture.

When a wet drop hits my nose, I ignore it. It cannot be raining. I can still see blue sky and fluffy white clouds.

The first group stands around a collapsible picnic table with their guidebooks handy, chatting with the CI staffers about their collected bounty. Looks like everything is edible, including the *bugs* still alive in a glass jar—yeah, no thanks.

Upon seeing me shudder, one of the young CI attendants says, "Crickets are delicious! You've never tried them?" I shake my head no. "Entomophagy is mainstream pretty much everywhere except North America. The Seattle Mariners have offered chili-lime roasted grasshoppers and matcha ice cream with toffee-brittle mealworm and chocolate grasshoppers on their menu in a few recent seasons." She grins, clearly satisfied she's grossing me out.

"Good thing I married into a hockey family, then," I say, just as another fat drop hits the top of my head. Followed by another and another. Patches of blue sky remain visible, though the wind has picked up a bit, bringing forward clouds that look a bit ill intended. The eastern sky is a purplish gray whereas thirty minutes ago, it looked clear and well-mannered.

Then, as if someone turns on the tap, a deluge.

Par for the course for April in British Columbia.

Group one is unfazed, cracking up as their bare arms are pummelled by heavy rain splats, untying their jackets at their waists to cover up. We do not have any sort of awning or canopy here on the beach—since the forecast said *nothing* about rain—but fortunately, this group of locals is accustomed to coastal spring tantrums.

My long-sleeve shirt readily soaks up her fill, though my vest repels well enough. Can't say the same thing for my hair. I wait until I'm bona fide drowned-rat status, the last person from group one to board the Zodiac back to the big boat, before snapping a selfie for Tabby.

"Your lucky finger was right," I type, sending the photo. It will take a few minutes to arrive thanks to the spotty Wi-Fi out here, but she'll have a good laugh. And I look forward to huddling inside the much bigger, warmer boat so I can maybe stop feeling sorry for myself for a minute and laugh with her.

❦

The big electric boat is dead. And no one knows why.

We have eighty-odd guests with growling stomachs, full bladders, and baskets full of dinner fixin's who need to get back to the resort. So much for a relaxing day out.

Ryan and I go into manager mode and call Revelation Cove for help, relieved that our phones still have battery life *and* we get service from the bridge. Tanner and Brad and the Vikings will need to drive our smaller, on-loan electric boat and two gas-powered boats to our location to transport the groups back safely. Even with our three passenger vessels, it will probably take two trips to get everyone home to the resort.

A small backup generator thankfully functions, so the bridge has radio and instrument power, allowing Captain Dubus to notify the Coast Guard that we're dead in the water. Fortunately, we're large enough to be visible, plus we're not anchored in a ferry lane or in a spot dangerous to other boat traffic. As I am not a nautical expert, I have no idea how they will get this vessel back to the resort or Thalia Island or wherever it needs to go, but the captain seems calm as he makes arrangements with whomever is on the other end of his phone call.

The guests are in a surprisingly chipper mood, even though the rain has not let up and most of them are soaked from the trip from shore. At least two rainbows have sprouted in the last hour between downpours, offering great photo ops against the deep gray of the moody sky.

"Are you going to be mad at me for the rest of the day?" Ryan whispers into my ear. We're waiting outside, under the covered portion of the stern deck.

"I'm not mad at you. I'm just . . ."

"Mad."

"Fine. Yes. I'm mad."

"And you're right. I should've told you." He leans against the wall, hands tucked in his pockets. His dark hair is a curly, tousled mop from the rain; the cuffs of his Levi's and the tips of his steel-toe Timberlands are soaked. "It's not like I'm intentionally keeping things from you. I think maybe I've sorta gotten into a habit of dealing with stuff while I'm on the mainland working, and because our time is always so limited, I don't want to bore you with administrative crap."

I make sure no one is within earshot, especially NORA or Trent Boullet. "Ryan, we are *married*. And I know that a significant portion of our five years together has been spent with us living in two different locations, but money and financial stuff and business dealings—that's more than 'administrative crap,'" I air-quote. "It affects me too. If we're having financial problems, I need to know so I can do something to help."

He reaches out his hand, inviting me to take it. When I don't, he cocks his head at me and then pushes off the wall, closing the distance between us. His huge hands are warm as he loosely encases my neck, his thumbs on my jawline. "Hollie Porter Fielding, I promise that if we are ever in a position where I need you to help more than you already are, I will let you know."

"Don't make fun of me," I bite.

He snorts. "I'm not! But you do so much already. You keep the Cove running when I'm not here. Hell, even when I *am* here. You're so much more than the marketing director—you're now the beating heart of our resort. Even my mom says so. The team relies on you so much, and I know you work your ass off, so there is absolutely nothing else I need from you." He leans down and rests his forehead against mine. "Except your smokin'-hot bod."

I try not to smile, and fail. "Jerk. Don't keep secrets from me."

He kisses me lightly. "I was never keeping secrets from you. And I promise to pull you in whenever these conversations happen. Honestly, it was never a case of not wanting you to know anything—I just didn't want to ask too much of you when you're already doing basically everything already."

I look up at my husband and see sincerity in his eyes.

"Hollie, I wouldn't be coaching if you hadn't encouraged me to. I know me being in Langley half the year is hard, but we're working on that, right? Next season, we'll be together and you can boss me around all you want without having to wait for a prescheduled FaceTime call."

"I don't want to boss you around."

"What if I beg?" he teases, smirking. Ryan then kisses me for real, turning us and pushing me against the wall so we're not in view of the guests inside waiting for our rescue.

19

I have to say—this group of guests has been an absolute pleasure to deal with, comparatively speaking. I mean, other than whoever is still shit-posting on Instagram. And those protesters who crashed the fashion show. And the asshole reporter. And the robot who's supposed to be sharing facts about *Orcinus orca* and not our guests' latest blood test results. (To my horror, Lara Clarke informed me via text that NORA told another guest they should have a prominent mole on their forehead checked out by a doctor ASAP. Harmony needs to teach her pet about *inside voices*.)

But as the asshole reporter so kindly pointed out earlier today, corporate bookings at the Cove are down. The hospitality industry is always changing, I've learned, and it's important to stay agile and ready to pivot. But, like, if I could book a whole year of eco-summits, minus the aforementioned crazy-pants bits, instead of a whole year of spoiled brides who yell at me when it rains or the wind ruffles their updo?

Yes, please. In an overcaffeinated heartbeat.

It took a couple hours to get the foragers back to the resort, but spirits remained high (thanks to the spirits we promised everyone upon their return to the island). Folks disembarked and then disappeared to their rooms to shower and change, excited for tonight's eco-cooking challenge. The dining room has been transformed, the tables rearranged to accommodate what looks like a set from a Food Network show, including four separate cooking stations complete with metal rolling racks holding the tools and ingredients contestants are allowed to choose from.

Chef Joseph and his sous-chef will be leading one of the four teams, but tonight, the Clarke Innovations eco-chefs are holding court—and everyone is anxiously eyeing the coolers they brought with them. Finally, they will reveal what Thalia Island magic lies within while also demonstrating how to make delicious, affordable meals.

Along the room's eastern wall, the ever-present but pared-down buffet has snacky offerings—more of those incredible blueberry oat bars *and* the brownies I cannot get enough of, cookies, fresh fruit, bowls of various nuts and trail mixes, sliced artisanal bread with fresh goat milk butter pats—things to tide people over until dinner is served. Once the event gets underway with the CI chefs supervising, Joseph's team will lay out our usual Pacific Northwest-inspired spread to complement whatever else is created tonight. Bottom line, even if you don't want morel mushrooms or fresh dandelion and bug salad, you will still eat. Plenty of nosh to go around.

Across the lobby, the fashion show catwalk has been removed and the ballroom is prepped for the after-dinner entertainment, courtesy of the Garden Gnomes. Even though Monday technically is Earth Day, tonight is the big banquet-party night since most guests will be checking out Sunday (tomorrow) to return to their lives and businesses, I hope full of inspiration and great ideas.

I'm in the main foyer, freshly changed and coifed for the evening —black slacks, kitten heels, and a lovely bamboo fiber shirt in a deep purple—I'm still working, so nothing too flashy for me. Also, I have a history of ER trips when I attempt heels of more than an inch. I don't know how she does it, but Lara Clarke must have ankles of steel.

The vendors' booths in the lobby and sitting area still buzz with activity as more people gather, collect their cocktails from the bar, and look for seats in the dining room. Though the cooking stations are set up along the western wall of windows, there won't be a bad seat in the house when it comes to watching the culinary action unfold.

I just wish the unfolding would get busy. I'm hungry, and according to the waistband of these pants, I have eaten too many brownies and oat bars in the last couple hours.

I tried calling my dad after we got home, but it went to voicemail. If his latest Facebook post is anything to go by, it seems he and Miss Betty are attending a drama festival put on by a community theater troupe in Lincoln City. I did not know my dad was a fan of *Sweeney Todd* medleys, but good for him for broadening his horizons in the name of love.

Dad's social media post was much nicer to look at than the latest one by Flat Earther, laughing about how the electric boat passengers had to be rescued by fossil fuel boats. I cannot imagine anyone from today being so willfully spiteful—but the photo from the IG post was taken on the beach where we landed, so someone among that group of smiling, happy faces is a double-crossing backstabber.

"Boo." Tabby slides in next to me. A spruce tip pokes from the cocktail glass in her hand. "Have you tried this yet?" She offers me a sip.

"Later. I'm staying sober until everyone is taken care of."

"Such a good little employee. I hope the boss pays you well." She winks.

I throw her a dirty look. "Just trying to get through tonight without any more major calamities." I stare at her glass and then lean forward for a sniff. "Is it good?"

"*So* good." She takes a healthy drink. "Tell me what happened today. Other than the mean Instagram post, which *has* to be one of the people in this room right now. Dicks." She sips again. "Did they get that big-ass boat started yet?"

"I don't know. I haven't seen the captain around, so I'm guessing not."

"I saw Finan Rowleigh head out with a couple other dudes to go help them. He's adorable."

"And *married*."

"I didn't say I want to see him naked. I just said he's adorable."

We watch and greet guests as they wander past the vendors' booths and funnel toward the dining room. The main door to the kitchen area opens and my own adorable husband walks out, a green Revelation Cove apron tied around his front. Under it, he's dressed like he's going to a hockey game—suit pants and white button-down with a tie, though his shirt sleeves are rolled to his elbow, and he's foregone the suit coat. (Suits are a hockey thing. Players and coaches always wear suits to and from the arena on game days. It's scrumptious to behold and even more scrumptious to disrobe.)

"Speaking of adorable," I say under my breath, watching Ryan approach.

"Horndog. How are you not pregnant yet?" Tabby teases, slurping the last of her beverage. "See you in there."

"Save me a seat!" I call after her.

"You're not going to help cook?" Ryan asks.

"Very funny."

He kisses my temple. "Jill emailed about an hour ago. Brand-new listing that hasn't gone out yet."

"I saw her email but didn't open it."

"You should. It's a nice place." Ryan kisses me again and backs away. "Lookin' good tonight, Porter." He gives me that sizzling smile that works even when I'm still a tiny bit mad at him.

But the mention of the real estate agent sending over something worthy of haste—that's interesting. I step out of the main foyer and walk into the wide hall that connects to the outdoor pool and hot tub deck. The walls in this corridor are decorated with framed, signed hockey jerseys from Ryan's career as well as signed, game-worn jerseys he's collected from his idols. Can't tell you how many times we've had people offer top dollar for the whole shebang, but Ryan's adamant they're not for sale.

If we were in financial straits, he'd sell the jerseys, right?

I pull my phone from my pocket and find Jill's email and click on the attached PDF:

"Brand New Luxury Living in the Heart of Langley, British Columbia!

"Nestled in the vibrant community of Langley, this stunning newly constructed four-bedroom, three-bathroom home is a portrait of contemporary sophistication and design. With an expansive 3,500 square foot layout, this residence promises an unparalleled lifestyle of comfort and convenience."

It goes on to list all its amenities: open-concept living space, soaring ceilings, engineered hardwood floors, and an abundance of natural light, state-of-the-art kitchen featuring quartz countertops, stainless steel appliances, smart home technology for security and comfort, and energy-efficient heating and cooling systems, just minutes from urban conveniences.

Thirty-five hundred square feet? Jesus, that's a lot of house for two people.

Does it come with a housekeeper?

Why is this one any different from the others Jill's sent—

"Hello, Hollie."

I about jump out of my skin when NORA greets me.

"You look to be absorbed in whatever you're reading."

"I am. I was." I darken my phone and tuck it away. "Can I help you with something?"

NORA turns and points in the direction of the foyer, right as Harmony's and Elsbeth's faces disappear. They're peeking around the corner at me but don't move quite quick enough to avoid detection. "I would like to invite you to join Harmony and her friend Elsbeth and myself to spectate the cooking competition. It is about to get underway."

Giggling floats toward us as Elsbeth's little face peeks around the corner again.

"Did the girls send you to ask me?"

"Yes. They have something for you," NORA says. "It is a surprise. Harmony asked me several times not to tell you what it is, and I promised her I would not."

"OK. Well, then I guess we should go see what mischief these two are up to now."

NORA *whish-whirrs* next to me as we walk, and just as we're nearing the threshold where the hall connects to the grand foyer, Harmony and Elsbeth jump out. Elsbeth is holding up a drawing of a sea otter, and Harmony bears a plate with frosted cookies—in the shape of sea otters and sea stars.

"Surprise!" Elsbeth yells. It echoes off our cathedral ceiling. "We made presents for you!"

"Wow, you guys . . ." I accept Elsbeth's picture and examine her work. "Els, this is beautiful. I love it so much."

"Harmony helped me draw it. She said she made you a painting, so she taught me how to do a better sea otter. See? I even got the nose right this time." And she did.

"It's perfect. I *love* it. I'm going to hang it right beside Harmony's painting."

"We also baked these for you," Harmony says, offering me the plate of cookies. "I felt bad about what happened, you know, getting your niece stuck in that tree. And also NORA planting all your seedlings upside down."

The otter cookies look way better than anything I could've ever made—maybe next Valentine's Day, Chef and Miss Betty should invite Harmony to bake the cookies. She certainly knows how to *flood* her icing. "These are so cute! How am I supposed to eat them?"

"Like this!" Elsbeth grabs one from the plate and bites off the otter's head, which, of course, sends her into another giggle fit.

"Would you like to sit with us during the cooking contest, Hollie?" Harmony asks.

Even though I told Tabby to save me a seat, I can't say no to these girls.

I pick up a sea star and bite into it. Yup, they taste as good as they look. "Mmmm," I moan. "Harmony, these are amazing." She grins. "Lead the way!"

I nod toward the dining area. Harmony takes Elsbeth's hand and NORA follows us. "Where did you learn how to bake like this?" I ask.

"Catrina from the island. She and her husband Tommy run the diner, and she's an awesome baker. NORA also helps with recipes," Harmony says, casting a quick smile back at her robot companion.

"Well, they're amazing. I cannot bake for shit—sorry—for crap. I think these and your brownies are my new favorite foods."

We pause at the entrance to the almost-full dining room, and I look around for an empty space to accommodate the four of us and maybe Tabby, once she sees where I'm sitting.

"I'd be happy to share my recipes with your chef," Harmony says. "The best part is, even though they're technically sweets, they're *very* high in protein. Like, so much protein. And it's better protein than what you would get from like a cheeseburger or whatever."

"Really? How is that possible?"

"Oh, it's the flour."

"Flour is made from wheat. I didn't think wheat was a great protein source, is it?" *What do I know? I hate cooking.*

I pop the last bite of frosted cookie into my mouth.

"Yeah, but it's not wheat flour. I only bake with cricket flour."

20

O ne of the waitstaff comes to my rescue, a glass of water in
hand. Because I'm standing at the opening to the dining
room, making a scene as I choke on the last bite of frosted sea star
that, like an idiot, I inhaled in shock.

Harmony takes the cookie plate and hands it to Elsbeth, then
pats my back with enough vigor to dislodge a lung. Tabby magically
appears and pulls me by the elbow out of view of the whole
gathering.

"Are you OK?" she asks as I gasp for air and then gulp the water
and focus on not squirting it out my nose. "Girls, why don't you go
find a table and Hollie will be in shortly? They're just about to
start!" Tabby says, her voice higher than normal. She often sounds
like she's just sucked helium when she talks to kids.

"I'm so sorry, Hollie. I thought you knew," Harmony says,
nodding to the plate that still bears four sea otters and one sea star.

I give her a thumbs-up and mouth, *It's OK*, my throat not yet
clear enough for me to speak.

"Go on," Tabby urges, and finally the two girls plus NORA
disappear into the dining room. My friend waits for me to finish the

water and encourages deep breaths so I don't tumble into another coughing paroxysm. "What the hell just happened?" she asks.

I hand her Elsbeth's picture and sit on a random chair someone put in the corner. "The cookies . . .," I utter, voice strained. "Crickets in the cookies. And the brownies and oat bars. Bugs. In everything."

"What?" Tabby looks as appalled as I feel.

"Cricket flour. That's what they're baking with." I lean my head against the wall and point my chin skyward. "This whole weekend, I've been eating bugs."

"And nobody told you? Nobody told *us*?"

I need more water.

"This is like that movie—you know, the one where the people live on a train that never stops because the world has frozen over due to climate change and they feed the lower-class people these bars made of ground-up bugs? It has Captain America in it," Tabby says. She slides the plate onto a side table and pulls her phone from her pocket.

"Is everything OK? Hols, you all right?" Ryan buzzes out of the dining room toward me. "I heard someone choking and coughing— should've known it would be you."

I flip him the bird; he grins in response.

Tabby explains what's just happened.

"Crickets are high in protein, babe," he says, chucking my chin. "Good for you."

"Not helping," I growl.

My husband reaches down and takes my hand. "Come on. We're starting."

Reluctantly, I allow him to pull me from the chair and follow him and Tabby back into the dining room.

"*Snowpiercer!*" Tabby shrieks, a little too loud for as close to my ear as she stands. "Sorry. *Snowpiercer*. They ate bugs in that too."

"Didn't that end with Captain America killing the dude running the train?"

Before she can answer, the Clarke Innovations head chef clicks on the mic and welcomes everyone to this year's Green It Up Eco-Cooking Challenge.

❦

I recover quickly enough—a couple of Salish Sea Spritzers help—and the cooking challenge gets underway to great fanfare. Lara Clarke again takes over emcee duties so the chefs can do their chef thing.

Since not everyone who participated in the foraging exercise will fit behind the cooking stations, the teams have chosen ahead of time who they'll send into battle. Three teams have been paired with one of the CI culinary specialists and the fourth is led by our own Chef Joseph. Rolling metal racks are filled with eco-friendly, sustainably sourced ingredients the contestant teams can use, plus the cooks get their choice of ocean-based protein (all of it Ocean Wise and/or Marine Stewardship Council (MSC) certified, provided by the Gilberts from Chinook Hook). The only other rule: each team's meal must also include the items they foraged during today's outing.

NORA provides a polite countdown that culminates with a tinkling starting bell, and then the teams are off. Our normally quiet dining room transforms into a frenetic, circus-like atmosphere as guests root for their teams and cooks yell back and forth at one another over steaming pans, whirring blenders, and even a few toppled silver bowls.

Lara's assistant Meg has taken on the role of photographer tonight, capturing the fun and excitement with the hefty lens of a DSLR looped around her neck. It dawns on me as I watch her that maybe *she's* the one who's been shit-posting on Instagram—she was on today's outing, she was on scene yesterday when the girls were stuck in the tree, and she obviously knows how to use a camera.

But the Instagram photos weren't great, certainly not taken by someone who wants their photography skills highlighted. And Meg looks like she's having way too much fun to be faking it. I doubt Lara Clarke would allow a flat earther anywhere near her late grandfather's empire. Those folks can only hide their crazy for so long.

The red-numbered digital clock hanging from one of the metal racks, originally set for sixty-five minutes, ticks down. As we grow closer to the finish line, the volume in the dining room reaches a pinnacle.

Finally . . . *Ding! Ding! Ding!* NORA again provides a pleasant chime to signal the end of the exercise.

"Time's up!" Lara announces, her voice swallowed by applause and cheers. As the teams finish plating their creations, Lara unhooks the mic, stopping at each station to invite the team's leader to explain their dish.

Team One does grilled Pacific sardines and a fresh herb salad with lemon vinaigrette and roasted cricket croutons.

Team Two does wild mushroom and goat cheese tartlets and Dungeness crab puffs alongside a foraged greens and seaweed salad.

Team Three has made seared Pacific halibut, spot prawns with a mint glaze, and scalloped new potatoes.

And Team Four offers pan-roasted black cod with sea asparagus and wild garlic sauce.

The Revelation Cove culinary team fills in the gaps with our cedar-planked maple salmon, a clam and kelp chowder, risotto, and romaine and spinach salad (for those with less adventurous palates). And while Joseph has spent a good portion of the last few days perturbed about the intruders in his kitchen, he looks to be having an absolute blast surrounded by his novice cooks.

Every table of eight will be served a portion of the eco-challenge dishes to share and sample, in addition to the full salmon meal provided by our kitchen. Once we're done, all the diners will vote on the four teams' creations, and the one with the most votes wins.

Fast-forward to me untucking my shirt so I can unbutton my pants.

I have never, ever, *ever* eaten such delicious food in all my life. If Apophis the Giant Meteor were to slam into the resort right this minute and incinerate my person, I would evaporate with an overfull belly and a stupid, gluttonous smile on my face.

And I'm glad I didn't know what was being prepared until we actually watched the magic happen. To me, sardines have always been those gross, greasy things that maybe looked like fish at some point but now come in a tin can, and usually I avoid most green vegetables, but I must admit—tonight's sardine dish was *chef's kiss,* and the sea asparagus with the garlic sauce? Kind of awesome.

Ryan managed to score a bowl of roasted crickets for our table, thinking himself hilarious as he popped a few into his mouth, grinning as they crunched under his molars. I told him he has to brush and floss his teeth for one whole hour before I will kiss him. Consuming crickets ground into flour is one thing—still not something I'm happy about—but taking the whole bug and throwing it down the hatch?

Shudder.

When a tiny leg gets stuck between two of his teeth, I raise my hand to summon another alcoholic beverage, sending my sister- and brother-in-law into hysterics. Elsbeth and Harmony have long since abandoned our table in search of dessert, and the dining room staff dip in and around tables to collect empty plates and refill water glasses.

I spot Trent Boullet at a barstool with a drink in one hand, his phone in the other as he watches the room. He looks like he's waiting for something exciting to happen—something more exciting than a bunch of green nerds eating crickets and fish. The suit jacket over his light blue shirt is new, but it seems that's as fancy as he gets. He could easily be taking photos to send to Flat Earther—I'll check later if there's a new post, and if the picture was taken from that angle, then huzzah! Guilty!

Through the open dining room doors, audible evidence that the Garden Gnomes are getting underway floats in, signaling the migration from this room to the next. Lara Clarke clicks on her mic one last time to remind everyone to vote before leaving. She slides the microphone back into the stand just as Finan walks through the dining room doors, Len Emmerich and Captain Dubus and crew right behind. Lara squeals and runs toward her husband, launching herself into his arms as if he's been absent for months and not hours.

Ryan sees it too, and when we look at each other, he grins and picks up my hand from the table, planting a juicy kiss on the back of it.

"You taste better than crickets," he says.

"I swear to god, if you start rubbing your legs together to chirp, you're sleeping on the couch."

21

The thought runs in a loop in my head as I primp and preen so I can spend the day shooing all these lovely people back to their own little worlds. We have one more morning session and then a closing ceremony to celebrate Earth Day (which is technically tomorrow) that ironically involves—you guessed it—planting trees.

Probably not going to ask NORA to help out on this one.

Last night after returning to our love nest, Ryan, the good lad, brushed his teeth for the allotted time, and after inspection to ensure they were free of cricket body parts, I allowed him to choose another page from the sexy funtime book. He chose the Feisty Fisherman because he has a pair of waders in our closet and I have a mermaid blanket that, when slid over my legs, turns me into a fin-bearing sea goddess.

Except our romantic role-play was interrupted when we sidetracked into a rather heated debate surrounding the mechanics of *how* Prince Eric might have had sexual relations with singer-songwriter and trinket-collector Arial, daughter of King Triton, if she'd remained in her natural state and hadn't, in fact, traded her pipes for legs.

Between his waders and my knitted fish tail, we concluded that interspecies intercourse would've been problematic at best, and once divested of our costumes, we aligned our compatible body parts and a climactic end was achieved for all parties involved with zero binding agreements made to voluptuous sea witches with great hair.

What we did *not* talk about last night? The latest house listing Jill sent over or anything further regarding our financial situation and if it is as dire as Trent Boullet would have me believe. I considered revisiting both topics this morning while we bathed, but shower time with Concierge Ryan is sacred and relaxing and romantic and I want to hang on to that as long as I can.

He's already out the door to address his endless to-do list, but in his wake, he's again left a pot of fresh-brewed coffee. I don't want to eat in the dining room this morning, so from the fridge I grab a yogurt and granola cup. Should probably make a bagel—the sniff test of the two bagels left in the breadbasket is borderline at best. I'll risk it.

I pop the bagel into the toaster and then turn to lean against the countertop to check any waiting or urgent messages. Out of the corner of my eye, though, I see the glass snap-top container that holds the remaining otter cookies from Harmony. Elsbeth's drawing is propped against the fruit bowl on the kitchen island.

They were so excited to give me these presents.

My phone set aside, I slide the snap-top bowl before me and open it. Ryan must've eaten the last sea star as I have four sea otters left, their little icing-decorated faces smiling up at me.

I cannot believe they're made with pulverized crickets.

I pick up one of the cookies. Sniff it. Turn it over, icing face down, and closely examine the backside of the cookie. Unlike the cricket leg stuck in Ryan's teeth last night, I find zero evidence that the smooth, baked surface of this sweet treat contains milled insects. Yeah, the flour is a little darker than bleached white flour, but I thought maybe it was because they added ginger or cinnamon or something to the recipe. And the brownies and blueberry oat bars? I can't deny I'm more than a little obsessed.

I flip the otter cookie back over and stare at the cute little whiskers Harmony painted on. She really did do a nice job, and it must've taken a lot of patience—

The toaster pops and scares the crap out of me and the cookie falls from my hand. (Yes, even though I activated the toaster, I forgot about it, and our apartment is really quiet with just me here.) I quickly pluck the bagel halves from their slots so they don't burn. Upon dropping them on to the cutting board, I note a patch of green mold festering on the bagel's inner surface. Plus it stinks now. Burnt mold stinks.

Damn it.

I lean over and pick up the otter cookie that broke into two pieces on impact, and rather than throw it away, I inspect for dust. Invoking the five-second rule, I pop the first half into my mouth.

Nurse Bob is never going to believe his daughter who he had to bribe with cash to put a single cheese-covered broccoli floret in her mouth is willingly eating crickets.

I dump the moldy toasted bagel in the green waste bin and finish the other half of my cookie, plus one more for good measure. Hey, Harmony said they're high in protein. That means they're more than just sugar. And they go great with my yogurt cup, so I'm calling this breakfast a win.

Before sliding into my boots, I swipe open my phone screen to see where I'm needed first this morning. Top notification is from the RevCove employee group chat—seems that the dismantled GreenMuncher, sitting outside the service entrance next to the kitchen, has recaptured the attention of Rhonda Raccoon and her bandit-faced offspring (the momma who launched herself at me out of the Christmas tree—you can hardly see the scar anymore).

The next is a text from my dad—a quick video of him and Miss Betty standing in front of a beachside candy shop where, in the window behind them, a dual-armed machine pulls saltwater taffy. I smile. Dad and I have visited that Newport shop a million times. I'm glad he's sharing it with her.

And finally, a text from Sarah with a link preview. I click on it and Instagram opens. It's a photograph of a toppled silver mixing bowl, its contents splattered over the dining room floor—from the cooking competition last night. The caption reads, "Hypocrites who harp about global food waste and yet this is how they treat dinner? #hypocrisy #climatehoax #redpill."

Flat Earther strikes again.

❧

When I get down to the front desk, Hannah throws her thumb over her shoulder at the closed back-office door. "Ms. Clarke and her bodyguard are in there. The big guy was pissed about something."

Shit.

I open the door and indeed find Lara Clarke clutching a coffee cup in Miss Betty's old wingback chair and Len Emmerich hunched over a tactical-grade laptop on the desk. "Everything OK?" I ask, trying not to sound sheepish, quickly glancing at my phone screen to double-check that neither of them attempted to contact me in the interim between me leaving our apartment and now.

"That prick Boullet is stirring up shit," Len growls.

"On Instagram?" I ask.

They both look at me. "No, he's written another sensationalized piece of garbage for the rag that employs him," Len says. "Did he post something on Instagram too?"

"No. I mean, I don't know if it's him. It's that Flat Earther account."

He-Man shakes his head. "I doubt that's Boullet. Too obvious." He opens Instagram on his phone and scrolls, his eyebrows furrowing like two blond caterpillars leaning in for a smooch.

"But it's probably someone here, right?" I ask. "It would have to be—with these photos and specific details about what's going on?"

"Fucking trolls," Lara mutters, lifting her mug for a sip.

Len snaps his laptop closed. "OK, well, we're not going to figure this out stewing in here." He checks the bulky watch on his wrist. "Your last session starts in ten. Finan's already in there with Dr. Aiken. We should get going."

Lara closes her eyes for a long beat and then stands. "I can do this." She looks right at me as she says it.

"You can totally do this," I reply.

She pours whatever liquid remains in her cup down her throat. I reach out to take the empty from her, but as she hands it to me, she lifts an eyebrow. "Do your bartenders work Sunday nights?"

"They do."

"You guys have karaoke here?"

I smile, very much liking where this is going. "I think something can be arranged."

I manage to catch the last twenty or so minutes of the final workshop on "Community-Driven Sustainability: Engaging with Local Stakeholders and Indigenous Partnerships." Finan is a dynamic presenter and listening to Dr. Aiken is calming and informative. She's obviously a total brainiac, but she's funny and approachable and it makes the heavy, even depressing information feel less hopeless.

Dare I say that with the culmination of this conference, the cyclical doom-and-gloom spiraling through my brain just three days ago is somewhat eased? Yeah, we're not going to save the world all by ourselves. But with every "green it up" step we take, it's a move in the right direction.

Oh my god, I sound like their rah-rah-rah marketing materials.

With the final slide presented, Finan, Lara, Drs. Aiken and Shalvis, the rest of the weekend's experts, and Clarke Innovations staff are granted a standing ovation in the packed ballroom. NORA and Harmony take the stage to invite everyone outside to lift a glass of kombucha at the tree-planting ceremony, although their speech is rudely interrupted when Acorn launches himself up the three short steps onto the platform and restarts his whole stranger-danger routine, barking and snarling at the robot.

Of course, this sets off the service-dog-in-training, sitting in the front row.

Ryan hurries onstage and picks up our resident golden retriever, throwing the still-barking canine over his shoulder and rushing out of the ballroom. NORA then reiterates the invitation for guests to gather outside—and I hold my breath watching her, hoping she doesn't decide now is a good time to tell everyone whatever deep, dark secret she's (illegally) uncovered this morning.

Our guests gather their things, chatting and exchanging promises to keep in touch as they slowly filter out of the ballroom and into the lobby-foyer. After yesterday's unexpected squall and then late-afternoon rally, Sunday dawned a bit foggy, a little damp, though the sun is trying her best to burn through the cloud cover. As much as I'd love to accompany the group down to the planting spot, I am needed at the front desk to help Hannah with the incoming tidal wave of checkouts.

Trent Boullet stands against the far wall, near the door that leads to the kitchens, his phone pressed against his ear, mouth moving. I watch him in between nodding polite greetings to attendees headed outside. He smiles and nods during his chat, clearly enjoying the conversation, and when the call finishes, Trent raises the phone above him, snaps a photo of the people slowly making their way outside, and then leans over his phone, thumbs flying.

Ha! Caught in the act.

Without a word to Hannah, I circle the front counter and march over to the mealy-mouthed muckraker. "Hey!" My voice startles him. "Are you the one who's been shit-posting all weekend? You have something you need to get off your chest, *Flat Earther*?"

Trent Boullet stares at me, wide-eyed. "I beg your pardon?"

"Are you the one who's been trolling the entire conference with your hashtag climate hoax, hashtag lib agenda nonsense?"

A sly smile crawls across his face.

It is at this moment I realize I have made a grave error in judgment.

22

"You can't go around accusing people of being assholes," Ryan says, zipping up the back of my dress. When he's done, I drop my freshly blown-out and curled hair (thanks, Tabby!) and turn to face him.

"I didn't."

He hikes an eyebrow. "I think you did. Now who knows what Boullet will say about *us* in his next article." Ryan moves to the mirror to adjust his tie. His ass looks delicious in his suit pants, but I must stay focused.

"He was standing there looking all smug and slimy with that stupid rat tail hanging over his shoulder, and just the look on his face . . . it set me off."

Ryan reaches for his suit coat on its wooden hanger hooked over the dresser handle and slides into it. He's preparing to escort me to the Sunday night party we threw together kind of last-minute for the CI people and the handful of guests who're staying one more night. I don't know what it is about my man in a well-made suit, but it's *very* distracting, and I am supposed to be defending my most recent spate of bad choices.

Awkwardly, I lower myself to the end of our bed so I can slip

297

into my shoes, cursing my recent dietary choices while concurrently thanking my uterine lining for exiting on schedule, even if she has to show off by puffing me up like day-old fugu. The Spanx shapewear under this hot little red number threatens to choke out my organs, but hey, as long as I look cute, right?

Ryan sees what I'm doing and kneels before me, taking hold of my right foot to slip on my shoe. He repeats the act with my left foot, running a slow hand up my freshly shaved calf.

"Sir, if you continue in such a manner, I will be forced to change our evening plans." I try to lean forward to kiss him and cannot due to aforementioned Elastane-nylon sausage casing.

Ryan smirks and closes the distance, his lips featherlight on mine. "Page 84, the Cocky Cordwainer. We should try that one next." He bites my lower lip and then rises, offering me a hand to stand up.

"That sounds extra dirty. And I don't know what a cordwainer is, but if it involves more of what you just did, I'd like to make a reservation on behalf of my vagina."

That earns me a loud laugh and a head shake. "How have we not been sued yet with that mouth of yours . . ."

"You love this mouth of mine," I say. "And don't give up hope on pending litigation. Night's still young."

The nice thing about an almost-empty, post-summit hotel is that the people who *have* stayed over are friends of Revelation Cove. Smitty and Audrey are checking out tomorrow, as are Rob and Randi Gilbert, all the Clarke Innovations team, and a handful of other longtime business friends of Ryan and Tanner's. (I've met them all, several times, while sober. Alas, do not ask me their names while unsober.)

It's kinda like a giant slumber party but for grownups and with an open bar and unfettered access to the fridge.

With the weekend's important matters concluded, and the slimy reporter long gone, the atmosphere is much more chill. Although

I'm not sure if a ballroom of liquored-up nerds is chill—more like New Year's Eve 2.0. We even moved the big rectangular cooking challenge clock into the ballroom where it hangs above the Garden Gnomes. They jam, we dance, and the clock counts down. Then at midnight, it will officially tick over to Earth Day, and we can raise more glasses to Mother Nature and renew our promise to stop patronizing businesses who still allow single-use plastic.

I'm also learning a lot about my new friend. The bolts that hold Lara Clarke in perfect place loosen quite a bit when plied with whiskey. Her husband is always close by, watchful and kind but not overbearing. As if he's afraid she will trip and fall. While doing my hair earlier, Tabby filled my ears with more intel she gathered from the Google and online sites about Lara's life—a wild and oft-absent mother, a doting but permissive grandfather, her own lifestyle as a spoiled party-girl heiress keeping many gossip sites fat and happy with content . . .

Talking to Lara tonight, I've come to know more about her from her own lips. She talks endlessly and lovingly about Rupert (her grandfather's right-hand man who basically raised Lara) and his husband Wes, about how her work on Thalia Island started as a stipulation of her grandfather's will, about how much she loves her life there and how she has the world's most perfect husband and how she learned a few years ago that Len Emmerich is her biological father and how weird it's been learning how to be a daughter of an overprotective bodyguard. She even pulls out her phone to flip through pictures of their dog, Humboldt, a bullmastiff who looks like he could take down a bear.

"He's harmless," she says. "All he does is slobber and sleep and follow Finan around the fields."

We talk about our moms (hers is far more interesting than mine), about how we met our husbands, about her past life as an impulsive brat and about mine as an aimless wanderer with an affection for sea otters. I tell her about rescuing baby Clara; she tells me that Clarke Innovations donates big money to Ocean Wise and the Vancouver Aquarium's Marine Mammal Rescue Centre.

"I spend so much time working, I don't have a lot of friends,"

Lara says, gently grabbing my wrist. "This has been so much fun getting to know you, Hollie."

"Aww, thank you! And I know! All we do is work, and then living on an island, it's not like I have access to big-city events. The few friends I have from my old life know I probably can't attend their events since I'm here running the resort."

"We should definitely hang out. You come to Thalia and stay with us for a week, not for work or to tour the farms, but just to relax." She leans in closer. "And we can go across to Vancouver and shop, but no one else needs to know that."

I share about how we're looking at buying a place in Langley to be closer to the arena for Ryan's coaching job.

"That sounds very suburban." She punctuates her words with a shudder.

I laugh.

"Are you in need of schools and such?" she asks, hiking a brow and nodding at my mostly flat midsection.

"Oh god, no, not yet. Much to our parents' chagrin," I add. "My dad lives in Portland, and Ryan's mom lives here at the resort, but she's, um, out of town right now. Visiting friends." I'm not sure I want to share that my father and Ryan's mother are dating—each other.

The Garden Gnomes launch into a cover of a Gwen Stefani song and Lara stops midsentence, launching from her chair. "We have to sing! This is my song! Come on!" She grabs my wrist and pulls me up, but before we can squeeze through the crowd to get to the stage, He-Man approaches and indicates we are needed elsewhere.

Lara groans and we follow her bodyguard/father out of the cacophony and into the slightly quieter lobby. My ears ring with the change in decibels. Finan and Ryan are already out there, waiting beside the front desk. Between them, Harmony stands with arms crossed over her chest, her cute sparkly purple dress paired with a rainbow-print fanny pack and the well-worn, once-white Converse high-tops she's worn all weekend—and a very sour look on her face.

"What's going on?" Lara asks. "Harm, you OK?"

The young girl looks up at Finan. He juts his chin, gesturing for her to answer.

"I'm fine." She plasters on a saccharine smile.

Finan clears his throat.

"*God*, fine." From the fanny pack, she pulls out a phone, awakens the screen, and hoists it in front of her so the adults can see.

It shows a photo—an Instagram post—of the Garden Gnomes playing onstage, the countdown clock visible above their heads. The caption reads, "Different rules for the rich! The world is ending? Let's party! #climatechangelies #naturalprogression #nocurve."

"*You* are Flat Earther?" I ask. It must sound meaner than I'd intended as Harmony shrinks into herself a bit.

"Not just me. NORA too," Harmony admits. Finan plucks the phone from her grip. "I mean, NORA handled the photos. We thought it would be good publicity for the event."

"By saying terrible things and undermining what we're trying to do here?" Lara demands. She sounds angrier than me.

Harmony looks up at us, one at a time. "You all know the world thrives on controversy. As NORA says, 'It's not the calm seas that receive the most attention, but the storms that rage upon them.' So, I thought, let's give the people a storm."

Len Emmerich scrubs a hand over his face and sighs.

"Remember after all the stuff with the cult went down, all the attention Thalia Island was getting? If you look at the data, you'll see how Clarke Innovations' stock prices went up, how more people started looking into what we're doing. CI's website visits skyrocketed, and plain, boring old people started engaging on what were pretty flat social media accounts. People want to know how to grow gardens instead of lawns—they want to know how to lessen their carbon footprint, even if they can't afford an electric vehicle. They're demanding change in their neighborhoods—no Styrofoam containers for takeout, asking for bamboo or wood cutlery, collecting used chopsticks to be recycled and made into new stuff."

Harmony takes a deep breath and fidgets with the zipper on her fanny pack. "I'm not just being a brat here. Flat Earther was a calculated effort to draw more eyes to our cause. And it worked, didn't it? Look at the engagement! Look at the people arguing in the comments!" She points at Finan who still has her phone. "We're not just in a bubble talking to ourselves. We've engaged a wider audience, sparked debate, and brought critical attention to what we're doing. Making noise attracts attention. If you guys don't get that, then you don't understand social media at all." She feathers the end of her ponytail across her upper lip as she looks into the faces of the five adults staring down at her.

"OK, well, that's too fucking smart for me," Finan says, handing the child her phone back. "But no more. Flat Earther is retired until we get home and talk to your dad about all this."

Harmony rolls her eyes. "He'll think it's genius."

"Did you have anything to do with the protesters?" I ask.

Len Emmerich answers for her. "No. We confirmed who they are. Members of Extinction Rebellion who dabble in anarchism. We've had trouble with them before when the summits are held in Vancouver."

"And you didn't anticipate they'd show up?" Ryan asks.

"We didn't think they'd have a way to get up here. It's not exactly accessible by SkyTrain," Finan says.

"Then how did they get here?" I ask.

Len Emmerich pulls out his own phone and scrolls, showing us an email—from a Sergeant Wes Singh. "This came in while we were waiting for the Coast Guard to recharge our dead boat."

Ryan and I hunch together to read the update from Sergeant Singh. According to this, the protesters (David X. Fairman and Lisa "Sunflower" Peterson) were given the funds and the boat by "some reporter" who also sent them instructions on what to wear to blend in and where to land their boat.

"HA!" I say, looking up at Ryan as I thrust Len's phone toward him. "I *told* you that guy was an asshole!" My husband smirks at me.

"That is why I was so upset when Boullet showed up instead of the journalist we approved," Lara adds.

"Too bad he's not still here. We could've let Len and the Vikings have a little fun," I say.

"He left just in time. That little fucker is terrified of me," He-

Man growls. "I'll find him, though. Off-duty, when the rules don't count."

"And out of view of CI lawyers," Lara adds, smacking her dad in his tight gut.

One of the ballroom double doors opens as a couple exits, headed toward the washrooms. Music—someone singing, *very* well—spills into the lobby, fading as the door clicks closed.

We all look at one another. "Who is *that*?" I ask. The group rushes toward the ballroom and Len throws open the door for us to enter.

Onstage, gripping the microphone, is NORA, belting out "Uprising" by Muse.

Harmony stands at the door's threshold, a shit-eating grin on her face. "I programmed her to sing. And this is her favorite song."

<h1 align="center">23</h1>

"Did you get a chill when Harmony told us NORA is a MUSE fan? Aren't their songs about existential dread and political unrest?" I spit my mouthful of toothpaste into the sink. Ryan chuckles behind me as he hangs up a clean hand towel.

"That child scares the daylights out of me. Now I see why Len Emmerich is so uptight all the time."

"Yeah, he didn't even have a beer or anything tonight."

"He's always on the job," Ryan says. "You done in here?"

I nod. He clicks off the light and I follow him out of the bathroom and into our bed. He slides under the covers and waits for me to assume the snuggle position before draping the blanket over my shoulders.

"Finan told me a bit about Lara's backstory with Len. It's a soap opera, their whole life." As Ryan talks, I trace circles in his chest hair. I've had just enough to drink tonight to loosen me up (and ease the menstrual cramps that are now going for Olympic gold), but not so much that the room spins. I don't know how or why, but turning thirty flipped a switch on my body's ability to recover from hangovers in a timely manner. And tomorrow, or rather, seven hours from now, is a workday.

304

Look at me being all responsible and shit.

Except I've lost track of what Ryan is talking about. I wait for him to finish and then prop myself on my elbow. Our room is dark but light sneaks in from the single lamp always left on in the kitchen.

"You are so beautiful. Did you know that?" I ask him.

He smiles and turns to face me. "What do you want? Or what did you do?"

I poke his chest. "Shut up. I'm being serious. I just wanted you to know that."

"Thanks, but you're the beautiful one in our alliance."

I lean close and kiss his plump lips. "I … thought I was pregnant."

Ryan's eyes widen and he pulls back a couple inches.

"I'm not—Aunt Flo is here—but the other day, I took a couple tests because I was feeling weird after the incident at the container greenhouses and somehow I got it in my head that maybe I was nauseated from being knocked up and then Sarah got me a bit riled and said I should take a test, just to be safe."

Ryan plays with my hair draped over my shoulder. "How did you feel? When it was negative?"

"Relieved." I think I see a hint of disappointment in my husband's eyes. "I mean, whatever—if it happens, it happens, but I'd rather us get a little more settled first, you know? Figure out what we're doing in terms of a house, get situated before the new hockey season starts, plus deal with promoting whoever is going to take my place here on-site when I'm in Langley with you."

He nods, his beard scratching against his pillow. He drops the curl he'd been fingering and flattens his palm against my cheek. "Babe, everything will work out the way it's supposed to. Babies or no babies. And we're going to find the perfect house for us. The resort will continue to kick ass, as will my hockey team."

"You've got it all figured out, don't you . . ."

"Page 17: the Sex-Starved Soothsayer." He pulls the sexy funtime book from under his pillow, and my laugh bounces off the ceiling. "Now, nubile young virgin, follow me into my cobwebby lair where I will ply you with food and drink and lie you bare on my animal skins where I shall teach you the ways of the wise old man."

Ryan tickles me and slides under the covers, yanking up my tank top so he can grab a handful of boob. "Wait! Ryan, stop . . . don't! Stop!" I yell at him, gulping breaths in my laughing fit. "No, seriously—I can't. Period, remember?"

He grins up at me from under the covers, his right hand still full of breast. "And orgasms are good for menstrual cramps." He scoots up and hovers over me, his interest in a horizontal tango obvious against my tingly bits. "I'm a soothsayer, remember? That means I know things."

I snort. "Then lead on, wise old man. I shall pay for your services in crickets."

Afterword by Toni Freitas
What is a circular economy?

**Toni Freitas, Lecturer in Circular Economy,
Programme Director, MSc Circular Economy,
University of Edinburgh**

Not just Hollie and Lara can save the planet—so can you! When people discover I work in the sustainability field, the question I get asked most often is, "But what can I really do to make a difference?" This is usually followed by a look of despair or exasperation and the unspoken question of, "What's the point?! It's all just too much!"

Tackling the climate crisis as an individual, couple, family, or group of friends in the face of the global scale can feel too daunting or impossible. But I promise, you *can* make a difference! Below are some ideas for you to consider in your daily lives, with a few facts thrown in as to why these are important changes. (I can't help it— I'm a teacher, and this is a teachable moment! Stay with me ...)

Consumption

We often think of "consumption" in terms of food only, but we are consumers of SO many goods and services in our day-to-day lives.

Afterword by Toni Freitas

This includes energy, clothing, food, and all the other stuff we buy. I specialize in circular economy, mainly because I wanted to find a practical way of combating climate change, and this framework makes sense to me.

The **linear** economy is the usual way we do things—take resources, make something with them, use it (sometimes only once!), and then dispose of it, maybe recycle it. The **circular** economy focuses more on designing out waste and pollution through the whole process, keeping products and materials in use for as long as possible, with as minimal environmental impact as possible. This includes thinking more about why and how we own things and considers more sharing, leasing, reusing, repairing, refurbishing, and recycling of existing materials and products.

So, what does that look like in the real world?

Food

You might be surprised to discover that farming animals is one of the biggest contributors to global greenhouse gas emissions, particularly methane (cow burps, not farts, are the main cause of this—ewww!). Meat and dairy production causes significant deforestation and at least 14.5% of planet-warming gases. This is nearly the same as all modes of transportation combined! Eating less (or zero) meat and dairy is something we can all do to help the planet, and we all know it is much better for our health too.

Avoiding as much food waste as possible is also a huge step to help with your individual planetary impact. We don't often think about how much energy, water, fertilizer, and labor goes into our food and drinks, much less our food waste, but think about every item in your fridge and cupboards. Wow! It takes a lot of resources to get that food to your home, measurable in both human hours *and* our hard-earned money. I know it's easy to lose track of what leftovers or vegetables we have in our fridge, or what is about to go out of date. Life is seriously busy.

But it's time to be a bit more mindful and get creative with what we have already spent our cash on; it will save you money and help the planet at the same time. Recent estimates suggest that 8% to 10% of global greenhouse gas emissions are associated with food and drinks that are not consumed—stuff that is *thrown away*. I include drinks because we don't often think of spoiled dairy milk as waste; we just pour it down the sink and it disappears, but there are a lot of emissions and resources within that milk.

To put food waste into context, if consumer food waste were a country, it would be the world's third-largest emitter; only China (21%) and the United States (13%) emitted more in the latest research. [Insert head-exploding emoji here.]

Clothing

The fashion and textiles industry is a biggie when it comes to global resource, energy, and water use. Did you know that approximately 1,800 gallons of water are needed to grow enough cotton for one pair of jeans and 700 gallons for one cotton T-shirt? Also, a whopping 85% of all textiles go to the dump each year globally. This is a *huge* waste of materials and resources.

Take a second to visualize your closet and dresser: How many items do you own, and how many do you actually wear? This is one area where a circular economy can help you. "Shop your own closet" is a phrase catching on, because we often have perfectly wearable or repairable items of clothes that we forget about or don't know what to do with (or if you are like me, are keeping because I might fit into it "someday" … Why do we torture ourselves like this?).

Many of us have not learned the skills to repair, mend, or upcycle/refashion clothing, so let's get to learning. There are lots of easy online tutorials out there, or perhaps you have friends or family with these skills or who are handy with a sewing machine. Consider the wonderful methods of "visible mending." Google it: SO many beautiful and fun ways to upcycle and repair clothes, and often you only need a needle and thread.

And not just women—men need these skills too. Why is it that some of the best-known fashion designers and tailors are men, but women are still expected to do all the mending at home? Let's break that cycle and get everyone of all genders, both friends and family, involved in considering how we can extend the life of our clothes.

For those items you no longer use but that are in good condition, numerous opportunities exist to swap, sell, or donate. And instead of replacing them with new, consider shopping for secondhand and vintage clothing or renting instead of buying, particularly formal wear (why do guys get to rent a tux, but women have to buy fancy, expensive dresses? Bah to that!). Look for secondhand clothing stores or apps or use Facebook Marketplace, or even host a clothing swap event in your area.

If you want to invest in clothing that is more sustainable or circular, try finding items made of natural fibers (bamboo, wool, linen, hemp, and recycled or organic cotton, if you can't find alternatives) or search for circular economy clothing companies; some even offer free repair services. There are some amazing companies innovating with waste from other industries, such as leather from pineapple or orange peel waste and even silk made from orange pulp reclaimed from the juice industry.

For all other consumer goods—everything from furniture to electronics to refrigerators to phones—the same principles apply. First question: Do you actually need it? Can you buy it secondhand instead of new, or even better, borrow it from someone? Can it be repaired or upcycled either by you or an expert? Can it be creatively used as something else? For instance, I have an old metal lampshade that looked awful in my hallway, but turned upside down, it is now a beautiful plant pot in my garden!

Your home environment

I am not going to presume anything about your living situation, so you can ignore this if it doesn't suit you or your family's health. The buildings we live in and use every day put an enormous strain on the planet. Buildings account for more than 21% of global greenhouse gas emissions, primarily due to electricity, heating, and cooling. If you can, consider a minor adjustment in your thermostat settings, particularly if you have good insulation in your house. Just a couple of degrees down for heating or up for cooling can make a huge different over the course of a year.

Can you and your family cozy up with blankets in the evening instead of having the house so warm you can wear a T-shirt indoors? Can you let a breeze in, instead of cranking on the air-conditioning in the summer? Can you slightly adjust the times your heating/cooling comes on? Or can you set specific times when you need heating or cooling instead of the system running all day? Just a few things to consider if you are able, and it might help save a few pennies too.

Outdoor environment

Bring on biodiversity! If you are lucky enough to have access to an outdoor area—a yard/garden, a deck or balcony, even a front step or strip of earth between the street and the sidewalk—then consider how you can help pollinators and local ecosystems by creating a diverse environment for them. Lawns can become wildflower meadows without much effort or money (and who likes mowing anyway?) and it looks stunning. You can get seeds for all kinds of flowers and grasses that are easy and cheap to grow. Also look for local seed exchanges and ask friends, family, or neighbors for seeds and plant cuttings.

Consider planting more for your weather and environment. If you have to water a lawn every day in the summer because it is too hot, perhaps it is time to reconsider how you can landscape to fit your local climate, including use of drought-resistant plants. Switch to native species of grasses, plants, and flowers or climate-friendly varieties, and consider choosing plants that flower or fruit throughout the year to help year-round biodiversity.

On the flip side, if you are in a cool place and you are constantly fighting moss in your lawn or on your roof, what about letting the moss win instead? (Because again, who likes mowing?) Moss is much more resilient to climate shocks and weather changes (it has been around for over 450 million years), it absorbs ten times as much carbon dioxide as grass, it improves soil, AND it fights air pollution. Moss is the unsung superhero of the natural world and deserves some kudos.

Depending on your roofing material, moss often does very little damage to a roof. Just make sure it isn't blocking drains or gutters. Of course, do your research—it really depends on what your roof is made of. Moss is absolutely beautiful too. Have you ever looked at moss up close or run your hand over it? It's like a silky-soft micro-forest . . . so calming.

Gardening does not have to be expensive or difficult, and there are so many wonderful websites and Facebook groups that give out lots of helpful advice. If you don't have a place to garden, then consider joining (or starting) a community garden group.

I know—some of the things listed above might take a bit of extra thought and time. But we are often willing to give that for our friends and family, so how about a little more time for our gorgeous planet? Just like you, she needs some TLC too.

Books for further investigation

To further guide and inspire you, as we are all book people here, I highly recommend reading these books by awesome women. And yes, I've listed all women authors/creators because climate change is NOT gender neutral, but that is another story . . .

- *Not the End of the World: How We Can Be the First Generation to Build a Sustainable Planet*, by Dr. Hannah Richie
- *The Future We Choose*, by Christiana Figueres and Tom Rivett-Carnac
- *Climate Optimism: Climate Wins and Creating Systemic Change Around the World*, by Zahra Biabani
- *Consumed: The Need for Collective Change; Colonialism, Climate Change and Consumerism*, by Aja Barber
- *Braiding Sweetgrass: Indigenous Wisdom, Scientific Knowledge, and the Teachings of Plants*, and *Gathering Moss: A Natural and Cultural History of Mosses* by Robin Wall Kimmerer

- *A Terrible Thing to Waste: Environmental Racism and Its Assault on the American Mind*, Harriet A. Washington
- For kids: *Bright New World: How to Make a Happy Planet*, by Cindy Forde (author) and Bethany Lord (illustrator)

Podcasts

If you are a podcast fan, here are some great podcasts, but there are many more:

- *Mothers of Invention*, with Mary Robinson and Maeve Higgins. Inspiring women from around the world, with a bit of humor too! I know, how can the climate crisis be funny? Just listen!
- *Drilled*, with Amy Westervelt. True crime meets the climate crisis!
- *The Circular Economy Show Podcast*, from Ellen Macarthur Foundation. I had to advocate for a circular economy one. (There are lots—look it up!)
- *Visible Women*, with Caroline Criado Perez. I had to throw this one in, because (a) she is amazing, and (b) the gender data gap is NEVER talked about. Read the book this podcast came out of too: *Invisible Women: Exposing Data Bias in a World Designed for Men.*

Thanks for letting me slide into your fiction world with some facts. Be well and love the planet.

~ Toni

Toni Freitas is a lapsed American from Vancouver, Washington, who has lived in Edinburgh, Scotland, for twenty-one years. After many career twists and turns, she is currently a passionate lecturer in Circular Economy at the University of Edinburgh. She recently created a master's programme in Circular Economy at

Afterword by Toni Freitas

the University's Futures Institute because it is the degree she wished she had been able to take. Shameless plug—check it out. You can do the degree from anywhere in the world!

In her spare time (in between taking too many photos of her beautiful cat, LV), Toni has found her happy place—and a moderate-to-severe plant obsession —in the garden.

*(*University of Edinburgh, Futures Institute: https://efi.ed.ac.uk/programmes/ circular-economy/)*

Hollie Porter's
Hat Trick
Christmas
ELIZA GORDON

Open
Me
First
ELIZA GORDON

MUST LOVE OTTERS
FROM THE AUTHOR OF DEAR DWAYNE, WITH LOVE
ELIZA GORDON

HOLLIE PORTER BUILDS A RAFT
SEQUEL TO MUST LOVE OTTERS
ELIZA GORDON

Hollie Porter
Saves the Planet
ELIZA GORDON

a Revolution Cove standalone novel
Love
Just Clicks
Is Frankie ready for her close-up?
ELIZA GORDON

I Love You,
LUKE PIEWALKER
THE FORCE
ELIZA GORDON

Dear
Dwayne,
With
Love
a novel
Eliza Gordon

FROM THE AUTHOR OF MUST LOVE OTTERS
WELCOME TO
Planet
Lara
ELIZA GORDON

Planet
Lara
TEMPEST
ELIZA GORDON

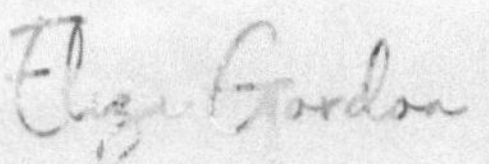

Planet
Lara
SANCTUARY
ELIZA GORDON

Find the Eliza Gordon books at the following retailers in e-book, print, and audio.

Did you know you can ask your local library to order in Eliza's books?

Visit elizagordon.com for links.

Amazon globally | Angus & Robertson | Apple Books | Audible | Audiobooks.com | Barnes & Noble | Biblioteca | Bold.de | Books-A-Million | Bookshop.org | Booktopia | Chapters/Indigo | Chirp | Everand | Google Play | Hoopla | Ingram | Kobo | Libby | Libro.fm| Mondadori | Overdrive | Powell's | Scribd | Thalia.de | 24 Symbols | Waterstones

SGA
BOOKS

www.ingramcontent.com/pod-product-compliance
Lightning Source LLC
Chambersburg PA
CBHW022018310726
48972CB00006B/1711